PRAISE FOR *BITTER CREEK*

"Peter Bowen is an American original. His mysteries are quirky and satisfying, while his diamond-cut prose slices clean to the bone."

—MARYANNE VOLLERS,
AUTHOR OF *GHOSTS OF MISSISSIPPI* AND *LONE WOLF*

"In *Bitter Creek*, Peter Bowen's new Gabriel Du Pré mystery, a long-hidden treachery is unearthed and, by the skin of some teeth, put to rest. Hooray for Bowen's irascible and humane detective! Hooray for storytelling that is astringent, syncopated, comic, and utterly its own."

—DEIRDRE MCNAMER,
AUTHOR OF *RED ROVER*

In Gabriel Du Pré, Peter Bowen has given the Métis a worthy hero in contemporary literature. Now, with *Bitter Creek*, we have a borderlands *lagniappe* of fourteen tales that collectively make their stand along the Montana Medicine Line (and in American letters) like a bison herd turned into a storm—fixed on the landscape of our imagination."

NICHOLAS VROOMAN, PHD, MÉTIS HISTORIAN
AND AUTHOR OF *"THE WHOLE COUNTRY WAS . . . 'ONE ROBE' ": THE LITTLE SHELL TRIBE'S AMERICA*

PRAISE FOR PETER BOWEN

"Peter Bowen writes mysteries that are truly mysterious—informed by Western legend, steeped in Indian superstition. . . . Riding with Du Pré is some kind of enchantment."
—*The New York Times Book Review*

"Bowen plays his language the way Du Pré plays violin: plaintive, humorous, wild, the sounds of the sentences as meaningful as the story."
—*The Washington Post Book World*

"In detective Du Pré, Peter Bowen gives readers all they can hope for: a hero as odd and surprising as the mystery he is called upon to solve."
—Water Kirn, author of *Blood Will Out*

"One of the most unusual characters working the fictional homicide beat . . . powerfully poetic but unsentimental."
—*Booklist*

"Bowen's writing is lean and full of mordant observations. His hardy characters . . . come to life, and his wry humor provides relief from the haunting, wind-bitten cattle-ranch landscape."
—*Publishers Weekly*

· Bitter Creek ·

· Bitter Creek ·

A Montana Mystery Featuring Gabriel Du Pré

PETER BOWEN

Cover design by Neil Alexander Heacox

978-1-4976-7658-9

Published in 2015 by Open Road Integrated Media, Inc.
345 Hudson Street
New York, NY 10014
www.openroadmedia.com

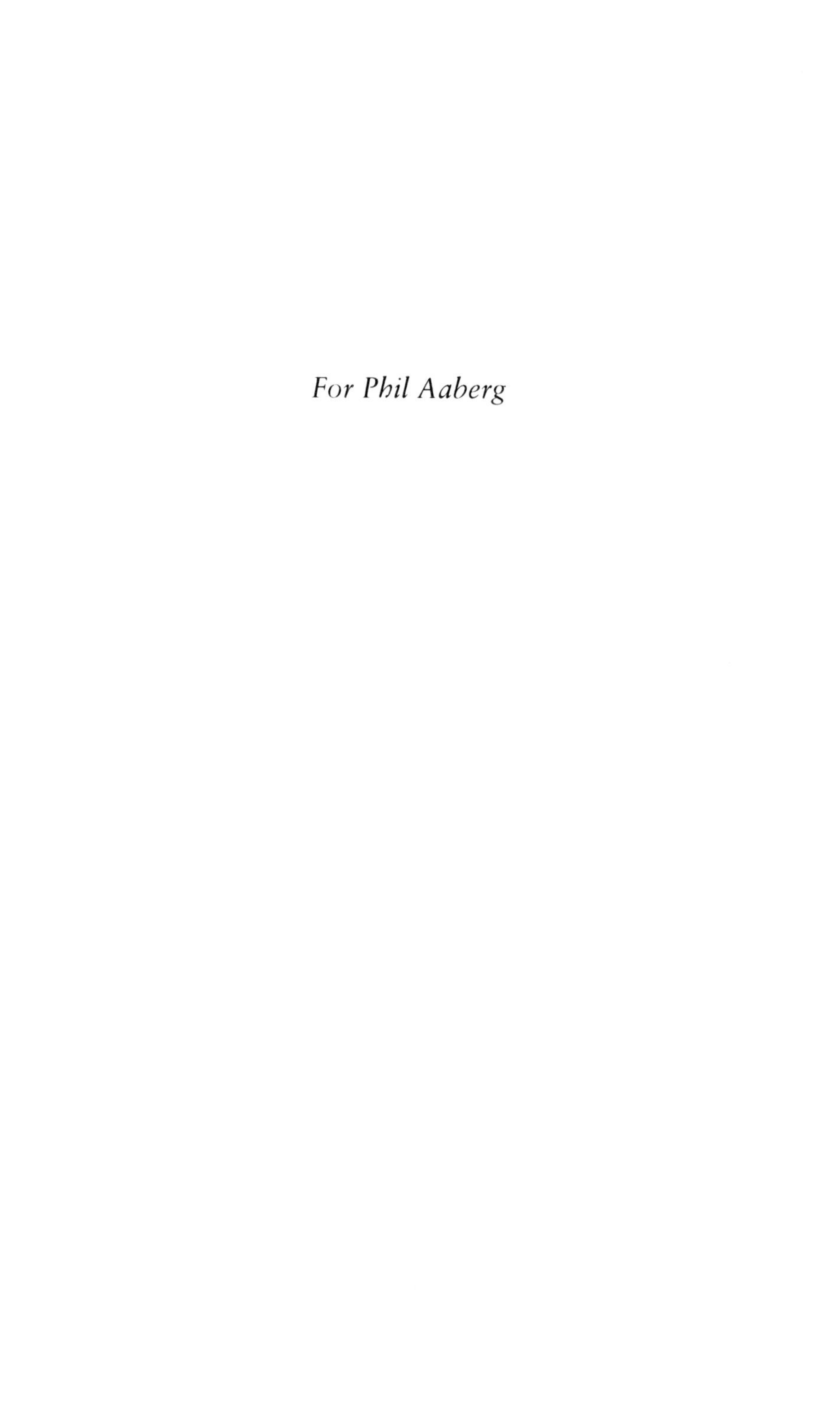

For Phil Aaberg

· Bitter Creek ·

· Chapter 1 ·

DU PRÉ'S SLEEP DISSOLVED; he heard bacon sizzling in a pan, he rolled to Madelaine and found her gone. The bedclothes were thrown back and her scent of musk and sage rose from where she had lain.

Du Pré yawned, blinked, sat up. He swung his feet over the side of the bed, reached for his shirt, underwear, socks, pants, boots.

He went to the kitchen, scratching the nape of his neck to spur his waking.

"Good morning," said Madelaine, half turning from the stove. "You were snoring. You never snore."

"Sometimes I do, yes," said Du Pré.

Madelaine put bacon and eggs scrambled with sharp cheddar cheese and chunks of green chilies on a plate, stuck a slab of buttered homemade bread on the edge, and handed it to him. He ate, staring at the food. "Not waking up," he said.

"Good night to sleep," said Madelaine, "the rain, that sound . . ." Du Pré nodded. A thick scent of lilacs wafted through the window.

"There is a car outside," said Madelaine. "Don't belong here." Du Pré nodded.

"Somebody is sitting in it," she said. Du Pré nodded. Madelaine poured two cups of strong coffee. She brought them and she set them down. "What I think is it is someone looking for Chappie, they maybe want some breakfast. We don't got a restaurant here . . ." said Madelaine.

"Chappie," said Du Pré.

"He is in a uniform," said Madelaine.

Du Pré sucked down the coffee, hot enough to make him cough. He nodded, got up, walked through the house and out the front door. The tortoiseshell cat looked up at him as he passed. He had a gopher that was almost dead but not quite.

The tan sedan was parked across the street. A man sat in it, bareheaded, looking at some papers.

Du Pré walked up to the car. The driver's window was down. "Madelaine wanted to know if you are hungry," he said. The soldier turned, startled. His left ear was deformed. When he raised his left hand, Du Pré saw that it was plastic.

"Oh," he said. He was young, in his early twenties perhaps, and he had lieutenant's bars on his dress uniform. Marine.

"She is happy to feed you," said Du Pré. "You are looking for Chappie?"

The man nodded. He reached across with his right hand to open the car door, swung his legs out, stood up. He reached for his hat and he put it on.

"Yes," he said, "I'm Patchen, John Patchen. I was Chappie's commanding officer."

Du Pré nodded.

"Come, eat," he said. "We go find Chappie then."

. . . who was drinking much last night and will still be passed out. Chappie cannot sleep but he can pass out . . .

"Kind of you," said Patchen.

Du Pré led him to the front steps, went up, opened the door.

Patchen went in and waited.

Du Pré led him to the kitchen.

"You are that Patchen," said Madelaine, smiling. She held out both her hands and Patchen offered his right and then reluctantly his false left.

Madelaine looked at him levelly for a moment.

"Chappie, him love you," she said. "You are here for him why?"

Patchen nodded.

"He . . . has been awarded a medal," said Patchen, "I thought he might not . . . come to the ceremony, so I came to ask him to do so as a personal favor. . . ."

"Medal," said Madelaine. She shook her head. She turned and heaped a plate with food and she pointed to the table. Patchen sat, and she set the plate in front of him. Du Pré brought him coffee.

"Chappie don't talk about Iraq," she said.

Patchen nodded. He began to eat, carefully, but he swallowed quickly and he began to eat a bit faster.

"This is very good," said Patchen. "I didn't eat in Billings and . . ."

"You been sitting out there since I got up at four," said Madelaine. "So, you come here, why you don't knock?"

"I didn't wish to disturb you," said Patchen.

Madelaine reached out and she patted his cheek.

"Chappie got very drunk last night," she said. "He did not say, he had a medal. . . ."

"I wrote him," said Patchen. "I . . . thought he wouldn't want it. But . . . his . . . friends are going back there in a week. . . ."

Madelaine nodded. "Find those weapons of mass destruction this time," she said.

Patchen looked stricken.

"I am sorry," said Madelaine. "You eat now, then we go and get that Chappie. . . ."

He began to eat again, but his eyes were wet.

"It is not you I am mad at," said Madelaine.

Patchen laughed.

"From what Chappie told me of you," he said, "I am surely glad of that."

Du Pré nodded, went out and rolled a smoke, looked up at the sky. A clear day. The golden eagles that lived on the cliff that rose yellow-gray halfway up the first mountain in the Wolfs were riding the high air. They flew lazily.

Then one folded its wings and tumbled down through the air and the other dove after.

Du Pré smoked, standing. Honeybees were gathering nectar and pollen from the lilacs. He glanced back at the house. A blob of color caught his eye.

A tiger swallowtail butterfly had just emerged from its chrysalis and was pumping up its wings. Du Pré bent close. The frail creature tensed a little, the wings filled a little more.

Du Pré split his smoke open, scattered the tobacco on the ground, put the little ball of paper in his shirt pocket.

"Good luck, you," he said.

He backed away slowly.

Patchen laughed, a rich laugh.

Du Pré could see the trailer Chappie lived in, back of the Toussaint Saloon, behind the ones that were rented as rooms. Chappie's blue heeler pup was running around, nose to ground.

. . . won't find no heel there to nip, Du Pré thought.

He went back in.

Patchen stood up.

"Have you a bathroom I might use?" he said.

Du Pré pointed down the hall. Patchen walked swiftly that way. "Chappie said he was a good man," said Madelaine. "I think he is." Du Pré nodded.

When Patchen came back, he got his hat from the counter and he put it on.

"Thank, you, ma'am," he said, and bowed a little.

"I let you and Du Pré do this," said Madelaine. "I don't think Chappie, him want to see his mother right now. . . ." And Madelaine laughed. So did Patchen.

"No," said Patchen, "me either."

Du Pré went out and Patchen came after him. Du Pré got in his old cruiser and Patchen into his sedan and Du Pré led him along the street to the turn that went back to Chappie's trailer. Du Pré stopped and he got out. Patchen did, too, and he put his hat on and he walked to the front door of the trailer and he rapped on it loudly. Nothing.

Du Pré sat on the hood of his cruiser and he rolled a smoke. Patchen banged again.

Du Pré looked at a pile of old lumber that sat a hundred or so feet away from the trailer. Something had moved in it or on the other side, a quick flash and then nothing.

Patchen banged on the door again. Nothing.

Du Pré whistled, soft and low, and Patchen turned. Du Pré pointed to the woodpile. Patchen nodded. He walked toward it.

When he got there, he stood very straight. Chappie rose up, shakily, filthy, his hair awry.

Then he changed. He snapped to attention, in his uniform of rumpled clothes and puke. He saluted. So did Patchen.

Chappie staggered out of his hiding place and he fell into Patchen's arms and the men held each other, shaking.

Du Pré nodded, got into his cruiser, and drove off.

Madelaine had dressed and she was sitting on the front steps, holding a mug.

"Find him?" she said.

Du Pré nodded.

"I maybe borrow your big new gun, go to Texas," she said.

"Talk to the guy was president," said Du Pré.

"No," said Madelaine. "Me, I do not want, talk, him."

· Chapter 2 ·

CHAPPIE'S HEAD LOLLED and he stank of stale booze and old sweat. He was holding his head as they rode along, moaning. Patchen sat in the back with him. He held a plastic bucket ready in case Chappie needed it. Du Pré roared up the rise to the benchland and he turned left toward the west. He accelerated and the heavy car flew when it crested the first low hill.

"Uhhhh," said Chappie, "ohhhh." He retched. Du Pré slowed by Benetsee's drive, turned, went slowly up the rutted track, stopped. Woodsmoke.

The cabin door was open. So the old man was back.

. . . I never know where he goes . . . this is good, maybe the stones are hot . . . Du Pré thought. He got out and helped Chappie, and Patchen got out and they walked Chappie past the cabin and down the little grade to the flat by the creek where Benetsee's sweat lodge stood.

There was a fire in the trench and the stones had fallen through the ricked wood as it burned fast and hot.

They could feel the heat radiating ten feet away. "Benetsee!" yelled Du Pré. No answer.

Du Pré and Patchen pulled Chappie's dirty clothes off

him. The fake leg fit over the stump of his right leg and it was held on by a fabric collar that closed with Velcro.

"You get in, too," said Du Pré. He tossed down the big beach towel he had carried from the car. "I hang your uniform up."

Patchen looked at him and then he nodded.

He stripped and handed his uniform to Du Pré, then removed the artificial arm and hand from the stump of his left arm.

Chappie wiggled backward into the sweat lodge. Patchen followed on his one hand and knees.

Du Pré looked for the steel-handled shovel that worked best to move the stones. He saw the rusty shaft leaning against the woodpile. When he grabbed it, he heard laughter, old and thin.

Benetsee was standing near the lodge, wearing only a pair of dirty jockey shorts.

"Eight stones," said the old man. He held the small brass bucket and dipper, full of water to the brim.

Benetsee watched as Du Pré carried the stones one by one from the fire trench to the sweat lodge, where he dropped them into the small pit to the right of the door.

When all eight had been set, Benetsee crawled in with the bucket and Du Pré flipped down the heavy canvas-and-wool blanket that covered the door.

Hissing, white tendrils of steam curled out from small gaps. Benetsee began to sing. More hissing.

Du Pré heard Madelaine's car pull in close to the sunken meadow. A door opened, closed, Du Pré looked up at her. She came down quickly.

"Du Pré," said Madelaine, behind him, "I brought fresh things, I think I go, not be here." She set down a black nylon duffel bag and she offered Du Pré a steel thermos. He took it, then she kissed him and went back up the little rise to her small station wagon.

Du Pré sat on a round of wood in the shade of the willows. He opened the thermos, unscrewed the cap, and laughed. Whiskey and water with one little chip of ice.

Du Pré rolled a smoke and he looked north toward the Wolf Mountains, rising high and blue and dark green and gray, snow up high, still thick.

. . . how many times I see this in June . . . it is June when the snow on the mountains is thick up high and gone the rest . . .

Du Pré heard Benetsee singing and then he heard the drumming coming from the sweat lodge where there was no drum; he felt the drum in the earth beneath his feet . . . heart of the people . . . More voices joined Benetsee's. The sound was not loud but it was everywhere. Du Pré swung his head round; there was no one place it seemed to be coming from now. Water hissed on the hot stones again. Steam white and curling came from the blanket edges. Du Pré drank more of the whiskey and water. He looked at the fancy watch Bart had given him. "You get in trouble you can always hock it," Bart had said. "It's platinum."

. . . rag-ass Métis retired brand inspector got a watch on my wrist worth as much as most people's houses . . . Jesus . . .

Du Pré finished the whiskey and water and the voices were still.

He had another smoke and then he had to piss, so he walked away toward the willows and brush downstream, took his leak on bare ground, and then he walked back to the round of wood he had been sitting on.

The blanket flipped up and fell back down. Du Pré went to the sweat lodge and he lifted the heavy wet cloth up and folded it back over the top.

Benetsee came out on his hands and knees, stood up, and walked swiftly to the edge of the deep pool nearby, where he stepped off the grassy verge into the cold water.

Chappie came next, his eyes blinking at the bright light, and he went on hands and knees to the water and he slid over the lip of the bank on his belly.

Patchen was last. He stood up as soon as he was clear of the doorway, his right hand over his eyes. Du Pré took his elbow.

"Over here," he said. "You jump in the water, I help you out." Patchen nodded. Du Pré led him to the pool and Patchen dove in, his right arm stuck out and the stump of his left held as though the limb was still intact.

He slid under the water and he kicked his legs and pulled with his one arm and hand.

When he came up for air, he went *whoooooooooo*.

Du Pré nodded.

. . . that water was snow yesterday . . . not so far from ice now . . .

Chappie was down at the tail of the pool. He was able to get up on the bank on his hands and knees. Du Pré took his leg and fresh clothes over to him, and a towel.

Chappie nodded, but his face was very far away. Du Pré went back to the deeper part of the pool. Patchen was swimming down deep, his head and back arching as he moved through the water, snakelike.

He came up for air. He blew water out of his mouth.

"One more dive," he said. His voice was weak.

He went down again. When he had reached the bottom, he turned like an otter and he rippled up to the bank and stuck out his right hand. Du Pré hauled him up. He handed him a towel and his folded clothes. The plastic and metal and cloth arm sat on top of the uniform jacket. Patchen picked it up and attached it with one swift set of movements, slung the harness around his back, and buckled it in front.

Patchen tested the hand once, fiddled with some adjustment, and then he dressed very swiftly.

Chappie had found a log to sit on while he put on his leg and then his pants, a shoe and sock matching the one on his artificial limb.

Chappie stood up, tucked in his shirt; he slid his belt round the loops, set the hook in the hole. His stained old hat was last.

They looked round.

"Benetsee?" said Chappie.

Du Pré shrugged and rolled his eyes.

"Old bastard is out there fucking muskrats," said Du Pré. "Him got to have his joke."

"I did see a muskrat," said Patchen.

A kingfisher flew downstream.

Skraaaaaaaak! it said.

They walked back up to Du Pré's old cruiser.

The cabin door was shut now.

Chappie yawned.

"I am hungry," he said.

"Good," said Du Pré. "Your mother, she will feed you."

Patchen and Chappie got in the backseat. Du Pré fished a flask out from the glove box and he had some whiskey. He rolled a smoke for the road, started the old car, backed and turned.

Benetsee was on the porch of his cabin; the kingfisher was perched on a peg on one of the posts that held up the little rain roof.

He did not look at them.

Du Pré drove away, down the rutted drive to the county road. He sped up on the graded gravel.

It took ten minutes to get to Madelaine's house.

Du Pré stopped and he shut the car off.

Patchen got out and he walked toward his sedan.

He turned just before he got to the car.

"See you tomorrow night in Helena?" he said, looking at Chappie.

"Yes," said Chappie.

Patchen walked back across the street. "Where is Bitter Creek?" he said.

"I don' know," said Chappie, looking at Du Pré.

Du Pré shrugged. "Don't know, Bitter Creek," he said.

"There is much here I do not understand," said Patchen. "Voices and drums close by and far away all at once. And a deep voice, a black voice, saying 'Bitter Creek' and that I hear and you do not. . . ."

"He is talking to you then," said Du Pré.

Chappie grinned at Patchen. "It means that voice wants you to do something that the living can do but the dead cannot—they want your help . . ." he said.

"You can just walk away," said Du Pré. "They will not bother you again."

"No," said Patchen, "I can't walk away. . . ."

"They know that too," said Du Pré. "Why they ask you. . . ."

"But we will help," said Chappie.

Patchen nodded. He nodded again to Du Pré and Chappie and then he walked to his car. He stopped.

"I am honored," he said, and then he got in his car and started the engine.

Du Pré and Chappie went into Madelaine's house.

There were good food smells.

. . . Chappie is cold sober . . . Du Pré thought.

He went back out to his car.

Patchen's sedan was gone.

· Chapter 3 ·

RAIN CLOUDS WERE BILLOWING UP over the top of MacDonald Pass west of Helena, and the mountain wind sliding down smelled of fresh water.

Du Pré and Madelaine and Chappie and Patchen stood in the parking lot near the Fort Harrison building where Chappie had gotten presented with his Navy Cross.

"Thank you," said Patchen. He hugged Chappie.

Du Pré rolled a smoke.

"Like everything else with this bunch," said Patchen, "it's a damn wonder they didn't have the ceremony in the dead of night. . . ."

Chappie held the case in which the medal had come in his right hand, or what was left of it.

"We're out of it," said Patchen. "But they aren't."

"Good bunch," said Chappie.

Patchen turned to Du Pré and Madelaine.

"I have to go back to Virginia for a bit," he said. "A month or so—family matters—and then I would like to come back. . . . That voice I heard in the sweat lodge haunts me, and I think he meant to . . . This is mine to pursue. . . . The other voices are of murdered people . . . aren't they?"

He looked at Du Pré. Du Pré and Chappie finally nodded, both together.

"Got plenty places, you stay," said Du Pré.

"I wouldn't want to impose," said Patchen.

"Christ," said Chappie, "you come, don't stay, you hurt our feelings. You are a friend. . . ."

"Apologies," said Patchen. "I have a plane to catch. I must go, and I thank you again, Gunnery Sergeant Plaquemines."

Chappie snapped to attention and saluted and so did Patchen and then they both laughed.

Patchen got into his rented car, started it, drove away. "So you saved his life," said Madelaine.

"So I am told," said Chappie. "Don't remember much but noise and fire and screaming. . . ."

They got into the big green SUV and Du Pré drove off. They stopped in Fort Benton and ate at a saloon and restaurant. The cheeseburgers weren't bad, but they weren't good either.

They walked down to the Missouri and looked at the keelboat that Hollywood had made for a film about the mountain men.

. . . once this shore was full of steamboats, so many saloons and so many people playing cards . . . they throw the used cards on the boardwalks, it's hard to walk on them, slippery . . . long time gone . . .

"Come on, Du Pré," said Madelaine. "We will be plenty tired we get home. I know you can see, steamboats, Métis in big canoes, Crows camped across the river there, . . ." Du Pré laughed.

They got back in the SUV and Du Pré drove across the bridge over the Missouri and up the long grade of the hills.

The grass was still green but would soon die and turn yellow and pale brown.

Two-lane blacktop, Du Pré got up to only about eighty.

"This thing a piece of crap," he said.

"Fifty-thousand-dollar piece of crap," said Madelaine.

"All the same, you," said Chappie, "I like it. Du Pré is not driving one-twenty like mostly. This thing feels like it will fall over one side or another. Me, I am having a drink now. . . ."

He fished makings from the cooler, poured Madelaine some pink wine, a ditch for Du Pré, one for himself.

"We are all illegal," said Chappie. "Used to be you drive Montana, go from bar to bar, get another road cup. Fucking yuppies. . . ."

Madelaine turned in her seat and she looked at her son. "That Patchen, he is a good man I think," she said.

Chappie nodded. "Hard for him," he said. "He is only out of Annapolis two years, thinks he will make his life, Marines, now he got to do something else."

"Like you," said Madelaine.

"Yeah," said Chappie, "I got more time in, I guess, but that bomb, change our plans. . . ."

"He is what, twenty-four?" said Madelaine.

"'Bout that," said Chappie.

They rode on, silent. The sun was still high, a few days before the solstice of summer. It would be light until ten and dusk until eleven at night.

"Why he coming back?" said Madelaine. Chappie was quiet.

"He don't say," he said. "But when we sweat, you know how it is, Benetsee's lodge there, old voices, dead people maybe, they are singing and he hear a voice, sings 'bitter creek bitter creek bitter creek.' When they sing, it gets cold in the lodge, and that lodge is so hot. . . ."

"I don't know Bitter Creek," said Madelaine. "You know, Du Pré? Why it get cold?"

"They were murdered maybe," said Du Pré.

"Patchen, he is ver' smart," said Chappie. "He show up, we are in Iraq, he looks about fifteen, you know, does the salutes, makes the little speech, asks to speak to me privately, says, at ease, now what the fuck do I do?"

Du Pré and Madelaine laughed. "I tell him keep his head lower than anybody else's, we are all trying that, we are in a fucking shooting gallery and are the rubber ducks. . . ."

Chappie made more drinks. "He is all right," he said. The road was deserted.

"Damn," said Du Pré. "It is like driving a milk truck."

"You want your Crown Victoria, the souped-up engine," said Madelaine.

"It has center of gravity under my butt," said Du Pré. "In this thing, it is over my head about ten feet."

In time they saw the lights of Havre and they picked up the Hi-Line that went due east. It was two-lane, too, and had heavy trucks lumbering along at sixty miles per hour on it. Du Pré passed when he could.

They got back to Toussaint at eleven, and Du Pré pulled up to the saloon, which still had lights on. They got out of the truck and went in. Susan Klein was behind the bar, and three men in worn work clothes were drinking draft beers. The men were spackled with bits of hay.

They had just quit working. This time of the year, when the hay was put up, days were sixteen hours.

The men finished their beers and walked out, nodding to Du Pré and Madelaine and Chappie as they passed by.

Susan looked up and smiled when they sat down. She fixed two stiff ditches and some pink wine and she set the drinks on the bar.

"All done?" she asked Chappie.

"Yes," he said.

"You did good," said Susan, patting his mangled hand. Chappie nodded.

The television behind the bar was showing ambulances

and armed men, burned walls, and tables and chairs thrown over.

The door opened and Bassman and Père Godin came in, bickering about something.

. . . shit, thought Du Pré . . . we play tomorrow night . . .

Bassman and Madelaine hugged. Bassman reeked of marijuana, like always.

Susan drew two beers and she set them up.

Père Godin looked round the empty room.

"We maybe should have left earlier," he said, looking at Bassman reproachfully.

"Old goat," said Bassman. "You got enough children. You got about two hundred children, old goat. Should cut your balls off so I don't have to listen to you bitch—no women you give children to here. . . ." Du Pré and Madelaine and Chappie laughed.

"It is seventy-three children," said Père Godin, "that is all."

"Kim come, too?" said Madelaine, looking at Bassman.

Bassman shook his head. "Come tomorrow," he said. "She had stuff, do, said I maybe behave so she doesn't have, shoot me tomorrow." Madelaine nodded.

"Me, I thought Montana land of fucking opportunity," said Bassman.

"Père Godin," said Madelaine, "you know anything, got 'bitter creek' in it?"

"Sure," said Père Godin, "know a song anyway."

Madelaine nodded.

Père Godin looked mournfully around the room. "Old horny bastard," said Madelaine. "What is the song about?"

"Little girl," said Père Godin. "Little Amalie, her people are being killed, her father throws her over creek bank, she hide, night come, she go on, find a few Métis, they go to Canada. . . ."

Du Pré turned on his stool. "Where you get that song? I never hear it," he said.

Père Godin grinned. "She sing it for me," he said.

"Why do I know before you say it has something to do with your dick," said Madelaine. "You, old goat."

"I hear it one time, thirty, forty years ago," said Père Godin.

"Three dozen children ago," said Madelaine.

"So," said Père Godin, "I am in love this woman . . . Suzette, I think, up in Canada, Manitoba, she take me to meet her grandmother Amalie. . . ."

Du Pré looked hard at him.

"Amalie she is not so old, she sing this song, 'bout the people running from the soldiers, think they are safe, stop rest, no fires, but the soldiers find them, the morning, start shooting, little Amalie she is thrown over the bank, hides, listens to her people being killed, gets away, eats berries, eats grubs she finds in a log, she smells smoke, finds people. . . ."

Du Pré stood up. "Where is this Amalie?" he said.

"Manitoba," said Père Godin. "She is still alive, I see Suzette maybe six months ago, ask how is our son. . . ."

. . . Jesus Christ . . .

"How old is this woman now, this Amalie?" said Du Pré.

"Amalie is maybe seventy, Suzette has my son," said Père Godin.

Madelaine looked at Du Pré.

"1910," he said.

· Chapter 4 ·

"*NON*," SAID PÈRE GODIN. "*NON non non*. After Suzette has my son she marries this fellow, somebody, they have kids, but this fellow say, he ever sees that Godin . . ."

"He cut your balls off," said Madelaine.

"Yes," said Père Godin, "I don't meet him ever, still have my balls, but I am told he is very large, has very bad temper."

"Père Godin," said Madelaine, "you got lots of husbands want to cut your balls off, dozens of them. Why are you so worried about one of them?"

"I only got this one pair, balls," said Père Godin, "not enough to go round, me and them, you see. . . ."

"This is important," said Du Pré.

"Excuse me," said Susan Klein, "but I don't understand why. . . ."

Du Pré looked at her. "That Black Jack Pershing, him sent here 1910, round up the Métis are living in camps, don't got cabins, little piece of land, he does, puts them in boxcars, it is January, sends them to North Dakota, many old people, children, they die. Métis then don't got Canadian, American citizenship. No one knows about this. . . ." said Du Pré.

"Oh, God," said Susan Klein, "I certainly never knew. . . ."

"But this Bitter Creek," said Du Pré, "it means that some Métis got away, were hunted down and killed. . . ."

"But in 1910?" said Susan. "I knew about the slaughters in the nineteenth century. . . ."

"Been plenty since then," said Du Pré. "See them on the evening news."

"God," said Susan.

"So we are finding this Amalie," said Du Pré, looking at Père Godin.

"It is too dangerous, me," said Père Godin.

"I cut your goddamned balls off," said Madelaine.

"Shit," said Père Godin. "Why am I born?"

"I need a toke," said Bassman. He walked out and then they heard his van start.

Père Godin ran to the front door. "Dirty bastard!" he screamed. "Piece of shit leaves me here to die!"

Du Pré and Madelaine and Chappie and Susan laughed.

Père Godin slumped. He walked wearily back to the bar. "How 'bout I tell you all I know of her, you leave me alone then," he said. He did not look hopeful.

"You find Amalie," said Du Pré, "that is all you must do."

Père Godin nodded. "See what I can do," he said.

Chappie came off the stool very quickly and he grabbed the old man by the shoulders and he lifted him up so they could see eye to eye.

"You do whatever you got to," he said. "Me, I will decide when it is enough. Now maybe I take you, Benetsee's, sweat, you listen the voices, your people. . . ."

"*Non*," said Père Godin. "Lot of women are mad at me, are dead, I don't want to hear them, you know. . . ."

"We are going now," said Chappie. He put his good left hand on the back of Père Godin's neck and marched him out the door.

"Well," said Susan Klein, "for once Chappie didn't finish his drink."

"I am going," said Du Pré. "It is hard, Chappie, hold on to his neck and steer the car. . . ."

He kissed Madelaine and he went out. He got into his cruiser and he started it and he drove back toward Chappie's trailer; his headlamps caught the two of them marching toward Chappie's pickup.

Du Pré slowed. Chappie opened the rear door and he flung Père Godin in and he climbed in, too.

"Thing is," he said, "you got to keep telling me things I like to hear so I don't break your neck. . . ."

"Jesus," said Père Godin. "It is just a song, damn me for saying I know it. . . ."

"No," said Chappie, "it is not just a song. . . ."

Du Pré turned round and he drove off toward Benetsee's, turned on the rutted track, parked by the cabin. There was a light on inside.

The door opened and the old man stood there, small in his clothes, a red kerchief round his head.

"It is Du Pré," he said, "got friends, come see me late at night. Must be important."

"We want to sweat," said Chappie.

"*Non*," said Benetsee, "got old pecker there, bring him here." Chappie got out, with his hand still on Père Godin's neck.

Chappie set Père Godin down on the porch in front of Benetsee. "My old friend," said Benetsee, "we walk, see the creek, have some wine . . ."

Du Pré went to the cruiser and he got a half-gallon jug out of the trunk and he unscrewed the cap and set it back and he handed the jug to Benetsee.

The two old men walked down the hill toward the creek. Du Pré sat on the steps and Chappie, taller, on the porch. Du Pré rolled a smoke and gave it to Chappie and he rolled one for himself and they smoked and looked up at the stars.

Thin veils of cloud sat high and still, a quarter moon hung low in the east.

"I wonder what happened," said Chappie. "What happened at Bitter Creek?"

"People were killed, buried there," said Du Pré.

"Lot of blood on this land," said Chappie.

"Blood everywhere," said Du Pré.

"Why the roundup, the Métis?" said Chappie.

"Whites want something they had," said Du Pré. "Or maybe the whites wanted to blame the Métis for something they did. . . ."

"Old woman must be a hundred," said Chappie.

"Me," said Du Pré, "I have this great-great-great-aunt up in Canada, she live to be one hundred twenty-one. . . ."

"I don't want, live that long," said Chappie.

There was sudden laughter from the old men down by the creek. "I like Père Godin," said Chappie. "He don't want to be a hero."

"*Non*," said Du Pré. "Him just want, fuck every woman on earth."

"Him ver' ambitious," said Chappie, "very commendable. . . ."

"Him got a pretty good start," said Du Pré.

"So," said Chappie, "I guess we got to find that Bitter Creek."

"Let them sleep, we do," said Du Pré. "They sing at us now until they can sleep, cross over, you know. . . ."

"I don' know why me," said Chappie.

Du Pré laughed. He went to the cruiser and he got a bottle from under the seat and he broke the seal. He had some whiskey and he gave the bottle to Chappie.

"That old Benetsee, him," said Du Pré, "I go along, he does not bother me until he does. Once him start, it don't stop. . . ."

"I don't see him so much I am growing up here," said Chappie. "I know who he is but see him maybe twice."

"You were lucky, a time," said Du Pré.

"Who is he?" said Chappie. "Him Métis?"

Du Pré shrugged. "Him old when Catfoot is a boy. . . ."

"Catfoot," said Chappie, "I remember him cursing one time, his drag line break. We were fishing nearby. Cussed pret' good. Taught me new words. . . ."

Du Pré nodded.

There was more laughter.

"They are having a good time, them," said Chappie. "I thought maybe we sweat, Bitter Creek people sing to Père Godin. . . ."

"It is west of here I think," said Du Pré, "that is where we will look."

"Why?" said Chappie.

"Most the Métis they are near Helena or up, Mussellshell country, maybe Judith Basin. . . ."

"This is, hundred years ago maybe," said Chappie.

"Long time to wait," said Du Pré, "in the dark."

"I don't know I know things," said Chappie. "Maybe they are in your blood. . . ."

"Yes," said Du Pré.

"So what we do?" said Chappie.

"Find Amalie," said Du Pré. "See if she remembers anything, where they left from, where they were, how long they were running. . . ."

"Find Amalie," said Chappie. "You think Père Godin help?"

Du Pré nodded.

More laughter from the two old men down by the creek.

"I go with you, we get to Canada," said Chappie.

Du Pré nodded.

"Madelaine says you always find stories," said Chappie. "You look for them?"

"It is like this," said Du Pré. "I see a little and want to know more. . . . But you stay here, I must go alone. . . ."

"You were not in the lodge," said Chappie.

Du Pré shook his head. "Heard many voices singing," he said. "But I think more than one person is too much for Amalie. . . ."

There was a popping sound from behind the cabin, like faint gunfire, and then a shriek of pure terror. Silence.

Du Pré put the top back on the whiskey. "We go now," he said.

· Chapter 5 ·

"THAT GODDAMNED GUINEA PRICK," said Booger Tom. The old cowboy's long white mustache twitched with rage.

Du Pré looked at him.

"Water buffalo," said Booger Tom. "Bart has bought some water buffalo and he is sending them here. I guess them danged yuppies like eatin' water buffaloes along with their mow-ray eels and roots and bark. You ever seen a water buffalo?"

Du Pré nodded.

"One dozen water buffalo arrivin' from Australia," said Booger Tom. "I was losin' lots of money for him with cattle and horses, which is what he likes the most . . . for losin' money . . ."

Du Pré said nothing. He rolled a smoke.

Booger Tom waved a computer-printed picture of a water buffalo. "Christ," said the old cowboy.

They were standing by the double gate at the bottom of the big pasture. A stock hauler appeared on the horizon, an eighteen-wheeler with a double-deck aluminum trailer.

"I never thought I'd see the damned day . . ." said Booger

Tom. "Hell, we could raise llamas. Or . . . what are them danged birds everybody's so hot on?"

"Emus," said Du Pré.

"These little bastards give it up and get to knowin' they are all gonna die one day, maybe the whole country ain't gonna be terrified a . . . satch-oor-ated fat. . . ." said Booger Tom.

"You know any place called Bitter Creek?" said Du Pré.

"Not offhand," said Booger Tom. "I mean, further south, but we don't got alkali here, we got caliche. . . ."

"There is bad water," said Du Pré.

"The fartwater you get near the Park," said Booger Tom, "stinks of sulfur and rotten eggs, but I don't know no Bitter Creek here. Know some in Arizona, New Mexico . . ."

The stock hauler crested the nearest hill.

"Water buffalo," said Booger Tom. "Bart buys these things just to piss me off. Place he got 'em from in Australia sent me about half a ream of helpful hints over the computer. . . ."

Du Pré nodded.

"Might not be the water," said Booger Tom. "Could be somethin' that happened there, or it could be Bateau Creek, place got a lot of good boatmakin' trees. . . ."

"The woman wrote the song is French," said Du Pré.

"Frenchy French or Prairie French like you?" said Booger Tom.

The stock hauler ground up the long drive and stopped. Booger Tom opened the gate and the driver took his rig on through. Booger Tom closed the gate.

Du Pré ruffled through the papers on the clipboard.

"Not much call for you do that anymore," said Booger Tom.

Du Pré shook his head.

. . . just big ranches here moving big shipments. None of the little people left . . . like everything else . . .

They went through the gate and up to the truck. The driver set the aluminum ramps under the swinging rear doors.

"Go ahead," said Booger Tom. "Goddanged water buffalo."

"Tell ya one thing," said the driver. "Easiest stock I ever hauled. They got off the airplane and went right on the truck, didn't have to use the prod or nothing. They seem smarter than cattle. . . ."

The driver swung the doors open and a water buffalo peered out at them. The buffalo moved to the ramp, walked down it, and came up to Booger Tom. They stood looking at the old cowboy.

"Whaaah!" yelled Booger Tom.

Other water buffalo came down the ramp and they spread out in a circle around Du Pré and Booger Tom and the driver.

The driver started stowing the ramps. The buffalo moved out of his way. He shut the doors, checked to see that everything was secure, got in the cab, and drove back to the main gate. He got down and opened the gate and drove through and then he got out and closed it.

Du Pré walked over to the fence, and he ducked through it, handing the driver the receipt.

"Like I said," said the driver, "they are easy to handle."

"Back off, ya sons of bitches!" yelled Booger Tom.

The water buffalo looked at him for a moment, shrugged, and went to nibbling grass.

The old cowboy strode down to the gate. Du Pré swung it open for him and then closed it and dropped the pin in the brackets.

Du Pré handed Booger Tom his receipt. He put the clipboard in the leather case and he slung the strap over his shoulder.

"I would admire a cup of coffee," said Booger Tom. "You want one?"

"Sure," said Du Pré. They went to the old man's cabin, a large one, and Booger Tom set water to heat. He dipped ground coffee out of a rusty Arbuckle's coffee can.

"Ain't made Arbuckle's for years," he said. "I miss it, like I miss old Nate's biscuits. Best camp cookie ever." Du Pré nodded.

The water boiled and Booger Tom poured it through the coffee and he waited while the last drops drained into the pot. He filled two cups and he set one in front of Du Pré.

Something heavy stepped on the front porch of the cabin. "Bart?" said Booger Tom. He went to the door and he threw it open. A water buffalo stood there, looking amiably at him. "You leave the danged gate open?" said Booger Tom.

"*Non*," said Du Pré.

"Jesus," said Booger Tom.

The water buffalo backed off the porch. He lifted his right front hoof and he tapped it three times on a stone that edged the flower bed.

"Tom!" yelled Pidgeon, Bart's lovely wife. "You have a fax!" Du Pré went out the door.

Pidgeon was grinning. She waved a sheet of fax paper. Booger Tom waited until she got to him. He reached out for the paper.

"You done read it already," he said.

"Yup," said Pidgeon. She walked over to the water buffalo. Booger Tom went in the house and found his spectacles.

"Hello, Eustace," Pidgeon said. She scratched a large ear.

The water buffalo nodded at the sound of his name. "When that dumb guinea yer married to comes back, I think I will kill him," said Booger Tom.

"Nah," said Pidgeon, "I'd cry and you can't stand to see a woman cry."

"She don't play fair," said Booger Tom, looking mournfully at Du Pré. Booger Tom glared at the sheet of paper. "'By now you will have met Eustace,'" he read, "'a good bloke. If he taps three times on the ground, he wants his beer, two gallons, warm.'"

Du Pré laughed. "I got to go," he said. "We are playing tonight."

Pidgeon looked at Du Pré.

"A Lieutenant Patchen called and asked me to tell you he is looking hard at army records," said Pidgeon, "and he will be back. . . ."

"'Eustace can open any gate not secured with a padlock,'" yelled Booger Tom. "I am gonna kill him."

Du Pré walked to his old cruiser and got in. Turning the vehicle around, he drove down to the county road. He stopped at the snowplow turnaround that sat on a bluff, where he could see clear to the line of hills above the Missouri River.

. . . Bitter Creek . . . Bateau Creek . . . or it could be something like Bittner Creek, somebody's name . . . or it could be something else . . .

The land rolled away for seventy-five miles, purple and ocher in the distance.

Light glinted on car glass on the highway far below.

. . . finding Amalie . . . we go and do that . . .

Du Pré got out and he sat on the hood. The sky was cloudy and the day cool, and it would rain toward evening. A vulture flapped up from the brush below, head bright red and slick with rotten grease from a deer carcass.

. . . the soldiers come here, round up the Métis, it is the hard part of the winter . . . who got them to do that? . . . why? . . . there are people buried somewhere out there . . . little Amalie . . .

He looked over to his right and saw a good-sized rattlesnake wind out from some stones. The snake was shedding and had ragged strips of old skin hanging here and there from its body. Du Pré watched.

The snake rasped against the rocks. The new skin looked

bright, browns and grays and blacks. Du Pré looked out on the land.

. . . it is very big and I am not so big . . .

He got back in the cruiser and he drove on.

A huge badger waddled across the road, glanced once at Du Pré's car, dodged into the grass at the roadside.

. . . lots of secrets . . .

The air was full of the scent of new-mown grass. A rancher on a tractor pulling a bailer waved and Du Pré waved back.

. . . lots of blood . . . land is full of it . . .

Du Pré got to the Toussaint Saloon just as Bassman and Père Godin were trundling the electronics in.

"You know you got to have a passport to go, Canada, now?" said Père Godin.

Du Pré nodded.

"Yes," he said, "it has been that way for a while now."

"Used to be we didn't know where the Medicine Line was," said Père Godin.

"Yes," said Du Pré, "but that is where Amalie's people were running to. . . ."

· Chapter 6 ·

DU PRÉ YAWNED as he passed the welcome sign.

The little Manitoba town was the usual welter of small houses, a couple of streets of slightly larger ones, and some grain silos near the rails.

He stopped at a gas station, filled his cruiser's tank, and got directions from a cheerful young woman.

The little house was set back from the street, some spruces growing close.

Du Pré looked at his watch. Two thirty. He was half an hour early.

The door opened and a heavy woman, white haired, wearing a loose housedress, came out and waved at Du Pré. He got out and walked up the little gravel path to the door. "I am Suzette," she said. "Old bastard Godin, he was too cowardly to come, I bet."

"He think your husband kill him," said Du Pré.

"My husband," said Suzette, "been dead fifteen years. So you are Du Pré, the fiddler."

Du Pré nodded. There was fiddle music playing in the house. One of Du Pré's records, a fairly old one.

"You drive a long way, see Amalie," said Suzette. "We go

to her now, you come back and eat, you wish. . . ." Suzette shut the door behind her. An orange cat came out of the shrubbery, carrying a young robin in its mouth.

Suzette moved surprisingly fast for a woman so bulky. Du Pré opened the car door for her and she slipped in neatly. He got in and started the engine.

"Next town, it is only seven miles," said Suzette. She pointed the way. The land was flat; some low hills rolled to the north.

They soon came to another little town, and Suzette pointed to the turns and they pulled up in front of a long gray building, single story, with ST. LUKE'S HOME set in block letters on a white sign on the lawn. "Suzette," said the woman at the front desk, "so you are here and this is that Du Pré."

"Yes," said Suzette. "But he is very shy. So we go and talk to Amalie . . ."

"She was awake not long ago," said the woman. "But you know she sometimes plays possum, she is awake but she won't let you know that."

"I stab her with a pin," said Suzette, "that works good." They both laughed.

Suzette led Du Pré down the hallway, to a door that stood half open. She went in and then she motioned for Du Pré to come. He followed.

Amalie was sitting in a chair by the window, the sun on her face. She was very old, her skin so wrinkled that her black eyes were almost hidden by old flesh. But the eyes were clear and there was intelligence in them.

"Suzette brings you Du Pré, Granmaman," said Suzette. "He is a ver' famous fiddler. . . ."

Amalie looked at her granddaughter and at Du Pré. "He comes to talk to you about your song, 'Bitter Creek,'" said Suzette.

The old woman flinched as though she had been slapped. "Aieee," she wailed.

Du Pré pulled up a chair, close, and he reached for her hands, writhing in her lap. "Those people talk to me," he said. "They want me, find them, help them sleep, been wandering long time, long time gone. . . ."

Amalie spoke, her voice a whisper, reedy, ancient. "What . . . you . . . want . . . to . . . know?" she said.

"I want to know what happened," said Du Pré, "from the beginning, from when you left to go to Canada. . . ."

Du Pré put a small tape recorder down on the little table by the window.

"For many years I forgot about it," said Amalie, "but now I think about it, I was so young then and I am so very old now. . . ." She breathed deeply.

"Suzette," she whispered, "could I have some tea, little sugar?"

Suzette bustled off.

". . . The day before we left it snowed," said Amalie. "It was very cold, and Papa came and told Maman we had to go, that there were soldiers after the Métis, we were not where most of them were so maybe we could get away. We were living in a lodge. . . ."

Du Pré nodded.

Amalie put her hand to her face and rubbed her eyes. "I helped, I was seven, I think, and we packed things and Papa put them in our cart, he had a gray horse to pull it and two more to ride. The lodge was big so Papa said we could not take it. We had blankets and some old robes, he wanted to go then, and we left while it was still dark. . . ."

Suzette brought the tea.

Du Pré waited while she sipped a little.

"Do you remember where you were?" he said.

Amalie shook her head. "I think there was a railroad near," she said. "I remember the trains, how they sounded. We began to travel, other people joined us, we went away from roads and rails, we went through country that was very beautiful and empty. . . ."

"Were there trees?" said Du Pré. "What kind of trees?"

Amalie thought. "First night we camped in cottonwoods. It was very cold. My brother coughed badly. . . ."

Amalie sipped tea.

"When we went on, I remember the land was pale colors, a little snow, we went along not very fast, the carts were noisy, they were worse if you pulled them fast . . . I got to ride . . . my brother lay beside me in the blanket and he coughed . . .

"We were very hungry and one of the men killed a cow, I remember the cow, brown, red-brown, and white, we roasted the meat and it tasted very good, we had full bellies that night, we had more meat in the morning and we went on. . . ."

Amalie sipped tea.

"It was so long ago . . . We went past a beautiful butte, I remember, pale red and yellow and white and gray, it was almost perfect, not broken on the sides like they usually are. . . . We camped and then we crossed a big river on a raft, one of the men rode across it and took a rope with him and the men pulled the raft back and forth. It was cold and the river splashed on me, it burned it was so cold. . . ."

Amalie sipped tea.

"That was the Missouri," said Du Pré.

"I think so," said Amalie. "It was wide and deep, the man who rode his horse across with the rope lost his hat and I watched it go down the river, there was not time to chase the hat. He kept rubbing his ears from the cold, I remember that. . . ." Amalie stared at her lap.

"We ate another cow the next day and we went on, we had the meat with us, we stopped near a creek. . . ."

Du Pré bent close. "Lots of willows?" he said.

"Yes," she said. "Cut into the land, too, we were camped down on a flat place. Next morning I was just up, rubbing my eyes, when there were sounds of horses, lots of horses, and then . . ."

Amalie looked at Du Pré.

"Papa grabbed me and threw me down into the willows, told me to hide, and then he . . . he jerked and fell and a man on a horse rode over him. . . ."

Du Pré waited.

"I dug into the willows, found a mat of dead ones the stream had piled under the living willows, I crawled as far into that as I could, put my hands over my ears but there were screams. . . ."

Du Pré waited.

"I saw two men on horses with long knives, the sabers, they rode down to the creek and looked right at me but they didn't see me. . . ."

"Soldiers?" said Du Pré.

Amalie nodded.

"The soldiers were black men," she said.

She sipped tea.

"Then it was quiet, I heard two men arguing, they were shouting," she said.

"What about?" said Du Pré.

"I could not speak English then," she said. "I remember one word, *cannon,* it might be a name. . . ."

She stopped, rubbed her eyes,

"I went to where the camp was and they were all dead and the men on the horses were gone. I found a little food, I looked back the way that we had come and I went the other way. . . . A few hours later I was walking across a flat place, I saw two horsemen, I ran, they came after and they caught me. . . ."

"Métis?" said Du Pré.

"No," said Amalie, "they were whites. They took me to a

house and a woman fed me, then they put me in a wagon and took me to Métis, over the border, and I stayed there. . . ."

"Where did you hear Bitter Creek?" said Du Pré.

"One of the men who caught me said Bitter Creek, that all those who did that would rot in hell. . . ." said Amalie.

"He called it Bitter Creek?" said Du Pré.

Amalie nodded.

"I didn't know where I was," she said.

· Chapter 7 ·

DU PRÉ AND SUZETTE STOOD OUTSIDE the front door of the old folks' home. Du Pré rolled a smoke, glanced at Suzette, who was looking at it hungrily. He lit it and gave it to her, made another for himself. "Good tobacco," said Suzette. "How is that old bastard Godin?"

"Old bastard," said Du Pré. "Plays pret' good squeezebox though."

"Him, do lot damage," said Suzette. "I meet couple other women, they say they got a kid of his, he has over a hundred. . . ."

"Two," said Du Pré. "Over two hundred."

"Over two hundred?" said Suzette. "I don' feel so bad then. He is like the weather or rivers, just is, no stopping. . . ."

. . . old bastard got something . . . Du Pré thought . . . how old is this Amalie, born 1903, must be hundred two, older even . . .

"You are her granddaughter?" said Du Pré.

"Yes," said Suzette, "Amalie have my mother she is fifty almost, my mother is some surprise you bet. . . ."

"She ever talk, you, about Bitter Creek?" said Du Pré.

"Not much," said Suzette. "She hear a fiddle sometime, she look away, eyes wet. Her papa plays the fiddle. . . ."

Du Pré nodded.

"She was ver' young," said Suzette. "Us Métis, got a lot of stories like that you know. . . ."

Du Pré nodded. "I find those people, bring them home."

"Tell Amalie that," said Suzette. "She is old, might die. . . ."

Du Pré nodded. "I go talk to her more."

"Give me another smoke maybe," said Suzette. "I let you alone a time." Du Pré rolled two for her, handed them over, fished a book of matches out of his jacket. It was a cold day, clouds in the west, heavy and black with rain.

Du Pré walked back down the hallway, through the door of Amalie's room. The old woman was awake, looking out the window and very far away. Du Pré sat down. "Wheelchair in that closet there," said Amalie. "I want to go outside."

Du Pré went to the closet, found the folding wheelchair, a sturdy one, steel and nylon. Amalie fished around in the drawer in the little table by the window, and she took out a small purse and a rosary. "Shawl on the hanger," she said.

Du Pré found the shawl. The old woman had very few clothes. Amalie looked round the room, her face set. Du Pré unfolded the wheelchair.

The old woman stood up, turned, sat down. She put her feet on the little platforms. She nodded to Du Pré. He bent over, his ear next to her lips. "I go with you, show you where," she said. "I am here long enough. I dream, my brother, he is coughing in the dark, I go and find him, give him rest you see. . . ."

Du Pré drew in his breath.

"What we do, you are taking me, a ride, you drop Suzette off. She talks too much. Give her a little money, she will go and play cards. . . ." Du Pré laughed. Métis gamble, all of them.

"I tell these people I be back day after tomorrow, Suzette don't got to know I said that. Little case in the bathroom, you get that." Du Pré found it. It had medicines and a comb and brush. "I go back to acting little tired, simple now," said Amalie. "That Suzette, talk too much. . . ."

Du Pré wheeled Amalie down the hall to the front desk. "Amalie!" said the woman. "You are leaving us?"

"*Non*," said the old woman, "I go for today, tomorrow, be back day after. . . ."

"Where will you be?" said the woman, tapping on her computer.

"Suzette's, she is my granddaughter," said Amalie.

"Just saw her . . . so . . . OK," said the woman. "We have all the information. Do you have your medications?"

Du Pré put the little case on the desk. The woman looked at them and the computer screen. "Have a good time!" she said.

Du Pré wheeled Amalie out the door. Suzette gave a start. "This nice man take us for a ride," said Amalie.

"OK," said Suzette, looking worried.

"You don't have to go," said Amalie. "I give you this twenty dollars you go and play some, your friends. . . ."

Suzette's face changed. It merely looked greedy. Amalie handed her a neatly folded bill and Suzette put it in her pocket.

Du Pré put Amalie in the front seat and the wheelchair in the trunk of the car. Suzette got in the backseat.

"Tell you what," said Amalie. "We drop you off, you want to go where?"

Suzette directed Du Pré to a café in the center of town. She got out in a hurry.

"Him take me back," said Amalie. "You not worry."

Suzette kissed her grandmother on her cheek.

Then she almost ran into the café.

"Stupid woman," said Amalie. "OK, Du Pré."

Du Pré laughed silently.

"Me, I will have trouble getting us over the border," he said.

"Métis having trouble getting over the border," said Amalie. "You are some sorry Métis you want me, believe that."

"It is different now," said Du Pré. "They want, passports."

"I want, smoke," said Amalie.

"Christ," said Du Pré.

An hour later he stopped at a self-serve station that was very large, and he parked out as far away from the cashier as he could.

Amalie kept down.

Du Pré got food from a fish and chips place a hundred miles farther on.

When they were halfway across Saskatchewan, Du Pré pulled over and he got out some whiskey he had bought the day before from a Canadian government outlet.

"You want, some of this?" he said.

"Sip," said Amalie.

Du Pré found her a paper cup. She put her nose in the cup and she drew a deep breath.

"1920s, we smuggle this over the border, my husband, he take horses, each horse carry eight cases booze," said Amalie.

"Yah," said Du Pré.

Du Pré came to the crossroads he had been looking for and turned south. Fifty miles on he turned west again on a two-lane blacktop, so narrow it had no place to pull off if you had a flat.

Du Pré crept across the border with the lights off, moving through a town that had only one light on and no police or border patrol cars waiting.

"Same way you come into Canada?" said Amalie.

"Yah," said Du Pré.

He waited until he was a hundred yards past the clutch of buildings before turning on his lights and speeding up.

They got to Toussaint at eight in the morning, and Du Pré pulled up to Madelaine's house.

He went round to the passenger door and opened it for Amalie. She stood up straight. She walked easily.

"You don't want the wheelchair?" said Du Pré.

"Sell it," said Amalie. "Ver' expensive them."

Madelaine was in the backyard digging in her flower beds. "Du Pré," she said, looking up. She had a smear of earth on one cheek.

"I have brought her," said Du Pré.

Madelaine got up swiftly. "Amalie?" she said.

Du Pré nodded.

Madelaine almost ran to the back steps; she brushed past Du Pré. Du Pré laughed, stepped down, went to the picnic table, had a smoke. He rubbed the back of his neck.

. . . not much sleep, two days . . .

He could hear the rapid rattle of Coyote French in the kitchen. "You are back," said Chappie, who had come on the path that went through the pasture and across the little creek.

"Yes," said Du Pré.

"You find the old woman?" said Chappie.

Du Pré nodded.

"Me, I would have liked to see her, hear her," said Chappie. Du Pré pointed to the back door of Madelaine's house.

"Jesus," said Chappie, "you bring her here?"

"Yes," said Du Pré.

Chappie sat down on the bench beside Du Pré. "She is . . . all right?" said Chappie.

"She is ver' fine," said Du Pré.

"My God," said Chappie.

A kingfisher flew down the creek. *Skraaaaak!* it said.

· Chapter 8 ·

DU PRÉ SHUT THE DOOR of the old cruiser and he went round to the driver's side and he got in.

Amalie sat in the passenger seat; she could barely see over the dashboard.

"We go, your daughter's?" she said.

"Him got two," said Madelaine from the rear seat. "Jacqueline has twelve kids, Maria don't got none yet, she is teaching in England."

"Twelve kids," said Amalie. "I have five, none of them worth much, I don't pick ver' good men. . . ."

She looked at Du Pré.

"Not my idea," said Madelaine.

The two women laughed.

"Ver' funny," said Du Pré.

He drove out to the house he had been born in that now held Raymond and Jacqueline and their children, all but Pallas, who was in school in the East.

Du Pré parked near the front door. The house was set back from the road, a simple frame house painted white with blue shutters and a long addition in the back for the children's rooms.

Du Pré opened both doors for the women, helped Amalie

out. She was still spry, and she went up the steps to Jacqueline who held out both of her hands.

Eleven of her kids were standing in the living room, hands clasped.

Jacqueline escorted Amalie to the dining room and sat her on a tall chair so she could eat easily from the table. The children filed in and sat.

"Raymond is working in Wyoming," she said. "Building towers for radios. . . ."

Amalie nodded.

"You want some wine, Granmaman?" said Jacqueline.

Amalie nodded.

She looked at the children.

"Ver' frightening," said Du Pré. "I will run now."

Everyone laughed.

"How old are you?" said Hervé, who was eight.

"Hundred and two," said Amalie, "and mean."

Madelaine and Jacqueline and Lourdes and Du Pré started carrying roasts of beef and elk, mounds of new potatoes, vegetables, pitchers of water and tea from the kitchen.

Jaqueline poured wine for Amalie and Madelaine.

"Don't worry," said Hervé when his mother shook her head at him, "we are making our own. . . ."

"Good stuff on the Internet," said Lourdes, "make wine out of just about anything."

"Dandelions," said Amalie, "make good wine from white grapes and dandelions, pineapple juice and dandelions work good too. . . ."

They talked and they ate, and then the children took the dirty dishes off and began to wash them.

Hervé came back with a bottle of pale pink liquid. He opened the screwtop of the spring water bottle, and he gravely poured Amalie four fingers in her glass. She sipped it. Hervé waited.

"You make this yourself?" she said.

Hervé nodded.

"Ver' good," said Amalie.

"Where you are doing this?" said Jacqueline, tapping her fingernails on the table.

"Snitches die horrible deaths," said a loud voice from the kitchen. "They are cut up and fed to dogs and skunks," said another.

"I cannot say," said Hervé. "You understand, Mama?"

"Uh-huh," said Jacqueline. Hervé scampered off with his jug of homemade wine. Amalie looked at Jacqueline. She passed her the glass. Jacqueline sipped it. "Wild plums," she said. "It is good."

"You will stay with us," said Lourdes. "We have your room ready."

"Ver' nice," said Amalie, "but I don't want, bother you."

Lourdes drew up a chair. She pulled close to Amalie. "We cry you don't stay," she said. "You come and see your room now. We work hard for you."

"They did," said Jacqueline. "They never know their grandmamas, were dead before they are born. . . ."

"I don' know," said Amalie. "There are so many of you, I never learn all your names."

"It is all right," said Lourdes. "Him, Du Pré, Grandpapa, he don't know all of them either. Had plenty of time, practice, too." They all laughed. "Come, we show you," said Lourdes. She led Amalie away.

"This is part," said Du Pré, "where I run, you know." He got up.

"You are going Benetsee?" said Madelaine.

Du Pré nodded. He went out to his cruiser and he got Amalie's little case and her shawl and he brought them back. Jacqueline took them. "We got plenty clothes," she said. "Anyway, we go and buy her whatever she needs. . . ."

Du Pré nodded.

He drove back to Toussaint and he went into the saloon. Susan Klein was there and her husband, Benny, the sheriff.

"Doo Pray," said Benny, "you are a wanted man."

Du Pré looked at him.

Benny pulled a sheet of paper from his pocket. "Some old woman named Amalie Montagne, last seen in your company," said Benny.

"Shit," said Du Pré.

"Some dinky town in Manitoba. I think what happened is somebody lied, you know, sayin' you kidnapped her. . . ."

Du Pré nodded.

"So I was wonderin' just what to do about it," said Benny.

Du Pré thought a moment. "Say you arrested me, beat me, rubber hoses, no sign of Amalie Montagne . . ." said Du Pré.

"It's true I ain't seen no sign of Amalie Montagne," said Benny. "Who is she?"

Du Pré slid up on a stool. Susan made him a ditch. "Old woman," he said. "In 1910 she is with her people, they are running to Canada, time Pershing round up the Métis who are poor, ship them boxcars to North Dakota, January, everybody but her is killed. . . ."

Benny looked sick. "Who done that?" he said.

"Don't know yet," said Du Pré.

"Where?" said Benny.

"Don't know yet," said Du Pré.

"Why were they killed?" said Benny.

Du Pré sighed. "Don't know. Old woman says she ate beef, they were hungry, killed couple cows. . . ." he said.

"Mother of God," said Benny. "In 1910?"

Du Pré nodded.

"How many?" said Benny.

"Thirty, few more," said Du Pré.

Susan Klein looked at Du Pré and at her husband.

"Where is she?" said Susan.

"Jacqueline's," said Du Pré. "Kids want her, for granmaman."

"OK," said Benny, "I'll tell them folks there ain't no sign of her and far as I know you ain't been in Canada. . . ."

"But you were," said Susan, "they have records at the border crossings. They will have taken down your license plate."

"Not there," said Du Pré.

"Good," said Benny. "Then how'd they know it? They got it on this here fax dingus."

"Her granddaughter, maybe the old folks' home . . ." said Du Pré.

"But you didn't cross where they seen you?" said Benny.

Du Pré shook his head.

"Homeland Security," said Benny.

"Not so good, them," said Du Pré.

"What happens when they find out she's here?" said Benny.

Du Pré shrugged.

"Hasn't happened yet, Benny," said Susan Klein.

"You gonna find out who murdered those people?" said Benny.

Du Pré nodded.

"Amalie ain't here then till we got to admit it," said Benny.

Du Pré nodded.

"Those murderers are all dead," said Benny. "Got to be."

Du Pré finished his ditchwater highball.

"She is not," he said.

"We oughta take that car of yours back over the border and torch the sucker, tell them it was stolen," said Benny.

Du Pré looked at him. Benny looked at Susan Klein.

"Benny," said Susan, "I married you because you are so smart. . . ."

"Oh, Christ," said Benny, "fuck me runnin'. . . ."

"After you get back," said Susan. "And that's a promise. . . ."

· Chapter 9 ·

DU PRÉ STOOD OUTSIDE the private-flight terminal in Billings. The little jet carrying Bart and Pidgeon and Pallas appeared, coming so swiftly out of the clouds it seemed to be going far too fast to set down. But it did, slowing to a stop two hundred feet away.

Pallas was first down the steps, then Pidgeon, and finally Bart, carrying a couple of heavy suitcases. He set them down on the asphalt and pulled handles out of scabbards and trundled them over to the big green SUV.

"Where's your old cruiser?" said Pidgeon.

"Stolen," said Du Pré.

"Somebody stole that wretched thing?" said Pidgeon. "Good thing for you Bart loves you and has another."

"Two more," said Bart.

"Couldn't find the keys," said Du Pré.

Pallas ran to her grandfather and threw her arms around him. They hugged for a long time. "I am here for two months," she said.

"Give me those," said Pidgeon. "There's more. . . ." Bart set the rolling suitcases on end, and he and Du Pré went back to the little jet. Bart went up the steps and in and he began to hand out sacks, shopping bags, and two more rolling cases, more shopping bags with thick cloth handles and the names of expensive stores on them.

Du Pré sniffed at one sack.

"Sopresatta," said Bart. "Real hard salami. What you get in the stores out here isn't fit for bait for trash fish. . . ."

Du Pré laughed.

They carried the rest of the stuff to the SUV. Pallas and Pidgeon each had soft drinks from the cooler Du Pré had brought.

"Whew," said Bart.

"She spend a lot of money?" said Du Pré.

"Pidgeon doesn't spend much," said Bart. "I try to get her to, but she just won't. . . ."

Bart got in the passenger door and Du Pré got in the driver's side. He started the big SUV. The little jet rose up off the runway, streaked into the clouds. "It is nice," said Pidgeon, "not to have to go through all the crap they put you through at airports now. . . ."

Du Pré drove down the steep road to the river flat Billings was built on. He turned on to the interstate and he speeded up.

"Water buffalo come?" said Bart.

"Yah," said Du Pré. "I was you, I be careful. Booger Tom got a bad temper."

"One of them does tricks," said Bart.

"He may be steaks and burger by now," said Du Pré.

"Oh, crap," said Pidgeon, "that old bastard loves animals."

. . . him only shoot people . . . Du Pré thought . . . like that dumb sheriff we have before Benny Klein . . .

"So," said Pidgeon, "what has happened since we've been gone?"

Du Pré told them about Chappie, Patchen, Amalie and her story.

"Mother of God," said Bart. Pidgeon and Pallas were silent.

"So we are going to find them, take them home," said Du Pré.

"There will be a lot of people," said Pidgeon, "who won't want this to come out. . . ."

"Yah," said Du Pré. The big SUV rumbled along.

"The keys are in the cruisers," said Bart, "I remember now. . . ."

"Not enough room all your stuff," said Du Pré. They laughed.

"How are my horses?" said Pallas.

"Fat," said Du Pré. "Need a good run, up to Canada and back." The telephone set in the console chirred. Bart picked it up. He listened a few seconds.

"Just a moment," he said, handing the phone to Du Pré.

"I ain't speakin' to that guinea bastard," said Booger Tom. "You saw that goddamned water buffalo you was here getting Bart's fucking land yacht there. . . ."

"Yah," said Du Pré, "he was in the pasture."

"Well, he ain't now," said Booger Tom. "He got into the grain room, opened the danged door, went in, shut it. He has his fat ass pooched up against it so I can't get in. He's eatin' real good. . . ."

Du Pré laughed.

"I quit," said the old cowboy. "He kin git another foreman. . . ."

"You quit twelve times the last two years," said Du Pré.

"I really quit," said Booger Tom. "I am going to be gone 'fore you git here. . . ."

"Why you run off before you kill Bart?" said Du Pré.

"Give me that goddamned thing," said Pidgeon, reaching for the telephone.

Du Pré grinned and handed it to her.

"Booger Tom," said Pidgeon sweetly, "it's me. Now what is this fucking bullshit about you quitting?"

She listened.

"You're whining," she said. "Cowboys do not whine. It's in the rules of conduct. Number six, I think."

She listened.

"So you got an animal smarter than you are. I have a cat like that," said Pidgeon.

Booger Tom's voice rose, crackling with electronic indignation.

"It's a first," said Pidgeon. "The Australians have a sense of humor. . . ."

She handed the telephone back to Du Pré.

"She don't play fair," whined Booger Tom.

"They don't," said Du Pré. "Them women, it is the way of their people."

"I think I will just shoot him," said Booger Tom.

"Then how you get the door open?" said Du Pré.

The phone went dead.

"I finally got him," said Bart, beaming. "I finally got him."

"Look at this simple idiot," said Pidgeon. "Now he has death following him on soft padded feet and he thinks it is a triumph."

"Booger Tom very vengeful," said Du Pré.

"Smart, too," said Pallas.

"I think I remember him once admitting he had a math degree from Dartmouth," said Pidgeon. "And the day he graduated he got on a horse and rode all the way to Wyoming. . . ."

"He lies a lot," said Bart.

They rode for a while in silence, looking out at the prairie flowers that soon would burn and be gone.

Du Pré found the road north. He sped up.

"We tried to get a plane to Cooper," said Bart, "but the flying service was booked."

"I hate those planes," said Pidgeon. "I think they are made of Styrofoam and duct tape. . . ."

"So this old woman is at Jacqueline's?" said Pallas.

"Yah," said Du Pré.

"It is an incredible story," said Pallas. "I have to do a paper over the summer. . . ."

"Pret' sad for a paper," said Du Pré.

"It is not over yet," said Pallas.

"Be careful," said Pidgeon, patting her.

A big coyote sped across the road in front of them, after a jackrabbit. The rabbit ran flat out past some sagebrush and another coyote took up the chase. The first coyote stopped and panted.

"Run him in a circle till he wears out," said Pallas.

"I will help in any way that I can," said Bart.

"Thank you," said Du Pré.

"America," said Pidgeon, "land of the free, home of the brave. . . ."

They stopped for gas at a roadhouse at a crossroads. The gasoline was well over three dollars a gallon. Du Pré filled both tanks and paid with a hundred-dollar bill and he got six dollars back.

They pulled into Toussaint at six, and Du Pré parked in front of the Toussaint Saloon.

They got out of the truck and went in.

Pallas ran ahead and she jumped into Susan Klein's arms. They hugged and laughed.

"My, you have grown," said Susan, who was not tall.

"Sea air," said Pallas.

The ranch folk at the tables grinned and Pallas went round to say hello to them.

Bart and Pidgeon and Du Pré got up on stools.

"I am back here," said Madelaine, "cooking, what you want?"

Pallas went to the kitchen; there were shouts and then laughter.

The television was on but the sound was not, Susan's firm rule. The day's budget of horrors crept across the bottom of the screen, the words often misspelled.

. . . three hundred dead in Iraq in the past week, mostly women and children . . . fifteen soldiers killed by roadside bombs . . .

Pallas came out of the kitchen and she sat by Du Pré.

They all had cheeseburgers and fries.

"Nothing as good as these," said Pallas.

"You have to grind your own meat," said Susan Klein. "Stuff you get elsewhere has a lot of cardboard in it."

Benny Klein came in. He sat on a stool next to Du Pré. "So I get this call from the Manitoba Provincial Police and I says, well, I got this stolen car ree-port made two a.m. last Saturday. Doo Pray was playin' for about two hundred folks in the bar you know, so . . ."

Du Pré waited.

"They said you had time get another car get there," said Benny. "I said I thought it was that car was done seen there, there was this long silence. . . ."

Benny sipped his beer.

"'Her granddaughter is known to us,' said this cop, 'I think that is where we need to look. . . .'"

· Chapter 10 ·

"YOU ARE USED TO SCREWING confessions out of bad people," said Du Pré.

"True," said Pidgeon, "in my stellar career with the FBI, I did just that. But there are ways and ways of interviewing people, Du Pré, and I have had a lot more practice than you have. . . ."

"She is right," said Chappie. "You look at this map, Du Pré, of the country there. Ver' big. If she could just remember where they were before they started running. We got four Métis trails there. Two of them, dip down into the Missouri Breaks, she was on one of those it might be underwater, them bones. . . ."

Du Pré nodded.

"I'm not going to be mean to Amalie," said Pidgeon. "She is a lovely person. She is not the one who did the crime. Other people did that. I've interviewed a lot of victims, too, Du Pré, many, many. . . ."

"She is right," said Madelaine.

"So I need to do this alone," said Pidgeon, "but I need to have you introduce me. . . ."

Du Pré stood up.

He and Pidgeon went out to the nice new old cruiser Bart had just given Du Pré. To annoy Du Pré further, he had sprayed new-car scent in it, the aerosol car dealers use.

"It'll stink of bad tobacco and good whiskey in no time," said Pidgeon.

Du Pré drove out to Jacqueline's.

Amalie was in the backyard. It was a very warm day; she sat in a loose cotton dress without her shawl.

"This is my friend Pidgeon," said Du Pré. "She wants, talk to you some about back then. . . ."

Amalie nodded. "Women as beautiful as her usually aren't too smart," she said, "or they are really smart, which one is it?"

"You were just leaving," said Pidgeon.

Du Pré shrugged. He walked back to his cruiser and he drove off to the road that led up to the bench where Benetsee's cabin was. He smelled woodsmoke when he turned in the rutted drive. He parked by the cabin.

A badger stuck its masked head up from a hole near the cabin's foundation, loose stones set on the ground. The badger drew its head back in.

Du Pré knocked on the cabin door. The old man opened it, grinning with his brown teeth.

"You are never here," said Du Pré. "Why you here now?"

"Most times I don't want talk, you," said Benetsee.

Du Pré sighed. He went to his cruiser and got a jug of bad wine and he came back and he sat on the porch and he rolled two smokes.

Benetsee brought out a quart jar and Du Pré filled it for him and he drank it all in one long swallow.

"Good," he said, holding out the jar.

Du Pré shook his head and he poured.

"This is all, you," he said. "I bring Chappie here, get him sober, you are here then you are doing this. . . ."

Du Pré lit a smoke and gave it to the old man.

"Where is Bitter Creek?" said Du Pré. "Under that water, the Fort Peck Dam?"

Benetsee said nothing.

A red-tailed hawk flew up to the top of a tall pine and perched.

"Don't know," said Benetsee. "I don't do this anyway, Bitter Creek people do this, they come, I don't ask them to. . . ."

Du Pré nodded.

"So you don't know where is Bitter Creek," he said.

"*Non*," said Benetsee.

"So what I do now?" said Du Pré.

"Be Du Pré," said Benetsee, "like you have to anyway."

"She is something, that old woman," said Du Pré.

Benetsee nodded. "She find it for you," he said. "She know where it is, just can't say yet."

"Pidgeon she is talkin' her," said Du Pré.

"Stones break," said Benetsee. "We go and get more."

"I am busy," said Du Pré.

The old man got up and he went to the cruiser. He got in and so did Du Pré. They drove east and then down a long grade. The ice had come and shoved stones along from Canada, some of them good rocks to heat. The Wolf Mountains were made of bad rocks to heat.

Du Pré stopped at a gate, got out and opened it, got back in the car, drove through, got out again, shut it, and got back in the car again.

They bumped along for three miles and came to a cut where the road ended. There was a wide place to turn around.

Benetsee jumped out and he scampered down into the gully. He looked at some round stones at the bottom, nodded, and lifted one and set it up on the bank by Du Pré. It was the size of a small head of cabbage.

Du Pré ferried the stones from the lip of the cutbank to the trunk of his car.

Benetsee selected an even dozen, then Du Pré grabbed his outstretched hand and pulled him up out of the cut. The old man did not weigh much.

They bumped back to the gate, the old car nearly running aground a couple of times on the transmission case.

Back at Benetsee's cabin, they carried the stones to the little grade, dropped them, and let them roll down to the flat.

"Good rocks," said Benetsee, "come from six, seven hundred miles north. . . ."

Du Pré nodded. They went back to the front porch and Benetsee had some more wine. "Why the Bitter Creek people choose Patchen?" said Du Pré.

Benetsee looked off in the distance. "Him need them, they need him," he said.

"How you know they are not underwater?" said Du Pré. "Not in the Breaks, under the water."

"They are not," said Benetsee. "Their voices don't sound under the water. . . ."

"So, what I do?" said Du Pré.

"Be Du Pré," said Benetsee. "Quit asking dumb questions. I got work to do, not answer dumb questions."

Du Pré got up and he went to his car and he got in, and when he looked back at the cabin, the door was shut. He drove back to Jacqueline's, half angry. He had some whiskey, a smoke.

Pidgeon and Amalie were still in the backyard, but now the old woman had her shawl round her shoulders. They were laughing. "They been laughing a lot," said little Nepthele. He was carving a cottonwood burl. The shape of a coiled snake was coming out of the wood.

Du Pré put on his reading glasses. "Snake?" he said.

"Yeah," said Nepthele, "big rattlesnake. Saw him on the rocks the hill there. . . ."

He pointed up to some jumbled flat rocks a half-mile away. "You make sketches?" said Du Pré.

"*Non*," said Nepthele, "I catch him, stick him in the freezer. Maman open the freezer, I forget to tell her. . . ."

Du Pré laughed.

"Snake, he is pret' cold so he can't move fast but she is still mad at me," said Nepthele. He looked ill-used.

"Woman don't like finding snakes, the freezer," said Du Pré.

"Yeah," said Nepthele, "that's what she said, kind of."

"He still there?" said Du Pré.

Nepthele nodded. "Froze now," he said.

Du Pré went to the low shed behind the house that held the two huge freezers full of elk and deer meat and beef and poultry and fish. Twelve kids ate a lot. He opened the first one and didn't see the snake. He opened the second and found it. It was a big diamondback, nearly six feet long.

The snake was coiled on top of a box of elkburger, five-pound lots wrapped in white paper. Its eyes were blue-white with frost. Du Pré shut the freezer.

He walked back to where Nepthele sat. The boy dug at the wood with his tool.

"Big snake," said Du Pré. "What you catch him with?"

"Snake stick," said Nepthele, "over there."

Du Pré found a cane with metal pincers at one end and a doublegrip handle and cables to work the jaws. He gripped it and he wiggled the pincers. He put it back.

"Where you get that?" he said.

Nepthele grinned. "People come, the university, look for snakes," said Nepthele. "I help them. . . ."

Du Pré nodded.

"They give this to you?" he said.

Nepthele nodded, looked intently at his carving.

"Du Pré," said Pidgeon, "I need to go home now."

Du Pré stood up. "I am glad, you are getting education," he said, looking at Nepthele.

"It is hard work," said Nepthele, "but rewarding."

Du Pré nodded. There had been a flyer on the wall at the saloon, offering a reward for the return of scientific equipment . . . and a camera.

· Chapter 11 ·

"THEY LEFT FROM NEAR HELENA," said Pidgeon. "Amalie remembered she went with her mother and father and brother to a Catholic cathedral, a big stone building in a city built on hills near the mountains. . . ."

Du Pré nodded. He steered round a dead deer sprawled half across the lane.

"They were over the river," said Pidgeon, "looking at the map, and they went to the west of the Bear Paws and then along the front. It must have happened near where Chief Joseph surrendered."

"She did not say anything about mountains," said Du Pré.

"From that side they don't look like mountains and it was winter and she said it was foggy," said Pidgeon. "They went to the cathedral for Christmas Mass. She remembers that, and she would have remembered moving a long distance, because it was cold and hard to do. . . ."

Du Pré nodded.

"It makes sense," said Pidgeon. "They would have tried to get to Fort Belknap, where they would have known people. Now if we just knew where, exactly, Pershing and his men were day by day. . . ."

"Patchen is looking," said Du Pré. "In Washington." He roared up the long rise to the bench road and he turned left and speeded up.

The turnoff to Bart's big house was a few miles down. Du Pré stopped and Pidgeon got out and checked the mailbox. She came back with an armload of envelopes.

"Ninety percent crap," she said, dumping the pile in the backseat.

Du Pré pulled up to the main house.

Bart was standing out on the porch, holding a glass of soda.

Pidgeon got out and she fished the mail from the backseat. She pecked Bart on the cheek as she went by.

"GIT, YOU SON OF A BITCH!" Booger Tom yelled. He was out of sight behind the machine shed.

"I think the finest thing I may have ever done is get those water buffalo," said Bart. "It has taken years from Booger Tom's face. He looks barely forty, though quite purple most of the time."

"GODDAMNIT, YA CUD-CHEWING BASTARD, GIT OUTTA THERE," Booger Tom yelled.

"So," said Bart, "when do you take her to see if you can find that place? I will help in any way that I can, just don't ask me to go and dig up bones. . . ."

Du Pré laughed.

"You and Benny," he said. "He has to call me, he has someone dead in a traffic accident."

"I understand," said Bart.

Du Pré drove back down the foothills to Toussaint. He parked at the saloon.

Madelaine was inside, sitting on her stool behind the bar, looking intently at her beadwork. "Du Pré," she said, "that poor old woman is living, all those savages?"

"They love her," said Du Pré. "They are not very savage."

"Amalie is from another time," said Madelaine. "They want to know about that. All those kids want to know things, they are a good bunch."

"I like them," said Du Pré, "farther away I am. Maybe one day they pack up, tear me to pieces like wolves. . . ."

"You love them too much," said Madelaine. "So many of them, it is hard for you. . . ." She laughed.

Du Pré went behind the bar, mixed himself a ditch. "I take her tomorrow, we go and look where I think she was," said Du Pré.

"How you figure that out?" said Madelaine.

"Maybe I don't," said Du Pré, "but we got to start."

"Long time gone," said Madelaine.

"That Pidgeon, she ask good questions," said Du Pré.

"They live on Moccasin Flat?" said Madelaine. "Helena, where the airport is now?"

Du Pré nodded.

"I don't know," said Madelaine. "Didn't used, live there winter, too much wind, went to Great Falls."

Du Pré nodded.

"What was the weather, 1910?" said Madelaine.

Du Pré looked at her.

"Pallas find it on the computer," said Madelaine. "She find anything on the computer."

Du Pré looked at his watch.

"I be here another three hours," said Madelaine.

Du Pré drove to Jacqueline's and he parked and walked round to the backyard. Amalie was not there, but Pallas was, sitting in a folding chair under the lilacs. She had a book open on her lap. "You are not riding your horse," said Du Pré.

"Little warm for him now," said Pallas. "Lourdes and I, we ride later; I am studying a little . . ."

Du Pré glanced at the book.

"Poetry," said Pallas, "different people. Some of it is good. . . ."

Du Pré laughed. "Amalie?" he said.

"She is sleeping. She got very tired. She is very old, Granpère, I don't know I want to get that old. . . ."

"Maybe she stay, see that this story is told," said Du Pré.

"Maybe," said Pallas.

"Can you find weather, 1910, for here, for Helena, last two weeks of January?" said Du Pré.

"Sure," said Pallas.

"Maybe tomorrow I take Amalie, we go and look, see if we can find something," said Du Pré.

Pallas nodded.

"I think maybe it happened near Bear Paw, where Joseph . . ." said Du Pré.

"Maybe," said Pallas, "I don't think you should go, tomorrow. I think we should talk, her, more first . . ."

Du Pré looked at her.

"She is ver' old, will get ver' tired . . ." said Pallas.

Du Pré nodded.

"Me, I am tired too, Granpère," said Pallas. "I don't want, go back there, that school. . . ."

Du Pré nodded.

"It is a fine thing, study with those people," said Pallas, "but I am there with other freaks. I am not like Maria, I don't want that. . . ."

"You don't have to," said Du Pré.

"Sometimes I just cry in my room," said Pallas. "Can't ride a horse there anywhere, there is no where. Everybody is standing on where. Too many people. . . ."

Du Pré laughed.

"I first go, I am happy, I am so smart so I am special," said Pallas, "but it is not my place, not my people, what will I do with it? Go some place, where I don't like it, study, maybe teach, something? I like it here. I miss spring. Fall. We went, hunted antelope once, remember?"

Du Pré laughed. "You shoot him, long ways," he said.

"Bart he has been so nice, I don't want to hurt him, his feelings," said Pallas.

Du Pré shook his head.

"Bart wants you be happy," said Du Pré. "He don't care where you are happy."

"He spends all that money, me," said Pallas.

"He has money," said Du Pré. "He knows what unhappy means. . . ."

"Yes," said Pallas.

"So don't go back," said Du Pré. "Bart have somebody get your stuff, bring it here."

Jacqueline came down the back steps with some iced tea and glasses on a tray. "So you coming back," she said. "That is good, I worry. . . ."

"Me?" said Pallas.

"You put on the I-am-so-happy," said Jacqueline. "I am your mother, I know when you are lying. . . ."

"It is all right?" said Pallas.

"Yes," said Du Pré and Jacqueline.

"Professor Goudge will be mad," said Pallas.

"So?" said Jacqueline.

"You are right," said Pallas. "He tell me I owe, my brain to the world."

"Him, full of shit," said Jacqueline. "Him just want to say, 'see, that is my student there.'"

Pallas laughed. "Yes," she said.

"Moondog, he don't like it there, bite the other horses, Bart has to fly him back here," said Jacqueline. "Maybe you come before you start biting people."

"I want to help, this story, Amalie," said Pallas.

"It is ver' sad story," said Du Pré.

"Whites do this," said Pallas.

Du Pré looked at her.

"People do this," he said. "All people do this, it is under the skin in the heart. . . ."

Pallas looked at her grandfather for a long time. Then she nodded.

· Chapter 12 ·

PATCHEN GOT OUT of the small SUV, one of the new run of smaller four-wheel drives. He had put two large containers on the top, black plastic, shaped to the wind. He had a pale brown leather glove on his artificial hand and wore mirrored sunglasses.

Du Pré held the door of the saloon open for him. Patchen nodded and he went on in. Chappie was sitting at the bar. He got up and he and Patchen hugged.

"So they throw you out?" said Chappie.

"Yup," said Patchen. "Found some stuff, but there everything you do is on a computer. This bunch of idiots we've got for a government is so paranoid now they don't like anyone looking for anything. I 'lacked proof of legitimate historical interest.'"

"Huh?" said Chappie.

"I was not there as a qualified historian. I am a wounded soldier, from their war that is not going as they thought it would. They are obsessed that one or another of us will say what a bunch of incompetent jerks they are," said Patchen.

"Everybody knows that already," said Madelaine. She had put down her beadwork, and was looking angry.

"But I did find out quite a lot," said Patchen, "and as I expected, having had dealings with these fools before, there is someone who is not yet of interest to them who promised to keep looking. . . ."

Chappie and Du Pré and Madelaine looked at him.

Patchen began, "Pershing and two companies of the Tenth Cavalry were sent at the request of the governor to remove 'undesirable noncitizens' from two places in Montana. They began on the twenty-first of January 1910, and they started shipping Métis out the next day from Helena, north to the Great Northern Line. They rounded up many in Great Falls. They sent the loaded cars out on the twenth-eighth. . . ."

Madelaine pointed to a glass.

"Oh, please," said Patchen, "a beer, any draft is fine. . . ."

"Eight days," said Chappie, "and it was over."

"Yes," said Patchen, "but I found one odd note on one report. A Lieutenant Albert, who was sent with six troopers to apprehend some undesirable noncitizens fleeing through remote country. . . ."

"What did he do?" said Du Pré.

"I couldn't find his report," said Patchen. "It should have been there. It was a separate event. . . ." Du Pré nodded.

"And I could not find the date when Albert and his men were sent. Which is very odd, since such departures should have been noted," said Patchen.

"Favor to somebody," said Du Pré. "Amalie's people were running, they kill and eat couple cows. . . ."

"Big rancher," said Madelaine.

"What I don't know, too," said Patchen, "is why they were classed as noncitizens. Indians were wards of the government then; it was pretty standard."

"Not Métis," said Du Pré. "They don't belong to either Canada or America then. Many don't belong until 1957."

"Because they weren't a tribe?" said Patchen. "They were half-breeds?"

"Mixed-bloods," said Du Pré.

"And that's all that I found, until I was more or less asked to leave before I found myself under arrest."

"Arrest?" said Madelaine.

"The charming fellow who came to my apartment said something about being ordered to active service in a place I would not like," said Patchen. "I resigned my commission the next day."

Susan Klein came in, and Madelaine gathered up her little plastic envelopes of beads and her threads and the piece of soft doeskin she was working in a fine beaded pattern. "So," said Madelaine, "you have not met Amalie and now you will. She is at Jacqueline's and she will be having supper, an hour or so, you come, too."

Patchen smiled.

"I'd love to meet her," he said. And then he looked sad. He walked outside, and he was there waiting beside his little SUV when the others came out.

"I ride with him," said Chappie. He walked across the street and the two men got in Patchen's car. Du Pré and Madelaine got in her little station wagon.

Jacqueline's house rang with shouts. The children were at war over some thing or other.

Du Pré glared at the place.

"You are being old fart," said Madelaine.

"I am old fart," said Du Pré, "ver' old fart, have to herd grandchildren. I need whip, chair. . . ."

Chappie and Patchen got out of Patchen's little SUV, and they began to walk toward the house, too.

Kids of all sizes came out of doors or around corners. Little Gabriel, named for Du Pré, aimed a kick at Nepthele. The boys fell to the ground, yelling.

Marisa and Berne followed. The girls were twelve and growing up—long-limbed twins, hair braided, both dressed in jeans and boots, both with hats that had chin-strings.

"We are going riding, Pallas and Lourdes," said Marisa or Berne—Du Pré could not tell them apart—"so that is four gone, Granpère, Gabriel and Nepthele kill each other, so half of us are no trouble. . . ."

"It is great help," said Du Pré. "I thank you." The two girls then ran to him and they hugged.

"Amalie is wonderful," said Marisa or Berne, "lots of stories. She is ver' sharp. . . ."

"Where are you riding to?" said Du Pré.

"Cooper Creek Canyon," said Marisa or Berne.

Du Pré looked at the sky. "Be careful," he said. "Rain hour before dark. . . ."

The girls looked at each other. "Thank you, Granpère," they said. They went through the hedge of lilacs to the horse barn. Du Pré and Madelaine walked round to the back of the house.

Pallas and Lourdes were there, both in their teens now, young women. Old Amalie was sitting in a camp chair; the girls squatted on their heels. Pallas got up. "We look again tomorrow," she said.

Amalie nodded. Her eyes were small and very dark in her old face.

Pallas and Lourdes came to Du Pré and Madelaine. "Pallas find a way, get pictures of the land," said Lourdes.

"It is on the computer," said Pallas.

"She show some to Amalie," said Lourdes.

"She say she doesn't see anything," said Pallas. "I am showing her square buttes. . . ."

"Good," said Du Pré. "You be careful, it will rain, don't get caught."

They went off toward the horse barn. Chappie and Patchen came slowly, shyly up to old Amalie, small and shrunken in her chair.

Du Pré got a couple folding chairs for them, and then he and Madelaine went in the house.

Jacqueline was fixing a huge pot of stew.

Du Pré sniffed.

"Buffalo," Jacqueline said. "Got nice stew meat, Martin place."

Du Pré nodded. The Martins were the largest landholders near Toussaint. They owned tens of thousands of acres and they leased many more.

They were trying to raise pureblood buffalo.

But very few Americans wanted to eat meat from a symbol.

Jacqueline added spices from big plastic bottles, some ground, some leaf. The bubbling stew smelled rich. The telephone rang. Jacqueline wiped her hands on her apron and she lifted the phone up and put it to her ear.

"Yes, he is here," she said. She handed the phone to Du Pré.

"Du Pré?" said Benny Klein. "Lissen, I'm calling on my cell. Four feds were just here, the office in Cooper. They're looking for the old woman and they're looking for you. . . ."

"OK," said Du Pré.

"I told them, far as I knew you was in Toussaint, since if I lied that'd blow back," said Benny.

"OK," said Du Pré, "we take care of it, thank you." Du Pré went out back to where Chappie and Patchen were talking to Amalie.

The old woman was lost in her story, and she did not look up.

Du Pré bent over, touched her lips with his finger.

"People are looking for you," he said. "We got to get you out of here."

Amalie nodded. She stood up.

"Where to?" said Chappie. "There are lots of possibilities."

Du Pré thought.

"Take her to Bart's, tell Pidgeon what is going on," he said.

The old woman went off walking strongly between the two maimed young men.

Du Pré went back in the house.

"Get the kids, tell them people are coming looking for Amalie," said Du Pré.

Madelaine and Jacqueline nodded.

"Federal people. That was Benny," said Du Pré.

"OK," said Jacqueline, "they don't say anything, I tell them they will take her away. . . ."

"I go after the girls," said Madelaine. "They are not gone too long."

"Where are you, Du Pré?" said Jacqueline.

"I go the saloon," said Du Pré, "be helpful."

· Chapter 13 ·

"BENNY SAID THEY WERE definitely looking for you," said Susan Klein. "Amalie's granddaughter had one of your CDs with your handsome face right on it. 'That's him,' she said."

Du Pré nodded, and he drank the last of his ditchwater highball. Susan made him another.

"So," she said, "what they're mad about is this: a hundred-and-two-year-old woman made it across our well-protected border. The Canadians, though not pleased, are delighted that Homeland Security of the good old U S of A looks like the jackasses they are. They're making noises about the awful abduction of one of their citizens, an ancient woman at that, but one doubts their hearts are in it."

Du Pré nodded.

"So what're you gonna do?" said Susan.

Du Pré shrugged.

"I've known you a long time," said Susan, "and you've got a bad temper, Du Pré, so as a friend, I ask you don't kill no more of them than you absolutely have to. . . ."

"*Any* more of them," said Du Pré. "You used, teach school, you know."

"I'm trying to forget," said Susan.

"Amalie Montagne, she is here because she wants, be here," said Du Pré. "Long time gone, many Métis were killed, she was there, she wants justice, she wants them to sleep. . . ."

Susan looked at him.

"1910," said Du Pré. "Somewhere out there, thirty-two people are buried."

"Madelaine told me," said Susan, "and I know the old lady wants to do right. Thing is, these bozos who are looking for you now, they work for our government, which, since that Patriot Act was passed, throws people in jail and forgets about them. . . ."

Du Pré nodded.

"Which I would hate to see happen to you," said Susan.

Du Pré shrugged.

"I don't think so," he said.

The television screen above the bar showed burning vehicles and shouting people, bodies covered in sheets, a man weeping as he stood near one of them.

"It's a good thing that bat-eared nitwit wasn't president when Pearl Harbor happened," said Susan. "He'd have invaded *China*. . . ."

The door opened and little Colette came in, the youngest of Raymond and Jaqueline's brood.

She smiled as she walked across the floor. She climbed up on a stool. "I am here, protect you, Granpère," she said.

"Good," said Du Pré, "I won't worry then. . . ."

"Us kids love Amalie," said Colette, "these people, want, take her away. . . ."

"Yes," said Du Pré.

"But they will not," said Colette.

Susan Klein put a glass of pop in front of Colette. The little girl sipped some, and she ate a couple of peanuts.

The door opened and four beefy men came in, all in slacks and open-necked shirts and blue windbreakers, government issue. One of them looked at a CD in his hand, nodded, and nodded to his companions.

"Gabriel Du Pré," he said, "we have some questions for you. . . ." They moved in a pack, the sort of men who have to do that.

"We have information . . ." the oldest of them said, "And. . . ."

The front door banged open so loudly everyone flinched.

FBI Special Agent Samantha Pidgeon walked in, wearing a dark blue suit, sensible shoes, white blouse, ID on a chain around her neck, and her business Glock 9 mm.

"Well," she said, smiling, "what have we here? Nice jackets. Got some fucking ID?"

The men looked baffled.

"ID," said Pidgeon. "It's usually plastic cards got your picture on 'em and other information."

The men drew out wallets, opened them.

Pidgeon looked at them all. "Don't suppose," she said, "you have a good excuse for being here at all. What's the deal, fellas? Du Pré is a poor half-breed so you can dispense with the rest?"

The oldest of the Homeland Security men was trying to say something, but his mouth would not work.

"See this?" said Susan Klein, pointing to a sign on the counter:

WE RESERVE THE RIGHT TO REFUSE SERVICE TO ANYONE WE DON'T LIKE MUCH.

"You have now been asked to leave," said Pidgeon. "Absent a signed warrant, that means you leave. . . ."

The Homeland Security men looked at each other.

"Get out of my bar, assholes," said Susan Klein, schoolteacher, retired.

"You smell that?" said little Colette. "Something is burning." Something was burning.

There was a sharp stink of burning rubber and plastic.

"Out," said Pidgeon.

The men began to edge toward the door. One of them peered through the window.

"Jesus," he said, "the car's on fire!" They ran out.

Two tan SUVs with the Homeland Security logo on the doors were parked across the street. The one on the left was burning. The one on the right, which was pulled up close, was not.

A man pulled keys from his pocket and he pressed the control for the automatic locks. He jumped into the driver's seat. He shoved the key into the ignition.

He looked at it, puzzled.

He tried again.

The burning SUV was burning harder.

"Get out of there, Sid," one of the men yelled. "Gas tank may go on the other one. . . ."

The man leaped out, leaving the door open.

The first SUV was flaming, fabric and foam, weather stripping, burnable materials in the engine compartment smoking and stinking. Flashing lights came down the street.

The volunteer fire department's one truck, a large one, whined up and men in rubber coats and steel hats jumped off and pulled out hoses. They stood, one lifted a hand to the driver, and water pumped into the flat canvas tubes. Hard streams shot out of the nozzles. Billows of stinking steam rose off the burning SUV. The fire was out in a very short time.

"You know," said Pidgeon, "I was you, I'd leave while I still had something to drive. . . ."

The Homeland Security men edged to the SUV. The man who had tried to start it peered at the ignition. He pulled something out of it. He put in the key, turned it, and the engine caught immediately. Du Pré glanced over at the empty lot next to the saloon.

Eight kids stood there, all Jacqueline's.

All eight had red kerchiefs wrapped round their heads. All eight had guns.

Colette had a shotgun somewhat taller than she was.

"Christ," said Du Pré.

Pidgeon looked over at the local militia. She began to laugh.

Du Pré strode across the packed gravel. "You!" he said. "You put those guns down." The kids looked at him.

Du Pré looked at the Homeland Security forces, who were backing away from the burning steaming SUV.

"It is bullshit, Granpère," said Alcide. "You know, Gabriel Dumont, he has the English where he wants them, kill them all, Louis Riel him say no. So the English get away and they hang Louis Riel."

"I'll hang you all if you don't put those damned guns down," said Du Pré.

"He is mad," said Armand. "Talking white, he is mad."

"They are getting away," said Nepthele.

"I shoot maybe a tire?" said Hervé. "Give them fighting chance?"

The Homeland Security SUV roared past, the men staring at the Toussaint militia.

Most of the children gave them the finger.

"Shit," said Alcide, "they are cowards, will not fight."

Du Pré looked at the brood of his grandchildren.

"You little shits," he said, "you get, my car. Keys are in. You put those guns, the trunk. . . ."

"Some granpère," said little Gabriel. "We ready to die, save you, all you do is bitch. . . ."

"Saving me, not starting a war," said Du Pré.

"They come back, there will be more of them," said Hervé. "More targets."

"Your mother skin you all," said Du Pré.

At the mention of Jacqueline's name, the troops became subdued.

Jaqueline's big van roared up.

She opened the door, and she glared at the Toussaint militia.

"What is this crap?" she said.

"Granpère," said Hervé. "Maybe they come take him, Amalie away."

"Into the van, now," said Jacqueline.

The troops laid down their arms after unloading them. No loaded guns in houses or cars.

The children sat in the van, very quietly.

Jacqueline turned to Du Pré.

"I start to laugh I am lost," she said. She was biting her lower lip.

Bart came out from behind the propane tank that sat next to the saloon.

He had a big video camera in his hand.

"You get it, honey?" said Pidgeon.

Bart nodded.

"That's a good thing," said Pidgeon.

"Who set the car on fire?" said Du Pré.

"It was already burning when I started filming," said Bart.

Du Pré nodded.

Alcide gave him the victory sign as the van pulled away.

· Chapter 14 ·

THE HELICOPTER DROPPED DOWN to two hundred feet above the land and well below the tops of the buttes to the north.

The pilot went lower, and he followed the bed of a creek that wound across the dry wind-cut land. There were some willows bunched here and there, but the creek did not run all year, so they grew where water gathered beneath the earth.

Amalie was in the front seat, staring intently at the square butte to the north.

She had her rosary in her hand, and she was moving her lips.

The pilot hovered above a dished meadow sunk down below the surrounding flat. Thick willows nearly hid the streambed.

Amalie looked at the butte again.

Du Pré pointed east by north and the pilot nodded and he moved slowly along the course of the ghost river. The deep cut it had made in the land went on toward Canada in that direction.

It was midmorning and there had been clouds to the east, but the sun now rose above them and the square butte almost glowed as the light hit the bands of color, buff and gray, pale red and pale green. Amalie sat forward in her seat. She pointed at the butte.

Du Pré tapped the pilot on the shoulder and he stuck his thumb up. The pilot nodded and the helicopter began to rise and then it turned and headed west.

A few minutes later, the helicopter began to descend toward two big green SUVs.

Bart and Madelaine were standing by them. Pidgeon was up near the big circular field where the helicopter would land.

The pilot cut the engines entirely as soon as he had set down and they waited until the blades slowed and stopped. Then Du Pré got out and he waited while the pilot unlocked the passenger door and he opened that and helped little Amalie down.

"That is the place I am sure," she said. "I prayed and I am sure."

Chappie and Patchen got out of one of the SUVs, Patchen with a rolled map in his hand.

"How did you figure this was the place?" he said, looking at Du Pré.

"It is the only trail they would have taken," said Du Pré. "They would not want to cross the mountains to the south. From Moccasin Flat, Helena, it goes north and then east of the Bear Paw Mountains, then on to Canada. All the old trails are buffalo trails. . . ."

"Amalie," said Madelaine, "if you are tired, we can fly back to Toussaint, it would be ver' easy."

"I wait, long time for this," said Amalie. "I am not tired."

Du Pré waved his arms over his head. The pilot nodded and he started the engine and the rotors began to spin and soon he lifted up.

"It's BLM land," said Patchen. "Could be leased, but the way the beef industry has been doing, I doubt it. That is pretty desolate country."

Du Pré nodded.

They got in the SUVs and began driving east on the rutted track that went up and over a huge hill before dropping down to the ghost creek. It rose in the badlands and it sank out of sight in them, too.

"That is the butte," said Amalie. "I am not sure until the sun is on it and then I am sure."

Her voice was strong.

The going was very slow, and it took more than three hours to wind and bump and lurch up and over the last rise before the odd pocket meadow hidden in the earth.

They drove for a time up the watercourse, where a flash flood once or twice in a century might run. A huge boulder finally blocked the channel and the sides of the creek bed were too high for the SUVs to climb.

Everybody got out but Amalie.

She was weeping.

Chappie and Patchen got metal detectors out of the back of their SUV. They climbed around the boulder and up a game trail that led to the meadow and the thick stand of willows rooted in an underground pond.

Rocks stuck up between bunches of grass.

Chappie and Patchen put on the earphones that were wired to the sensors in the metal detectors.

They started to walk a grid. Du Pré rolled a smoke.

He lit it and he looked at the butte.

He looked at the ground.

He walked past Chappie and he went to the end of the willows and he looked back, waved, and walked on.

The creek bed narrowed and cut deeper. Du Pré looked for tracks, old tracks.

He walked up a short rise. There was a wind-carved set of pale rocks; the creek had sunk beneath the land.

. . . they have carts they don't come through here for sure . . .

Du Pré knelt and he looked at the tracks of deer and a bobcat. Mice.

Du Pré walked toward the huge butte. He climbed up a couple hundred feet and he looked out at the land to the east.

He shook his head and climbed down. He walked back to the place where Chappie and Patchen had been using the metal detectors. They weren't there. He went on and found them standing by the two SUVs.

Du Pré went up to Chappie and Patchen. "It was not through here, they come," he said.

"How can you be sure?" said Patchen.

"Bad land," said Du Pré. "You are using horses, ride, pull carts, they have to have grass. Métis would have gone a trail had grass. . . ."

"She was so sure," said Patchen.

"Not a diddle on these," said Chappie, nodding at the metal detectors.

"Last time I had one of these on," said Patchen, "I was learning how to find land mines."

Du Pré looked at the sun. "Maybe other side, the butte," he said.

Patchen unrolled the geodetic survey map. "No way to get there," he said, "unless we go all the way back to the road. There's a ranch marked on this. She was sure it was to the north of where they were?"

"Long time gone," said Du Pré. "She remembers things, maybe not quite right. . . ."

"We have to keep trying," said Chappie.

"I talk her," said Du Pré. He went to the SUV that Amalie sat in. He opened the door and bent his head close.

"Amalie," he said, "there are many buttes, Montana, I don't think this, the one. You remember, horses graze while you are traveling?"

Amalie nodded. "Men cut grass for them, cut those big bunches with long knives," she said. "I remember that."

Du Pré nodded. "We have done enough, today," he said. "We go on back now. Get some rest, try someplace else tomorrow"

Amalie began to cry.

"Do not cry," said Du Pré. "It is long time gone. We find the place; it is just not easy."

"I remember the butte," she said. "It looks like that."

"We find other buttes," said Du Pré. "We keep looking."

"I am sorry," she said.

"*Non*," he said. "It was . . . ninety-five years ago . . . you are young, we just look more."

"Worthless old woman," she said.

"Stop," he said.

"I am sorry," she said.

"Montana is a big place," said Du Pré.

He shut the door.

Patchen and Chappie were stowing their gear.

They all gathered in between the two SUVs.

"It is not here," said Du Pré. "This is a bad piece, land, there was no trail here."

"Could there have been back then?" said Pidgeon.

Du Pré shook his head. "Might be other side, the butte," he said.

"Time we get back to Toussaint it will be well past supper," said Bart. "I should have had the helicopter wait. Awful hard on Amalie."

"Well," said Pidgeon, "'nother day, 'nother try."

They all got in the SUVs and they traveled back to the road and drove north for an hour on a two-lane blacktop to the Hi-Line, and then they headed east.

When they got back to Toussaint, Amalie was sound asleep. Du Pré carried her into Jacqueline's.

The old woman did not wake.

He went out and got in the big green SUV and drove back to the saloon.

The rest of the search party was there, waiting for him.

"We'll find it," said Bart, holding up a glass of club soda.

They drank, and Susan Klein began to bring out food.

"I made you cheeseburgers, fries," said Madelaine, coming out with an impossibly large load of platters balanced on her arms.

"It was not going to be easy," said Patchen. "It would have been very strange if the first place we went was the right one. . . ."

It was dark when Du Pré and Madelaine got to her house. The coyotes began to sing the hunting song. The music went on for five or so minutes and then ended.

There had been a death in the land when the song stopped.

· Chapter 15 ·

DU PRÉ DROVE THE LEAD SUV over the road, barely visible in the grass. A washout appeared and he carefully edged around it, getting out to check and see that no transmission-eating rocks were hidden in the vegetation.

The square butte was due north of them, perhaps ten miles away.

The road had not had any vehicle over it in many years. In places where it crossed shallow marshes thick with sedges, it was invisible; just the tracks coming up out of the dark green told Du Pré where it went.

They drove back and forth down a steep hill, the top-heavy SUVs leaning uncomfortably close to the angle of repose. They got down to the bottom of the hill.

The road went on across a sage flat, and there was a fence beyond.

A ghost creek ran out of the saddle between the square butte and another some miles to the east.

Du Pré saw some movement in the landscape.

A white pickup truck was bouncing down the saddle, and coming on pretty fast.

By the time that Du Pré got up to the place where the fence crossed the watercourse, the white pickup had pulled up.

A tall gray-haired man in a battered Stetson stood by the truck, smoking a cigarette.

Du Pré pulled over and he got out. The other SUV came up behind and stopped, and Chappie and Patchen emerged and began to walk to Du Pré.

"Good mornin'," said the rancher. "And how may I help you?"

"We are looking for an historical site," said Patchen. "It might be a bit farther up toward the butte there."

The rancher nodded.

"Going to have to ask you to stay off the property," he said. "I have noticed that when a feller like me wakes up one mornin' and finds he's got a historical site or some critter like the black-assholed prairie rat on his land, he shortly don't have his land no more. I think I shot the last of them pesky black-assholed prairie rats this very morning."

"Sorry you feel that way," said Patchen.

"I am sorry I got to," said the rancher. "Times is like that."

"It is like that, yes," said Du Pré. "I see this is BLM land on the map."

"Bureau of Land Manglement," said the rancher. "Me and mine been leasin' this since the Taylor Grazin' Act went through in '33."

"Would you consider a payment for the privilege of looking?" said Patchen.

"Well, no," said the rancher. "You see, it still leaves me with a problem. It ain't that I mind you lookin' for this here site, just if you actually found it, I would be up to my pecker in college professors and government historians. And I just don't like either one of them. . . ."

Patchen nodded.

"And that is final and I got work to do," said the rancher.

"I am sorry to have to be like this. Had a neighbor found this stone bone on his property and it was off some critter been dead about a billion years and stood about twelve stories tall and now he ain't there no more. Last thing he said to me as he headed out for good was 'I shoulda left the danged stone bone in the ground but I got curious and wanted to know what it was off of . . . .'"

"I see," said Patchen.

"So," said the rancher, "I wish you well and the road is back that way. I fly over this often enough, saw ya headin' up and so I done drove over here to let you know how things is. I am as interested in history as the next fellow, but not if I got to lose my ranch over it. I ain't bright enough do anything else. . . ."

He touched his hat and got in his truck and he drove back up the long grade to the saddle between the buttes. Amalie was sitting in the first SUV. Her beads were running through her fingers. Du Pré got in.

"That rock over there," she said, pointing to a reddish chimney sticking up only fifty feet or so from the prairie. Du Pré looked at her.

"Past that rock there is willows, down behind that hill," she said. "I am so sorry; this is the place, I have been wrong." Du Pré nodded.

"We can't go on his property," said Du Pré, "until we can get some permission."

Amalie threw up her hands. "I wish I could remember better," she said.

Du Pré looked at the map. There was a depression past the rock, a large one that ran east and west. But it was well out of sight.

The sun had passed its zenith. It would take the rest of the daylight to get out of the land and back to Toussaint—and daylight went until ten p.m.

Amalie suddenly threw her car door open. She slipped to

the ground and started walking toward the fence. Du Pré ran after her.

"It is there," she wailed, pointing to the red rock. "My papa went up on that to look before we went around it. . . ."

"We have to do some things before we can go there," said Du Pré. He led her back to the big SUV and helped her in.

When they got to the county road three hours later, Du Pré stopped because the SUV behind flashed its lights.

"There's a shortcut here," said Patchen, pointing to the map. "Save forty, fifty miles. . . ." And he pointed to a gravel road clearly marked on his map. "And a roadhouse, post office," he said, "called Pardoe."

"OK," said Du Pré. "Maybe they have food, we eat there." Patchen pulled round Du Pré and drove off and Du Pré followed. They went west for a couple of miles and then the road turned north, running along an old river channel, a giant river from the age of ice, that now carried only the wind.

The road was well maintained and they made good time. The butte that might be the one in Amalie's memory passed by on the right, a huge thing, the north end of which tapered abruptly down to a jumble of massive rocks spalled off the cliff by ice and cold and time.

They came to a crossroads and Patchen stopped for a moment and then he turned right and speeded up. The road followed the contours of the land, heading east and north. At one point it became a narrow track between two jutting chimneys of rock, barely wide enough for two cars to pass each other.

Beyond, they could see a broad flat basin, one that had some water, for there was a big grove of cottonwoods by the road ahead.

When they got to the cottonwoods, they found a roadhouse, a white frame building set back in the trees. The paint was new and white, and the shutters and window frames were forest green.

They got out of the SUVs and Du Pré helped little Amalie down and they went in.

It was not a large place, and just beyond the main room there was a window in the wall that had no glass in it and beyond that, rows of boxes for mail.

A young woman came out of the kitchen.

"Afternoon," she said. "Evening, I guess, days are pretty long now." She had black hair and very dark blue eyes and pale white skin. "I'm Lily and I own the place, for my sins. . . ." And she laughed.

"Are you serving food?" said Patchen.

"Yup," said Lily. "Meeting here of the Stockman's Club, so I'm roasting some beef. Should be plenty, but not for half an hour or so. Prime rib and fixings for fifteen bucks. . . ."

They gave Lily drink orders and she filled them. As she left the bar headed for the kitchen she stopped. "We have a little museum past the post office there," she said. "Just open the door on the left. It ain't big but we like it." And she was gone. They heard her whistling in the kitchen.

Amalie walked to the little hallway that led to the restrooms, and she was gone for five or so minutes and then she came back.

"I am a little stiff," she said. "Think I will go in the museum." Du Pré got up with his drink and he followed her. He opened the heavy wooden door.

The room beyond was larger than the one that held the bar. There were some old guns on pegs, and some saddles on stands, and a buffalo head that had seen better days. Sunlight streamed in windows on three sides of the room. The fourth was the wall that separated the bar from the museum and the post office.

That wall was full of photographs above the wainscoting.

Amalie looked at the saddles a moment, and she turned then and walked toward the wall of portraits.

Off to the left there was a round-framed portrait of a young blond woman in a high-necked lace blouse and an embroidered jacket. She looked at the camera coolly, as if she knew she was a lovely woman and that was the way things should be.

Amalie approached the portrait slowly.

She stopped four feet from it and she stared.

She moved closer.

"Du Pré. Du Pré," she said.

Du Pré came over.

"It is her," said Amalie. "It is the lady who bathed me, held me, the warm house after the cold. . . ."

Du Pré nodded. "You are sure?" he said.

"The brooch," said Amalie. "She gave it to me but I would not take it. . . ."

An intaglio brooch, white on a dark background, was pinned above the woman's left breast.

"Her name was Elizabeth," said Amalie.

"Elizabeth Pardoe," said Lily, behind them, "and the gentleman there is Ellis Pardoe, her husband, and that one with the old gun is my great-grandfather, Hoeft—he hated Pardoe and Pardoe hated him, about like usual in those days, when two men wanted to own everything about them. . . ."

Long time gone, thought Du Pré, but not very . . .

· Chapter 16 ·

AMALIE WEPT. Du Pré held her as she sobbed silently, her face buried in his shirt. She collected herself in time, took a hanky from her pocket, blew her nose.

"I am all right, "she said. "I am sorry."

They looked round at the photographs. Amalie pointed to one of a man of perhaps thirty, dressed in a suit with a vest and a derby hat. He had a cane with a big gold head.

"That is one of the men," said Amalie. "I remember he put me in front of him on his horse when they took me over the Medicine Line to Canada, to some Métis, the Gardipees, them."

Du Pré nodded.

"He smelled like lilacs," she said. "I remember that."

"If you want to eat," said the young woman, "come on and do it. We may have more appetites than we got chairs and tables, and they usually get here a little before six. . . ."

Du Pré followed Amalie back out to the dining room. Chappie and Patchen were at a large table set for four. Du Pré pulled out Amalie's chair. She was so tiny she could barely see the tabletop. Du Pré found a child's seat at the side of the bar, one meant to be set on a chair. He brought it back and helped Amalie up on it.

"I am never very big," she said, "but smaller now. . . ."

The young woman brought platters with slabs of prime rib on them, a bowl of mashed potatoes, butter and rolls, four salads, and a carafe of water. She set down another bowl of horseradish.

"Spuds are full of sour cream," she said. "We like good clogged arteries hereabouts." She bustled back to the kitchen.

Someone else was back there now, as well. There was talk and then laughter.

The four ate rapidly. The beef was excellent and so was the rest of the food.

Du Pré got up, took the check, went to the bar. Another woman came out of the kitchen, and Du Pré started.

She looked so like the woman in the photograph that Du Pré blinked. He gathered himself and handed the woman the check and a hundred-dollar bill. "It is all right, the change is about right for a tip," said Du Pré. "But could you tell me who the woman in the photograph is who looks just like you?"

The blond woman smiled at him.

"Elizabeth Rhodes," said the woman. "She came here to teach and she married Ellis Pardoe and we are still here. I am a Pardoe, or was till I married old Macatee." She laughed, rich and pure.

"Thank you," said Du Pré. "I maybe come back here, it is a nice museum. . . ."

Then the ranchers and their wives and children began to come in the roadhouse, and there were shouts and shufflings, kids squirmed and got loose and ran outside to play.

The gray-haired man Du Pré had talked to earlier across the fence came in, looked levelly at Du Pré.

"Hello again," he said. "Mister Du Pré, we need to talk, outside and in back if you don't mind."

Du Pré nodded. He followed the rancher out. The man walked to a shed and around behind it.

"For good reason," he said, "I am going to sound discouraging for a while, not long. People here won't want this raked up, but it should be. One of them is a man named Bonner Macatee, who my daughter is divorcing. His family was part of this, as was that of the woman who owns the bar, the dark-haired one, Lily Hoeft Sandberg. Small place like this everybody is related to everybody else. But you keep going, you do that . . . and I should go. . . ." And he walked quickly away. He left a faint scent of rotten garlic, his eyes were red.

He is poisoned, Du Pré thought. What is this?

Chappie and Patchen and Amalie had already gone outside.

Du Pré joined them. They got in the SUVs. They were ready to head north toward the Hi-Line.

"That other woman look just like my Elizabeth," said Amalie to Du Pré. "It cannot be her, for that woman is young. . . ."

Du Pré nodded.

"Maybe she knows something," said Amalie.

Du Pré nodded. He sighed, then got out of the SUV. He waved to Chappie and Patchen.

"You take Amalie home," he said. "I am staying, I think I had better."

Chappie and Patchen nodded. "OK," said Patchen. "What should I tell Madelaine?"

"Be back tomorrow," said Du Pré. "I have a sleeping bag. . . ."

He helped Amalie from his SUV to theirs.

"It is her, I know it is her, him smell, lilacs," said Amalie. She yawned. The food and the long day had exhausted her. They drove off.

Du Pré went back to his SUV and he fished some of his CDs out of his battered leather musette bag. He put them in the pocket of his shirt. He rolled a cigarette and smoked it, looking out across the little basin. It was good cattle country.

He went back into the roadhouse and he sat on one of the six stools at the tiny bar. The two women were very busy, and it was twenty minutes before the blond woman came over to him.

"A ditch," said Du Pré, "double maybe." She poured it and he put a five-dollar bill down. "I look in your museum more," he added.

"Open till we close," she said and went back into the kitchen.

The people in the roadhouse were happy; they joshed and they ate; they drank some but not very much. And then one by one or family by family they went back out. Du Pré stayed in the little museum for an hour, carefully looking at everything.

He went back out to get another drink, and there were only six or so people left in the big room. One of them was the gray-haired rancher.

He ignored Du Pré.

The young dark-haired bartender got caught up enough to draw herself a draft beer. Du Pré put one of his CDs on the bar.

"I would like to come here, play," he said.

She picked it up.

"Oh, I've heard of you," she said. "But we can't pay you much of anything. . . ."

Du Pré shrugged.

"We have open date two weeks Friday," said Du Pré.

"Sure," said the young woman. "We don't have much live music. We have a few people play bad rock music but they can't find the time to rehearse. . . ."

Du Pré laughed.

"See you then," he said.

He went out. It was getting on to dusk, the light failing. The door opened and shut behind him.

"Why do I have the feeling," said the gray-haired man,

"that you ain't gonna go away till you find a black-assholed prairie rat?" He rocked a little, side to side; his balance was poor.

Du Pré turned. The rancher was smiling with his mouth but not with his eyes.

"You know why," said Du Pré.

"No, sir, I do not," said the gray-haired man.

Du Pré opened the door of the SUV. He found a box of wooden matches in the transom cabinet. He nodded to the gray-haired man. The man came close.

Du Pré set the box on the hood of the SUV, after sliding the cover off. He took out a match and he broke it and he put it down. Another. Another. Another.

Sixteen in all. He lifted them carefully one by one and and he put them in a row, six groups of five and two alone.

"Broken matches," said the gray-haired man.

"I am going to go from here soon," said Du Pré, "and then I will be back. I am Métis. I bring my band, I bring reporters, I bring the old woman. She was a little girl, her father throw her into the willows, she get away, the only one. . . ."

The gray-haired man looked at Du Pré and then away. "It was a long time ago and they are all dead," he said. "The people who did that awful thing are all dead."

"The blond woman, Mrs. Macatee," said Du Pré, "she is your daughter."

The gray-haired man nodded. "There are plenty of folks here would like to see . . . those matches . . . stay hid," he said.

"They will not," said Du Pré.

"I'm Jackson Pardoe," the rancher said, "and you are that fiddler, Gabriel Du Pré."

Du Pré nodded.

"So that was the little girl my great-grandfather and Elizabeth's brother saved," said Pardoe.

Du Pré nodded.

"There were others, two Pardoes, who were there . . ." said Pardoe.

"Who helped with the massacre," said Du Pré.

"It's been mostly forgotten," said Pardoe. "Was till you showed up."

"It is not forgotten," said Du Pré.

"Some blamed the soldiers, black troopers," said Pardoe. "But that never made any sense to me. . . ."

"No," said Du Pré. "Lieutenant Albert . . . ?"

Pardoe nodded.

"In 1931 he came back here," said Pardoe.

Du Pré rolled himself a smoke and he lit it.

"He shot himself down by the creek," said Pardoe, "and I heard some of the others who were there met bad ends. . . ."

Du Pré nodded.

"I should have done something long ago," said Pardoe. "I can't say knowing what I know helped me sleep."

"We do something now," said Du Pré.

Pardoe nodded, and he went back into the roadhouse.

· Chapter 17 ·

DU PRÉ PULLED UP to the Toussaint Saloon a little after eleven. He went in and found the place packed with people, most of them related to him. All Jacqueline and Raymond's children were there, looking lost, and Madelaine and Chappie and Patchen and Booger Tom and Bart and Pidgeon.

. . . she die, Du Pré thought. The old woman die . . .

He saw the big clumsy priest, Father Van Den Heuvel, sitting alone at a table near the wall. He had some papers in front of him. "She die?" Du Pré said to Madelaine. Madelaine nodded.

"We are driving back," said Chappie, "she is tired, we put her on the backseat, blanket and pillow, and she is quiet. We don't even know when. She is alive when we leave the roadhouse and she is not when we get here. . . ."

"So she is at Cooper?" said Du Pré.

"No," said Father Van Den Heuvel, "the coroner came here. He signed off. There was no reason for an autopsy, she was very old and she died of that. . . ."

Du Pré nodded.

"So," said Booger Tom, "we was waitin' for you to wander back so we could get the coffin made."

Du Pré leaned over and he kissed Madelaine on the cheek. "I be up, most of the night," he said. "See you in the morning, or when I get done."

Everyone got up.

Bart and Pidgeon and Du Pré and Booger Tom went out, and Du Pré and Booger Tom got in one big green SUV and Bart and Pidgeon in the other.

"Quite a gal," said Booger Tom. "Guess she did what she had to stay alive to do. . . ."

Du Pré nodded.

He drove out to Bart's where he had his wood shop set up in a big metal building behind the machine shed.

Booger Tom yawned and headed for his cabin; Du Pré went to the wood shop, opened the door, turned on the lights.

He breathed deeply. There was a scent of wood, new lumber, which had been trees not long ago, a smell of oil and solvents. It was chilly in the building.

Du Pré started a fire in the big double-drum stove he had welded out of scraps and two oil barrels. The big steel assembly began to throw out heat at once. He went to a clipboard and he got a pencil and he drew some lines on the dusty paper, nodding as he made some notations to the side. The door opened and Du Pré turned.

Bart came in, carrying two big mugs that steamed. "Coffee?" he said.

"Thanks," said Du Pré.

"And may I help?" said Bart.

"Sure," said Du Pré. He went to the wood rack that held the pine boards and he began to pull them out and look at them, inspecting both sides, and then down the edges to see how straight they were. "I need ten of these at thirty inches and ten at thirty-six," said Du Pré. "You cut them on the chopsaw maybe. . . ."

Bart lifted the stack of boards easily and he carried them over to a workbench that had a miter saw on it. He found a steel tape, made a mark on the platform that the saw set in, and began to cut.

Du Pré pulled out a sheet of plywood. He took a steel ruler and began to make marks and pencil lines on the wood. Then he took a circular saw and cut out the top and bottom, set them together, and planed and sanded the rough spots.

Bart brought the cut boards.

Du Pré went to a rack and he pulled out some bracings cut and beveled for a set joint. He took a gauge and set it to that and then he handed it to Bart.

"Give me those," he said, pointing to the shorter boards. Bart handed them to him. Du Pré marked the ends for the bevel cuts. He did the same with the longer boards. Bart carried the boards back to the miter saw and he began cutting the ends so they would fit properly.

Du Pré took a nail gun out of its case, filled it with ringshanks, put the hose and gun and air compressor together, and he turned the power on. The compressor blatted for a few minutes and then shut off. He found glue and a staple gun and he filled that with staples.

Bart brought the boards back and he held pieces while Du Pré slathered glue on the joints and then nailed them off. The coffin went together piece by piece; sometimes they had to stop and shave and fit the wood.

Du Pré put the bracings at the joints, and he stapled them off. They now had a top and a bottom to the coffin. They set them together. They fit with a few places in need of sanding.

"You must make a lot of these," said Bart.

Du Pré nodded. "Catfoot make them, he show me," said Du Pré. "Amalie is ver' small, this is not much bigger than a coffin for a kid. . . ."

Bart nodded. He kept sanding, squinted at the place. Du Pré found some strips of wood, thin ones, and he stapled and glued them around the joint. He took a drill and a countersink set and he drilled holes for the screws that would hold the coffin lid and base together. He went to the miter saw and he trimmed the strips and he brought them back and stapled them on. Then he screwed on six brass handles, simple ones, plated steel.

Bart looked at his watch. "We have been at this for five hours," he said. "How can that be?"

Du Pré laughed. "Woodworking, goes slow. Now you know why houses are expensive," he said.

It was light outside. They carried sawhorses out and then the two parts of the coffin; Du Pré painted the raw wood with oil. It smelled of lemons.

Then they walked up to the main house. Bart dug round in the fridge and he began to make breakfast. Du Pré made some coffee and he took his outside and sat on the steps and smoked and watched the light come up on the land below.

"Got her planter ready?" said Booger Tom. "You shoulda seen them two. They get back to the saloon, figure they'll buy Amalie a glass of wine and when they try to wake her up she won't. . . ." Du Pré nodded. "And them kids of Jacqueline's, they all was cryin'," said Booger Tom. "She sure got to a lot of people here. . . ."

"Yah," said Du Pré, "you, too. . . ."

"Yes," said Booger Tom, "me, too. . . . We're gonna find that place now for sure, yes?"

"If it is there," said Du Pré. "Long time gone, she pick other places, think it is there but it was not."

"And this one is on some feller's ranch," said Booger Tom.

"Jackson Pardoe," said Du Pré.

"I know him," said Booger Tom. "Has a good rep, fellers workin' for him said he was OK."

Du Pré nodded.

"Pidgeon printed up what seems to be knowed about all this," said Booger Tom. "I can't figger out how it got kept quiet all these years. It was 1910 fer Chrissakes. . . ."

Du Pré nodded.

"People will about disgust you," said Booger Tom.

The door opened.

"Chow," said Bart. "I'll even feed that old fart, just this once."

"What is we havin'?" said Booger Tom. "Guinea hash?"

"Eggs carbonara," said Bart.

"Guinea hash," said Booger Tom.

"You can go eat with the coyotes, you miserable old goat," said Bart.

"I *like* guinea hash," said Booger Tom.

They went in.

Pidgeon was up and there were four places set at the big round table by the bay window. Bart filled plates and brought them. They ate in silence.

"Wonderful, honey," said Pidgeon.

"Thank you," said Bart.

"It was only mildly toxic," said Booger Tom.

Pidgeon looked at the old cowboy.

"I found you in here," she said, "ripping off some prosciutto the other day. If memory serves, you whined at me until I gave you the recipe."

"Never trust no woman," said Booger Tom.

Pidgeon got up and she began to clear plates and put them in the dishwasher.

"Well," said Du Pré, "I go and get Amalie, take her to the church, I guess."

"I'll help with the coffin," said Bart.

They went out and put the backseat down in the SUV, and they picked up the coffin together and slid it in.

"We have to find her people," said Bart. "Amalie came home and we have to bring them home too. . . . Good that Suzette made no trouble. . . ."

Du Pré nodded and he got in the big SUV.

· Chapter 18 ·

FATHER VAN DEN HEUVEL BLESSED the little gathering, and as his hand moved, the coffin was lowered down into the grave. There were lilacs yet and many were tossed into the grave.

A hundred people attended, almost all of them from nearby.

Du Pré looked at the crowd, the chief mourners, Jacqueline's children, who had known Amalie so briefly, their window to the past now closed.

A man stood at the back of the crowd in the little graveyard by the Catholic church. He wore a tan windbreaker and a soft hat of pale wool and dark glasses.

"Come to our house if you like," said Jacqueline, "We will have food and drink, talk about Amalie. . . ."

People began to drift away. They got in cars or trucks and drove off, many to the work they had interrupted to come.

A man driving a little front-end loader came down the street. He waited for the crowd to leave before driving in to fill the grave.

Du Pré and Madelaine walked out of the churchyard together, her arm in his.

As they passed the stranger in the tan windbreaker, he

spoke. "Mister Du Pré," he said, "I wondered if sometime today I might have a few words with you?"

Du Pré and Madelaine stopped.

"I'm a writer," the man said, "Michel DuHoux, from Toronto. . . ."

"What you write?" said Du Pré,

"Magazine stuff, a couple of books," said DuHoux. "I heard a little about Amalie. . . ."

Du Pré nodded.

"So I wanted to talk to you," said DuHoux.

"OK," said Du Pré.

"When would be good?" said DuHoux.

"Come to my daughter's. You can follow us, we are in that car there . . ." he said and pointed to the new old cruiser. Du Pré and Madelaine got in and she looked at him.

"I talk my cousin, up in Manitoba," said Madelaine. "She say there is a lot of stink, the TV, about Amalie. That granddaughter of hers. . . ."

"Suzette," said Du Pré. He rolled a smoke, lit it, gave it to Madelaine for her one puff.

"She is claiming kidnapping, how the Americans steal old ladies from Canada," said Madelaine. "Cheap papers are having articles about it."

Du Pré nodded.

"So you watch out," said Madelaine.

Du Pré nodded.

He drove off, and a small station wagon, the sort that has four-wheel drive but is so light it does not help much in mud or snow, pulled out and came up behind them.

"Maybe he is a bad guy," said Du Pré. "If he is, we should know it soon."

"Ah," said Madelaine, "the kids."

Du Pré nodded.

He parked where he could get out easily and he waited for

DuHoux. The man parked beside Du Pré's cruiser, and when he got out, he took off his hat.

"Michel DuHoux," he said, offering his hand to Madelaine.

"Madelaine Placquemines," said Madelaine, offering hers. He bowed, just a little. They walked on into the house.

Jacqueline and Pallas and Lourdes were bustling around setting up food, a big pot of buffalo stew, a potato salad, fry bread, and chokecherry preserves.

. . . him got Indian blood, Du Pré thought, looking at DuHoux's skin, his long ear lobes.

When he got inside, DuHoux took off his dark glasses. He had gray-blue eyes.

"You are Métis," said Du Pré.

DuHoux nodded. "Pretty assimilated," he said, "so much so I was raised an Episcopalian in America. In Charleston, South Carolina."

Du Pré nodded.

"There are quite a few of us there," said DuHoux. "Troublemakers, I guess. Deported from Canada by the British after the French and Indian War. . . ."

Du Pré nodded.

"They take the French there, New York, Virginia," said Du Pré.

DuHoux nodded.

"So you are Canadian now?" said Madelaine.

"Yes," said DuHoux, "I began to not like America very much. It seems to have lost its way. . . ."

Father Van Den Heuvel came in, suddenly, tripping on something or other and falling on his face. The house shook. He was a very big man. He got up, brushing dust from his priestly garb. No one laughed.

"I haven't shut my head in the car door this year," he said, looking round the room.

"Still got six months," said Pallas.

Everyone laughed, including the big priest.

"How did you meet Amalie?" said DuHoux.

Madelaine laughed. She laughed and laughed until she choked and she had to go and get a glass of water.

"Père Godin's pecker," said Du Pré.

"Oh," said DuHoux.

"He is old goat," said Lourdes. "One, those men charm women, have so many babies he needs a box of cards for them all. . . ."

"I see," said DuHoux.

"It is a little more than that," said Du Pré.

"Yes," said Lourdes, "but if it is not for Père Godin's pecker, you don't know dick about any of it. . . ." And she smiled and walked away, shaking her hands above her head, triumphant.

"Suzette Murphy is an interesting person," said DuHoux.

"Murphy?" said Du Pré.

"I assume he was a drunken Irishman," said DuHoux. "Man'd have to be stoned to put up with that horror. . . ."

"You talk, her?" asked Du Pré.

"I listened. The burden of what she said was she was sure there was money she was owed in all this . . ." said DuHoux. "I didn't sense there was a great deal of filial devotion to her passion."

Du Pré nodded. "There is a song . . ." he said.

DuHoux looked at him and nodded. "Why the willow roots are red," he said, in French. Du Pré looked at him. DuHoux smiled. "I studied literature," he said, "and one of my courses was in the songs of the Métis. They were largely illiterate until the last century, of course, so the songs were their records."

Du Pré nodded.

"The little girl thrown by her father over the bank into the willows," said DuHoux, "where she hides and then makes her way alone. . . ." Du Pré nodded.

"Often it happens," said DuHoux, "that a folktale or a song has a very real basis, or a great poem. Wasn't Schliemann's explanation for his discovery of Troy that he found the directions in the *Iliad*?"

"Good poem," said Du Pré, "I remember one line I like. . . ."

Madelaine came back then, with a cup of pink wine. She had a tall glass of whiskey and water for Du Pré. "You want a drink," said Madelaine, "there is booze, the kitchen."

"Thank you," said DuHoux. He made his way through the crowd to the back of the house.

"So?" said Madelaine.

Du Pré shrugged. "He seems all right," he said.

"Seems," said Madelaine.

"I do not know," said Du Pré. "He comes a long way, speaking to that Suzette creature. . . ."

"She don't sound, good person," said Madelaine.

Du Pré shook his head. "*Non*," he said, "she is not."

"What he want?" said Madelaine.

Du Pré shrugged. "Story maybe," he said.

"That is what you want," said Madelaine.

DuHoux threaded his way back through the people, all talking.

"Before I forget," he said, "What was the line you liked from the Iliad?"

". . . of all things which crawl upon the earth," said Du Pré, "there is none so dismal as man. . . ."

DuHoux nodded, and sipped his drink. "Suzette wants money," he said. "And when she hears of Amalie's death, she will become insistent. The, uh, gutter journals will wonder why the old woman died here. . . ."

Du Pré nodded.

"But Suzette will overreach," said DuHoux. "She's been doing that all her life. She served three sentences for theft, the last one just six years ago."

"Amalie deserved better," said Du Pré.

DuHoux nodded, sighed, looked up at the ceiling.

· Chapter 19 ·

BASSMAN GOT OUT OF HIS VAN and he walked round to the passenger door and he opened it and Kim got out. Père Godin got out of the sliding door on the side.

"He is coming along," said Madelaine. "Opens your door for you."

"He always did," said Kim. "It was a couple other things we had to work on. . . ."

"Du Pré," said Bassman, "I got to get a beer. These woman, they kill me and skin me, I don't got to stand here and watch. . . ."

Du Pré laughed. He led Père Godin and Bassman into the Toussaint Saloon.

Susan Klein was behind the bar. It was midafternoon and there was no one else in the place.

"Beers," said Du Pré. "Whiskey ditch, me." Susan pulled beers, mixed a stiff one for Du Pré.

"Women are out there ruining my good reputation," said Bassman.

"That," said Susan Klein, "would take some doing. So Kim came?"

Bassman nodded.

"She's awfully nice," said Susan Klein. "Better'n you deserve."

Bassman looked hurt.

"I come in here, safety," he said. "Now look what happens."

Susan reached over the bar and patted his hand.

"It'd been me," she said, "your fat ass would be so full of buckshot you'd sound like a gravel crusher when you walked."

Bassman grinned. "Good to see you," he said.

"Uh-huh," said Susan, "and here is the redoubtable Père Godin. Who should have been shot years ago."

"Have beer," said Père Godin, "then you be nicer."

"You haven't played here for a while," said Susan. "Maybe you'll get lucky tonight."

Madelaine and Kim came in laughing.

Bassman looked at them, his face very long. "There is no escape," he said.

"Quit whining," said Père Godin, "Help me bring in the stuff, I am old and weak. . . ."

Du Pré and Bassman and Père Godin went out to the van.

"I am going Bolivia and change my name," said Bassman. "They need bass players, Bolivia. I hear that. . . ."

"Not far enough," said Du Pré. He picked up Père Godin's two accordion cases and he walked toward the back door of the saloon.

When they had set up the equipment, Du Pré went to the bar and he yawned.

"I got to sleep," he said, "I am too tired, play tonight."

Madelaine nodded. "You go to my place, I get you up, time for supper, get ready to play."

Du Pré nodded. He went out and he drove to Madeline's and he went in and took off his clothes and he crawled into the bed and he was asleep before his head hit the pillow.

Du Pré woke to the sounds of cooking, oil bubbling, good smells. Chicken.

He yawned and he went to the bathroom and he showered and he came out rubbing his hair with a towel.

Madelaine had laid out his clothes, a new shirt she had made, Red River shirt with brass buttons and white piping.

"It is a nice shirt," he said, when he came into the kitchen. "I put it on after dinner, so I don't drip on it."

Madelaine nodded.

Du Pré fished his watch out of his pocket.

Seven o'clock.

"Play at nine thirty," he said. " I slept a long time."

"Come and eat, Du Pré," said Madelaine. "I have to go, help Susan. You don't lie down again. . . ."

They laughed.

"I am late," said Madelaine, half an hour later. She slipped out of the bed and she dressed in a hurry and she went out buttoning her shirt and then tucking it in.

Du Pré heard the jingle of the silver and turquoise she wore as she put on rings and bracelets and the squash-blossom necklace he had found in a pawnshop in Spokane. An old one, faint hammer marks from the smith's peen in the silver.

She went out.

Du Pré ate chicken and mashed potatoes and gravy and home-canned long beans and he washed the dishes, then cursed.

. . . damn fingers be soft, they hurt end of the night . . .

But he didn't like leaving a mess.

He put on the new Red River shirt and buttoned it; he had a little trouble with the cuffs, set tight so they wouldn't get in the way of his playing.

He put his fiddle in the old rawhide case and he went out and he walked up the street toward the saloon. It was perhaps a quarter of a mile from Madelaine's.

There was already a crowd there when he came in, people eating and laughing.

Many hollered at him and a couple of people got up to come over and ask for favorite tunes.

Du Pré nodded at the requests and then he forgot them.

Père Godin was fooling with one of his accordions; he had a small screwdriver in his hand and he was peering at something and muttering.

"Goddamn thing," he said. "I wish, me sing better, I don't have to play no damn accordion. . . ."

Du Pré laughed.

He waved at Madelaine, who was busy mixing drinks and ferrying food to the tables.

Du Pré set his fiddle out on top of the old piano so it would be the same temperature as the room when he tuned it.

He went outside, saw Bassman and Kim sitting on folding camp chairs back by the trailers that Susan Klein rented as motel rooms. Bassman had a spliff as thick as a broomstick, half a foot long, and he was drawing the sweet smoke deep into his lungs.

Kim took a dainty puff and she choked. "I don't know how that man can walk with that in him," she said to Du Pré. Her eyes glittered a little.

"Good for lungs," said Bassman. "Like gravel in a bird gizzard, good smoke chews up the air, makes it easier to breathe. . . ."

Du Pré laughed. He took his flask from his hip pocket and he had some whiskey.

"Could I see that?" said Kim. Du Pré handed it to her. It was worn, pale gray, covered in rawhide, with a steel cap that unscrewed.

"My father give that to me," said Du Pré. "Catfoot made the flask, put the rawhide on it. . . ."

Kim nodded and she handed it back.

Du Pré waited while Bassman finished as much of his dope as he wanted. He carefully pared the burning coal from the end with his pocketknife and he put the huge joint in a cigar case, a single one meant for a panetela.

When they went in, they found the place was packed, save for the little dance floor out in front of the bandstand.

The crowd whooped when the three got up on the little stage. Du Pré turned on his amplifier and so did Bassman, and Père Godin jiggled his microphone, which made thudding pops.

Du Pré started with a two-step, and Bassman joined him, lazily thumping, and Père Godin nodded through one full round of the song and then he joined in, too.

People got up to dance.

Du Pré looked out at the crowd.

He saw DuHoux standing at the back, near the front door. He had on a leather jacket and the sunglasses, even though the bar was dim.

They played for an hour, people coming on to the dance floor and going off.

They finished with a fast jig, and Père Godin went out on the dance floor and danced while he played; people backed away, clapping.

The set done, Du Pré shut off his amplifier and he put the fiddle up on the piano.

He got a tall drink from the bar and he went out the back door for some air. It was still a little light, still dusk even though it was ten thirty.

"Du Pré?" said a voice.

Du Pré turned.

A man stood there, a big man in his thirties. The man smiled. He stepped forward and without warning he swung and hit Du Pré full on the chin. The glass flew out of Du Pré's hand and he fell back.

"Don't ever come to Pardoe again," said the man, who was walking away.

Du Pré shook his head. He had seen stars.

An engine started and a truck drove off. Du Pré got up and he staggered out past the saloon to see what it was. But the truck was gone. Du Pré fell to his knees, puking. He felt hands on his shoulders.

"Du Pré!" said a voice. He turned and looked. DuHoux.

"Somebody hit me," said Du Pré.

DuHoux helped him up. "I bet I know who," he said. "Bonner Macatee, he tried to pick a fight with me earlier, I don't know why. . . ." People were coming outside now.

Du Pré rubbed his jaw. "I am OK," he said.

"Did he say anything?" said DuHoux.

Du Pré nodded. "Stay away from Pardoe."

"That son of a bitch," said DuHoux.

· Chapter 20 ·

JACKSON PARDOE WAS WAITING at the gate that opened on to the track that led to the place Amalie had sworn was the place where the massacre had happened.

Du Pré was in the first SUV; there were three more behind him and then three other cars.

The gray-haired rancher waved them through. Du Pré stopped and he rolled down his window.

"Somebody don't like you," said Pardoe, looking at the bruise on Du Pré's jaw.

"I am sorry I don't give more notice," said Du Pré, "but he hit me last night so I got to be here today. . . ."

Pardoe smiled.

"My son-in-law," he said. "Bad temper and he don't like this. I don't like it either. . . ."

"Nobody like it," said Du Pré.

"You know how to get there?" said Pardoe.

"Straight ahead, then left fork after the next gate," said Du Pré.

"Put you right there," said Pardoe. "I will be down in a while."

Du Pré drove off and the others followed.

The pasture was huge, four or five square miles, and at the south end it tapered to a point fifty yards across, set between two hills cramping together.

Du Pré opened the gate. A few Herefords looked idly at him but they were far away and made no signs of moving. Du Pré drove on, stopping far enough away so the last person could shut the gate.

It was DuHoux, who had some trouble with the wire-and-post set. But he got it in time.

Du Pré got back in the big SUV and he drove on, up a long grade to a ridge and over it.

The butte was south and west a couple of miles. Du Pré could see the track.

He looked off to the northeast.

. . . good grass, water, they would come through here . . .

He drove on, bumping down a switchback on a road that stones had worked up through. He had to drive at a very low speed, the SUV lurching this way and that as it went over the rocks.

At the bottom he pulled away, leaving room for the others. Only the SUVs came down the hill, the drivers of the cars had left them up on top.

Du Pré waited until they were all down. Then he drove on, over the ancient riverbed, the ghost river that had flowed to the north in the time of the ice.

A couple of miles later Du Pré went round a huge boulder and he stopped.

. . . there it is . . . the creek, the willows . . .

A hidden dell, thick with grass, willows with their bright green leaves shaking in the little breeze.

Du Pré pulled farther on and he stopped. He got out and he walked down toward the willows.

He turned round and looked back.

Chappie and Patchen, DuHoux, Bart, Pidgeon, and most of Jacqueline's kids were standing together, quietly.

Lourdes ran over to her grandfather.

"So, did you hear the music, Granpère?" she said.

Du Pré shook his head.

"We leave you alone to hear the music and you don't," said Lourdes. "That is not too good. . . ."

"It might not be here," said Du Pré. "Maybe getting hit, spoiled my hearing."

The sun was very hot now, the morning cool had gone.

The others walked down to Lourdes and Du Pré.

Chappie and Patchen had the metal detectors out, and they were putting on the backpacks and earphones.

"What are we looking for?" said Lourdes.

"Old cartridges," said Du Pré.

She nodded.

Pallas was over by the willows.

She waved at Du Pré.

He walked over to her, Lourdes close behind him.

She pointed.

There was a flat dell below, a couple of hundred feet long and half as wide, set in against the prairie. It could not be seen until you were right up on it.

The willows grew very thick, and Du Pré could see the glint of running water.

There did not seem to be a good way down. The bank was about ten feet high and sheer.

Pallas wandered back, put her arm around her grandfather. "Music, my ass," she said. "You want to see if somebody shoot, it will be you and not one of us."

"You are ver' smart," said Du Pré. "You marry that Ripper, he has my sympathy."

"Maybe I don't," said Pallas.

Du Pré looked at her.

But she walked away then, looking very sad.

Du Pré waited for Madelaine and the others to catch up and then they all walked along above the dell, looking for a place to get down to it easily.

Lourdes got impatient. She dropped over the edge and slid down in a shower of earth and stones. She laughed and she ran out into the dell. Then she stopped and looked round.

Du Pré and Madelaine had found a path finally, almost at the south end of the dell, where it was easy to step down. Du Pré went down first. He offered Madelaine his hand and she took it and stepped down. They walked toward Lourdes.

Pallas had gone over the edge, too, and she was waiting with her sister.

"Jesus, Du Pré," said Madelaine, "it is cold down here."

Du Pré nodded.

The day was hot but the air was chilly in the dell. Madelaine shivered and she grasped her upper arms with her hands. The girls were shivering, too. Du Pré felt icy sweat on his spine. He walked round, looking.

It seemed ordinary, a place for a camp for a few days, with grass and water and dead willows for fires. He looked up at the butte, rising sheer two miles or so away.

The rock layers were uneven, broad cream bands, narrower red or green ones, a few thin dark lines.

The four of them met in the center of the dell.

The air was very cold, seemed to be coming up out of the earth. Du Pré could feel the flow. Then the cold air stopped suddenly and it was as hot as it had been when they were up above.

"This is it," said Madelaine. "Place gives me the creeps."

. . . long time ago I am in Idaho, go across a little pass, my tire blows, I stop, change it, it is very cold there in high summer in the desert, middle of the day . . . feel like someone is watching me all the time . . . stop at the next bar, ask, they say there was a massacre there . . .

Long time gone then, more than a hundred years.

The little creek was only a couple of feet wide, narrowing as if it had cut into the earth. Du Pré walked to it and he bent down and dipped a palmful of water.

It was fresh and cold and a little bitter.

He looked round.

Chappie and Patchen were walking along the rim above the dell. They swept the flat round metal plates over the earth.

Chappie stopped.

Alcide knelt and he dug at the ground with a screwdriver.

He picked up something.

Another.

Another.

Two other kids were over with Patchen.

They were finding things, too.

Du Pré and Madelaine walked back to the place they had come down and they climbed up and then back to where the kids and Chappie and Patchen were workng.

Alcide handed Du Pré a dark tube.

A cartridge.

Du Pré scraped the end with his pocketknife.

A .30-40 cartridge.

Bart and Pidgeon were off near a huge rock, Pidgeon pointing to something.

Alcide handed Du Pré another shell.

Du Pré scraped it.

Another .30-40 cartridge.

He looked at the place where Alcide had been digging.

He bent down.

Six old spent cartridges sat there, fused together by water and time. He picked them up. Same as the others.

"Guess we set up camp," said Chappie. He had taken off the earphones.

Du Pré nodded.

He saw a flash, out of the corner of his eye, up on the butte. He looked for a while but he didn't see another.

· Chapter 21 ·

DU PRÉ AND THE REST of the party were standing by the SUVs having some snacks and drinks when two tan government pickup trucks came over the hill and down the track toward them. “Ah, shit,” said Du Pré.

The lead truck stopped and a woman got out of the passenger side, young, dressed in a tan-and-brown uniform. She had a pistol on her hip and a badge.

“Gotta stop what you’re doin’,” she said, “right now, and turn over anything you may have found. . . .”

“It’s private land,” said Patchen, “and we have permission.”

“It is leased by Mister Pardoe,” said the woman, “but owned by the people of the United States. It seems you are conducting an archaeological dig without the proper permits. . . .”

Three other people got out of the pickups, but only the woman was armed.

“You leave now,” she said, “after handing in whatever you might have taken, I’ll let it go. Don’t leave, you are in violation of the law and there will be consequences.”

“This is bullshit,” yelled Alcide. “Our people, they were murdered here and we will find them. . . .”

The young woman flinched. "It's the law," she said. "There are many interested parties wanting to dig on public lands. Indian tribes, the EPA, private organizations . . ."

Alcide stalked off to where he had been digging and he began to stab at the earth with his screwdriver. Du Pré went after him.

"*Non*," he said. "We got to go. We come back, but we got to go now."

Alcide looked up. He was crying.

The few .30-40 shells they had found had been put in a small soft cooler. Du Pré took it to the young woman. She looked in. "This is it?" she said. Du Pré nodded.

"You do not have to leave," she said. "You have every right to be here. You simply cannot dig for artifacts here. Understood?"

She got back in the pickup and both the trucks left, with the shells. The soft cooler had been set on the ground.

Jackson Pardoe's white pickup truck wound slowly down the track and stopped. Pardoe got out, shaking his head.

"Somebody must have called them," he said. "It wasn't me. . . ."

Du Pré nodded.

"We go now," he said. "But there is a ver' important story here. Some people will not want it told."

"I wish I had never heard of it," said Pardoe.

He got in his truck and he drove back up the track.

Everyone else got in the SUVs and followed.

"I did not give them everything," said Alcide, holding two cartridges out for Du Pré. He was in the backseat with Madelaine and little Gabriel.

Du Pré laughed.

"It is not a gun I know," said Alcide, "U.S. .30-40."

"Thirty-forty Krag," said Du Pré. "It is a lever action gun like the little thirty-thirty you used for the deer last fall."

"Soldiers carried those?" said Alcide. "Don't shoot very straight, lever action."

Du Pré laughed.

He came up over the hill and down the winding road cut deep in the hillside, got to a more level place and went on. The stones jutted up, sometimes a foot. The going was very slow.

At the top of the next rise, they could see the green gate that opened onto the county road. Pardoe's white pickup was there and another, a newer one with double rear tires, steel gray.

When Du Pré got to the gate, Pardoe swung it open. The gray truck was gone. Du Pré pulled over and he stopped and got out. The other SUVs came out and turned east. Du Pré waved them on.

"Macatee was the one who called the Bureau of Land Management," said Pardoe. "He was bragging on it to me. Said he was gonna tangle this up in a whole lot of knots. Called somebody named, so help me, Medicine Eagle. . . ."

"Bucky Medicine Eagle?" said Du Pré. "That asshole? Last I know he is selling vision quests, guaranteed, fifteen hundred bucks. . . ."

Pardoe nodded. "Sounds about right," he said. "Used to be you leased land from the BLM they didn't give a shit what you did to it; now they come round, check the grass, see if there's a mine there shouldn't be, count the black-assholed prairie rats. Indians are fed up with having their people dug up and carted away as specimens, and I can't blame 'em. I made a big mistake, Du Pré, I got m'self born a hundred years too late."

Pardoe took a small cigar from his breast pocket, bit the end off, lit it. "You may never get to find what you are lookin' for," he said. "There are lots of people here don't want it found. My son-in-law for one. He's got a lawyer on it. Government's in on it."

"These things," said Du Pré, "they are in the way, but not for very long. . . ."

"I have a couple things you might be interested in," said

Pardoe. "Other people will be pretty soon, too, and it might be better you just took 'em now." He walked to his pickup truck and he looked carefully round at the land.

He took a worn brown leather case from the footwell on the passenger side. It was about the size of a pastry box. He handed it to Du Pré. "This would need to go someplace safe after you look at it," he said, "and that ain't here. I didn't give it to you. . . ."

"I see to it," said Du Pré.

Pardoe turned, and he looked levelly at Du Pré. "Good luck," he said. He walked to his truck and got in.

Du Pré held the case against his body, walked to the SUV, got in. He handed the case to Madelaine. She looked at it.

"Him," she said, "he maybe is killed over this."

Du Pré looked at her.

"I don't know why I said that," said Madelaine. "Others went to the roadhouse. We get something to eat, go on home. Bart is calling that lawyer, that Foote. . . ."

Du Pré laughed.

. . . this will not take long, Bart will own it . . .

They drove along in silence for a long time. Then they crested the hill and saw the roadhouse, white in the green of the cottonwood trees.

The other SUVs were parked in front, and a few pickups. Du Pré pulled in and parked and they got out and went in. The kids and Bart and Pidgeon were at two big tables pulled together, covered in plates pretty well picked clean.

"I never see you drive that slow, Du Pré," said Madelaine.

Bart got up and he paid the bill. The kids went outside.

Pidgeon was looking furious.

Bart came back to the table and she got up. As they passed Du Pré, he looked at her, raising an eyebrow.

"You'll see," she said. "We're going."

Du Pré and Madelaine and Alcide and little Gabriel sat down at a table.

There were menus in a holder next to the salt and pepper.

The dark-haired woman, Lily, Du Pré had spoken to about playing at the roadhouse came out of the kitchen, pulling an order pad from her apron.

"Lots of business," she said, smiling and looking sad at the same time.

Du Pré looked at a table off in a corner where it was fairly dark. The man who had hit him was there. He would not look in Du Pré's direction.

They ordered their food. Lily looked at Du Pré, smiled sadly. "We decided to not have live music here," she said. "Too rowdy for us. I'm sure you understand."

Du Pré nodded.

"I'll get your CD for you," she said. She headed back toward the kitchen.

Du Pré went to the bar.

The blond woman came out of the back, smiling.

She was wearing dark glasses.

"Drink?" she said.

"Ditch, a glass of red wine," said Du Pré.

When she bent to fill the tall glass with ice Du Pré could see the bruise around her left eye.

. . . that son of a bitch . . .

Du Pré took the drinks back to the table. Lily brought sodas for Alcide and Gabriel. And she brought the burgers and fries.

They ate and Du Pré paid. Lily handed him the CD he had left.

"I'm sorry," she said, smiling.

Madelaine and the kids had gone outside.

Du Pré walked to the man who had hit him in Toussaint. "We will be back," he said. "Soon."

The man gripped the table so hard his knuckles showed white.

"Do not hit your wife again," said Du Pré, and he walked

out. He got through the front door, and perhaps ten feet on, when he heard Macatee crash through.

And then Jackson Pardoe was there, with a gun.

"You cowardly son of a bitch," said Pardoe, pointing the pistol at Macatee's head.

Macatee went white.

Du Pré moved up to them quickly.

"Pardoe," he said, "*non*. You would not like Deer Lodge Prison. . . ." And he reached for the gun and pulled it slowly from Pardoe's hand.

"Not like this," said Du Pré. He whirled, his right foot shot out and Macatee yelped, his left knee dead, and he began to fall. Du Pré punched him in the throat, and the big man folded up choking for breath.

"Like that," said Du Pré. "Now take this and go home." He handed Pardoe his gun.

Pardoe nodded and walked toward his truck.

· Chapter 22 ·

THE HEARING WAS TO BEGIN in ten minutes. Du Pré and Bart were outside the Federal Building in Helena, and Du Pré was smoking a last cigarette.

A Cadillac stopped down at the no-parking strip at the bottom of the steps.

A man wearing fringed and beaded clothes and moccasins got out. He took an eagle-feather headdress from the backseat. He put it on. The Cadillac pulled away.

The man in the costume came up the steps, slowly, the moccasins sliding on the dust.

He was very intent on his footwork, and he got quite close to Bart and Du Pré.

"Bucky!" said Du Pré. "How is that child molesting that you do?"

The man moved away, headed for the doors.

"I take it," said Bart, "that is Mister Medicine Eagle."

"Him," said Du Pré.

"We better go on in," said Bart, looking at his watch. Du Pré tossed his butt down on the steps. A tendril of blue smoke curled up from it. He followed Bart into the building.

The hearing room was on the second floor, and it had about forty people in it.

Du Pré looked round.

Macatee was there.

A few white people stood around Bucky, mostly young and looking very lost.

Three rumpled fellows in tweed and beards. Experts brought in for testimony.

"They are pretty good about these things," said Bart, "being on time I mean. . . ."

The time passed, and another five minutes. The tweedbags looked at one another and their watches.

"It worked," said Bart. "If the usual folks had filed out of that door, I would be worried. . . ."

Du Pré nodded.

The young lawyer who had come to run him away from Bitter Creek came out of the door. She was wearing a suit and heels. She put a folder down on the podium and she opened it and she cleared her throat.

"The Bureau of Land Management has concluded," she said, peering very intently at the podium's stand, "that it has no jurisdiction in this matter and that the area in dispute is privately owned. . . ." She shut the folder and she almost ran for the door. She went through it and it had closed before any murmuring began.

"Jesus Christ!" yelled Bonner Macatee. "This is . . ." And he stopped and he looked round.

Du Pré nodded and smiled.

Bonner Macatee got very red.

Bucky and his disciples looked stunned. All dressed for a protest and nothing to be ill-mannered about.

Du Pré laughed.

"Poor Bucky," said Du Pré, "gonna protest moving sacred bones without paying him to burn sweetgrass and chant. . . ."

"OK," said Bart, "that is that. We have more pressing problems. But I did arrange for a security team to go in the moment this was done. . . ."

"It is nice, being rich," said Du Pré.

"Not always," said Bart.

They went out a side entrance to a parking garage and found Du Pré's old cruiser.

They got in and Du Pré backed out and went down the ramps. He paid at the gate, an old man taking his money and giving him a receipt.

Du Pré found the expressway north. He sped up to the limit and kept it there. He passed four highway patrol cars in the next forty miles. They were on the on-ramps, just waiting.

The cell phone in Bart's briefcase trilled and he fished it out and opened it.

"Oh, fine," he said, "thank you."

He listened a moment.

"That will be fine," he said, "though you could have gone ahead without checking with me. . . ."

He listened some more and then he laughed.

"He's right here," said Bart. "Just a moment. . . ."

He handed Du Pré the phone. Du Pré put it to his ear. "I take it things went satisfactorily," said Charles Foote, Bart's utterly ferocious lawyer.

"Yah," said Du Pré, "I don't suppose you tell me how you did that."

"In negotiations," said Foote, "one may offer something the other party wants a great deal, or . . ."

"Something they don't want," said Du Pré.

"Uh, yes," said Foote.

"Which was . . . ?" said Du Pré.

"Well," said Foote, "it would be a violation of the agreements reached for me to be specific, but let me merely say that there was once an administration that managed to obtain office by illegal means, and that there was a reason the voters did not want them in the first place. We have had, of course, criminals in every administration, and people who were not very bright. What was perfectly astounding about these people is that they were *all* stupid and they uniformly thought nothing of breaking the law. Perhaps they were too limited to grasp the laws. One must be kind. In any case, it is currently felt there are a few things that would best be left unsaid. Permanently. And to that end . . ." Foote became silent.

"Yah," said Du Pré.

"Not that government lawyers are in any way trustworthy," said Foote, "so you may expect difficulties. I don't know what they will do, but they do tend to do things so imbecilic no one with any brains could possibly expect it."

"OK," said Du Pré. "You coming out to hunt?"

"Birds," said Foote. "I have not forgotten the business with the deer. If there are a few birds to shoot, I will come in the fall. . . ."

"OK," said Du Pré.

"Do call if you need me," said Foote. "I expect that you will."

"Here is Bart," said Du Pré. He could see red lights flashing up the road. It took three or four minutes to come to the big eighteen-wheeler overturned in the center barrow pit.

The cab of the tractor was crushed and medics were holding something up.

A bag of fluid.

Bart mumbled something and he shut the phone back up.

"I don't even want to know," he said. He glanced over at the wreckage. "Poor bastard."

Du Pré passed the cop waving the flashlight and then he speeded up.

"I suppose," said Bart, "we can just go to the site. . . ."

"Yah," said Du Pré.

"We can have the security people there as long as you want them," said Bart.

"Jacqueline will not let her kids go back there," said Du Pré. "She is worried, too dangerous. . . ."

"She might be right," said Bart.

"People are very angry," said Du Pré.

"That they are," said Bart. "I'm angry. I am angry that over thirty people guilty of being poor were murdered in my country in 1910 and no one did anything about it. . . ."

"Yah," said Du Pré. They rode on in silence.

The sun slanted down toward the western horizon; it was nearing the solstice, and there were hours of light left.

Du Pré turned east on a two-lane road and he speeded up, back in his element.

They passed a cattle hauler, but that was the only traffic on the road.

Bart began to snore, slumped against the door.

. . . Elizabeth Pardoe, schoolteacher, husband, help little Amalie, get her to Canada . . . two men come looking for the child, men who were the killers of her people, they don't want a witness . . . couple years later, Pardoes they go to where the Métis were killed . . . cannot find the graves . . . the bodies have been moved someplace . . .

. . . she teaches school . . . he runs the ranch . . .

. . . no one says anything, no one ever says anything . . . Elizabeth Pardoe paints, watercolors, paints the country . . . paints one place over and over . . . little canyon, little creek, small cabin . . .

Du Pré rolled a smoke and he lit it. When the blue fog wafted to Bart's nostrils, he sneezed and he sat up straight.

"Whew," he said, "I really zonked out. . . ."

Du Pré drove on.

"Well," said Bart, "at least we can start digging in earnest. I got some help from a private firm. They did work in Yugoslavia, gathering evidence for war crimes trials. . . ."

"Send them home," said Du Pré. Bart looked at him. "The bones will not be there," said Du Pré.

· Chapter 23 ·

DU PRÉ AND BART GAPED at the floodlit gate that led from the county road to the bloody ground of Bitter Creek. Du Pré pulled over.

Several television stations had trucks there.

Chappie and Patchen were standing by an upended trunk that held a square of plywood, and on that were some folders and papers. They were both in uniform.

A young blond woman was holding a microphone to her mouth and speaking to a camera held by a man balancing it on his shoulder.

A generator purred off in the darkness, a cable snaked to some arc lights on stands near where the two marines stood.

Patchen had taken off his artificial arm and his left sleeve was pinned up.

Chappie wore his leg but not his eye. The scarred red mess the shrapnel had left glowed in the harsh light.

Du Pré stopped in back of one of the TV trucks. The doors were open and lights played on the inside from monitors.

Another crew from another station went to the two soldiers and another reporter, this time a young man, asked questions.

"I'll be damned," said Bart. "Manipulating the media. . . ."

Du Pré laughed. He reached under the seat and he pulled out a flask. He had a drink. He put it back and he got out and rolled a smoke and sat on the hood of the cruiser.

Two of the three TV trucks were loading up and in moments they all were turned round and headed back toward the highway. Du Pré and Bart drove on into the lighted patch. Bart got out.

"Whose idea was this?" he said.

"Mine," said Patchen. "I thought that if more people knew about what we were trying to do, there would be less trouble over doing it. . . ." Bart nodded.

Chappie was over by one of the SUVs, putting in his artificial eye. He took off his uniform and he put on jeans and a heavy cotton shirt and his boots.

The generator suddenly stopped running, the lights began to fade.

Patchen walked back from the dark, along the cable. He climbed into the SUV.

"Well," said Bart, "I now own a massacre site."

"Yes," said Chappie, "one of the security people told us."

"Where are they?" said Bart.

A dark-haired man in a dark windbreaker stepped out from behind one of the three SUVs.

"We're here, Mister Fascelli," he said. "I'm Knowles and there are four more people here. Mister Foote called. . . ."

Knowles had a thin white wire running from his collar to his left ear. He stopped and half turned.

"Right," he said.

He motioned to Du Pré and Bart to go to the SUV.

The last of the lights failed and it was dark save for the interior light in the SUV Patchen was in. Then it went out.

Du Pré and Bart walked to the dark vehicle and stood.

Knowles took a pair of night-vision binoculars from his jacket. There was a faint green light radiating from the lenses.

He put them to his eyes and he looked across the road. "Yes," he said, "I see them, two of them. . . ."

Du Pré leaned against the SUV.

"It's off Bart's land," Knowles said, "but it would be nice to know who they are and why they are traipsing about in the dark like that. . . ."

Du Pré looked around under the starlight. He turned so he was looking out of the side of his vision. A movement, black to black, as something went from one shadow to another.

"Go," said Knowles.

Du Pré saw another movement, this one near the road, just a flicker.

Knowles was still looking through the binoculars.

"Six. Sixteen. Forty," he said.

More dark and silence and waiting.

"Be right there," said Knowles.

An engine started and another SUV, this one large and black with dark windows, came out of the shadows in back of the now dead lights.

It went out the gate and straight through the fence on the far side of the road, the barbed wire parting with loud pings, and then the big truck lurched as it roared over the rough land.

Headlights and rack lights flared.

Du Pré glanced to his left and saw flashing blue lights, far away, cresting a hill, and then they were gone as the speeding police car dropped into a bank of shadows.

Two men leaped out of the rear doors of the black SUV and they grabbed at the ground, lifted up two people, hustled them to the SUV, and stuffed them in.

The lights went off, and the big truck turned around and roared back to the place it had torn through the fence. It crossed the road and pulled up close.

The doors opened and three men in black jumpsuits got out; they went to the rear of the SUV and opened those doors and pulled two men out.

Du Pré saw the flashing blue lights, closer now.

He walked to the men, standing now, blinking in the light.

Bonner Macatee and another man Du Pré did not know.

One of the men in the black jumpsuits held out a rifle, which had a huge night-vision scope on it.

"Russian," he said. "They aren't too bad if you can get the damned batteries to keep a charge."

He dropped the rifle on the ground.

Knowles looked at Macatee and his friend, just standing there now. The security men in the black jumpsuits had melted back into the darkness.

"Odd time to be huntin' gophers," said Knowles.

Macatee looked straight ahead. The other man looked everywhere. He was scared.

"So," said Knowles, "out for a little killin'?"

"I told you this wouldn't work," said the second man. "Dammit, Bonner. Look, we was just going to shoot close, not at. . . ."

He looked at the blue lights, on top of another hill, a faint sound of a siren.

"Shut up, Clay," said Macatee. "They can't do anything."

Du Pré heard a clicking sound, metal to metal. He looked across the road. A man was stretching the wire back over the hole the SUV had cut through it.

Du Pré walked up to Macatee.

"What we look for, this will be found," he said. "You should quit, before somebody gets hurt. . . ."

Macatee stared straight ahead. He would not look at Du Pré.

Knowles cocked his head, listening.

"Oh, no," he said, "let him by. We don't need to get into a war with the local law. . . ."

The blue lights came up over the last hill.

The big SUV suddenly blazed with lights, and the cop car began to slow.

It pulled over to the verge and the siren died.

A huge bald man got out, big head and belly, thick arms. He reached in the car after he stood up and found a cowboy hat and he clapped it on his head. He walked very slowly over to where Macatee and his friend stood.

"Name's Rudabaugh," said the huge man. "Sheriff of this county. I see you got Bonner Macatee, who I just happened to be lookin' fer. . . ."

"No law against being out at night on open land," said Macatee.

Knowles lifted up the rifle with the Russian night-vision scope on it. He handed it to the sheriff.

"Bonner, you dumb son of a bitch," said the Sheriff. "People get sent to Deer Lodge Prison, shit like this. . . ." He dropped the gun and stood on the scope, which crunched.

"Haven't done a thing," said Macatee.

"Eleanor says otherwise," said Rudabaugh. "Said you beat up on her. Got a good shiner, too. 'Gainst the law, Mac, so I am arrestin' you for assault. . . ."

The other man backed away from Macatee.

"Clay," said Rudabaugh, "I 'spect you got one or another of your vee-hickles parked some hidden spot. I was you, I would go and find it and go on home. It's late and my acid reflux is painin' me and my temper ain't too good. . . ."

Rudabaugh reached out for Macatee's arm. Macatee pulled it away, angrily.

"Mac," said the sheriff, "I don't want to have to break yer fucking neck but I will. Yer under arrest. Turn around and give me yer danged wrists or I will do it on the ground while I stand on yer neck. . . ."

Macatee breathed deeply. He turned and crossed his wrists, and Rudabaugh clipped silver handcuffs on, clicking them tight.

He took Macatee's arm and led him to the car and stuck him in the back.

Then Rudabaugh walked back.

"He ain't the only hothead round here," said the sheriff.

"You know why we are here and what we are doin'?" said Du Pré.

"Oh, yes," said Rudabaugh. "And as a matter of the peace, I wish you was not. Matter of right and wrong, I am glad you are. Easy for me to say, my people didn't get here till 'bout 1920. . . ."

"So what do you think?" said Knowles.

"I'm just the sheriff," said Rudabaugh. "I don't think."

He looked at Du Pré levelly.

"Hear you are good at figurin' things out," he said, "but take care with this one, 'cause not everything is what it seems. . . ."

Du Pré nodded and Rudabaugh went to his cruiser.

· Chapter 24 ·

DU PRÉ STOOD BY THE LITTLE CREEK, looking at the willows in leaf. A small breeze made the long thin leaves dance, and caddis flies wobbled through the air, pale brown and numerous. He looked down at the creek.

The bottom was clean now; a heavy rain in the night had run so much water over the stones they were scoured and shining.

He jumped over the little rivulet and he walked along the flat. A meadowlark flew up, flapped a few times, and settled back in the tall grass.

A cutbank rimmed the flat on the south side of the little creek. It was six feet high where it began, to the west, and came down to about half that at the east end.

There was an odd cut in the bank, one made a long time ago, about ten feet wide.

A ramp had been dug, and left to the weather, but there was little rain here and the land above the cutbank didn't cover much ground. Other low spines lifted up, not much water collected, so not much moved.

Du Pré saw something, brown, curved, thought it was a root. He bent over and he grasped it with his fingers. An old hayhook, one of the long ones the man on top of the rising stack used to reach down and grab bales and pull up. The steel hook was rusty. A few shreds of gray wood still sat in the socket of the handle. A brilliantly green beetle crawled out of a crack, opened its wing cases, flew away.

Du Pré walked up the little ramp.

He looked south.

A faint track, double, one made long ago by wagon wheels, the thin iron tires pressing down the earth.

The grass was new, the color of the grass on the track just a little lighter than the grass beside it.

Du Pré walked on to the top of the little ridge, looked out over the huge land.

Rolling hills cut with rocks and knees of reddish stone, odd banks of clay left by glacial lakes, compacted nearly to the density of plaster, cut only by the wind.

A few miles to the south there was a small line of big hills, and dark green foliage in their watercourses, deeper clefts than the rocks here had.

Du Pré looked up when a shadow passed overhead. A big vulture lazily floated along a hundred or so feet up, looking for the corpse of something.

Du Pré walked back, brushing the duff and some of the rust from the hayhook. He went down the bank, saw another hook, pulled it up. A long one, top-stack hook. He held them out, nodded. He sighed.

. . . pull a bale, pull a dead body on to a wagon . . . but they don't like it; when they are done they toss these over, don't want to touch them again . . .

He made his way up to the little bench. It was covered in lines made of strings and pegs and had little flags here and there, with notations on them.

A dozen people in shorts and many-pocketed shirts were down on the ground digging carefully with long awls, and when they found something, they carefully brushed the dirt from it, leaving it in place.

Chappie and Patchen were sifting soil through screens, then stirring the dust, picking out something here and there.

Du Pré made his way over to a white-haired man, whose skin was burned so dark by years of sun he looked as though he was made of walnut. His eyes were very blue in his dark skin.

Du Pré held out the two rusted hayhooks, light now with time eating at the steel.

"Uh-huh," said the man. "In Vietnam the Vietcong used those to drag its dead to the river. Whack them into the back of the neck, made it easy to pull. . . ."

Du Pré nodded.

"They took all the bodies," he said.

"No human bones here yet," said the man, "just the left-over ordnance. But I can tell you what happened. The shooting started back there. . . ." He pointed up the creek.

"We found some old cartridges by that red chimney," he said. "That was where it started, and then there were more back there. Some people had got in front of the refugees. They were trapped. Then the real shooting started, but it was up close. Several shotguns, the old shells, the ones that were all brass with a paper plug in the end. But then it gets odd. . . ."

The white-haired man nodded toward a folding table that had some large sheets of paper on it.

Du Pré followed him over.

"These are piles of thirty-forty Krag cartridges," he said. "There are six of them, they are about twelve feet apart, they all held twelve cartridges but the two places you say you dug shells from. . . ."

Du Pré nodded.

"The other cartridges are a mix," said the white-haired man, "and they are set as one would expect in a massacre where the killers were moving to get a better shot, or closer to the people who were hemmed in. But this group seems to indicate six men firing twelve shots twelve feet apart. . . ."

Du Pré nodded.

"And absent the bones," said the white-haired man, "we are done here today. If we could find the grave we could find out more. . . ."

"They moved the dead," said Du Pré.

"Obviously," said the white-haired man. "And now we must move on. A site in Guatemala. There just seems to be no end of demand for our specialty."

Du Pré walked up to one of the big green SUVs and he put the hayhooks in the back. He went to the big barrel of water, flipped on the spigot, and he washed his hands.

He moved to where Chappie and Patchen were sifting soil.

"I am going, go over to the roadhouse," he said. "I have some things to think about."

"This team is leaving," said Patchen. "And we heard there will be a piece on this on the evening news—that right-wing idiot who was here last week. . . ."

"Yah," said Du Pré.

He walked to the SUV he had driven down from the road and he took it as far as the gate, and then he left it and got in his old cruiser, which was too low to get over the rough ground.

He drove off with the windows open. The meadowlarks were trilling.

Du Pré rolled a smoke and he lit it and he speeded up.

When he got to the two-lane blacktop, he cut loose and he soon was going over a hundred. He slowed as he approached the tops of the hills and speeded up if it was clear ahead when he could see.

The hidden dell opened up when he got to the top of the last hill and he could see the roadhouse white in the green of the cottonwoods.

He pulled off the road.

A number of cars and trucks and SUVs were parked there, more than he had ever seen there before.

Du Pré sighed and he pulled the old cruiser round and he parked over the road, pointed back the way that he had come.

He looked at his watch.

Almost five.

He went in.

Heads turned, and people either stared or looked away.

Eleanor Macatee was behind the bar. Her eye was not so discolored now, but there was still a faint splotch of green where Bonner's middle knuckle had hit hardest.

"'Lo, Du Pré," she said. "You know, we used to have meetings where we talked about what might bring the tourists . . ."

Du Pré nodded.

Half of the people in the bar were reporters.

Eleanor made him a whiskey ditch, and Du Pré put five dollars down, and after he drank that she made him another. He sat at a table, quietly drinking.

Clay, the man who had been with Macatee, sneaking through the night with the rifle, got up and went out in some hurry. Du Pré looked at his watch.

He went back to the bar and got another drink; he rolled a smoke and looked at the TV over the bar. It had no sound on; some talking head was mouthing words.

The little strip of news at the bottom said *Twelve US soldiers killed in Iraq.*

"You want the sound on, I can do that," said Eleanor Macatee.

Suzette's round face appeared.

Du Pré nodded.

"My grandmama she is kidnapped, taken down to America, she die there, it is terrible," said Suzette, "I am heartbroken. . . ."

"Why was she taken?" said the talking head.

"She knows, a massacre done there by American soldiers," said Suzette.

"But there is no record of any such massacre," said the talking head.

"She see it," said Suzette, "it happen, 1910."

The talking head smirked.

Chappie and Patchen appeared on the screen. They looked ill at ease and the wind was harsh enough so that they squinted. "A massacre occurred here in 1910," said Patchen, "and we are trying to find what evidence might remain."

"Who killed those people?" said the interviewer, the wind making her jacket flap.

"U.S. Army soldiers," said Patchen, "we think."

"In 1910," said the interviewer.

The two talking heads appeared again.

"At a time when our troops are fighting in Iraq," said one, "there are those who dishonor them. . . ."

"Outrageous," said the other head. "It makes me sick."

· Chapter 25 ·

MICHEL DUHOUX SLID UP on the stool next to Du Pré. Eleanor Macatee came down the bar, DuHoux pointed to Du Pré's drink. She made him one.

He put some money on the counter.

Eleanor took a bill, brought back change. Then she went to the kitchen.

DuHoux sipped his drink.

"I'd rather have a martini," he said.

Du Pré nodded.

"Suzette is certainly acting like Suzette," said DuHoux. "I suppose she will keep shrieking as long as anyone will listen to her. But for reasons having nothing to do with what she wants, she may actually be helpful. . . ."

Du Pré looked at him.

"Do you know anything about Canadian history?" said DuHoux. "We don't really have much. Even our scoundrels are, by the abysmal standards of the rest of the world, rather nice. We are, someone said, the people your mother wanted you to hang with in high school. . . ."

Du Pré laughed.

"Louis Riel," said DuHoux, "our single great blazing

character. He founded a nation that did not last long, gathered a people, helped them know who they were. . . ."

"He was," said Du Pré, "nuts."

"Absolutely," said DuHoux. "Paranoid schizophrenic. Little chats with God. Her Majesty's servants hanged him. Today we would put him in a nice quiet place and keep him away from sharp objects. . . ."

"Gabriel Dumont," said Du Pré. "Him, come down here, riding with one of my great-grandfathers."

"The little general and his marksmen," said DuHoux.

"So the Canadian Métis will use Amalie, their politics," said Du Pré. "Use Suzette, too, but she will be more trouble than she is worth."

"You do know Canadian history," said DuHoux.

"Company of Gentlemen Adventurers of Hudson's Bay," said Du Pré, "and then they built a railroad."

"Amalie was not who she said she was," said DuHoux.

Du Pré looked at him.

DuHoux took out a packet of Player's cigarettes. He shook one from the packet and he tapped it on the ashtray before lighting it.

"You know who she was?" said Du Pré.

DuHoux nodded.

"The winter of 1910 was especially harsh," said DuHoux, "and indeed little Amalie did survive the massacre and indeed she was taken to Canada, and given to some Métis. But little Amalie was full of visions not of this world, and so the next summer the Métis, unable to cope with her, and with the help of a priest, committed her to an asylum for the insane."

Du Pré sighed, had a mouthful of his drink, rolled a smoke and lit it.

"So who is the woman we buried, the churchyard, Toussaint?" said Du Pré.

"The daughter of a woman who worked at the asylum, cleaning and cooking, who came there when Amalie had been there a year or so. The woman's name was Thérèse Malveaux. Amalie died a few years later of tuberculosis. Thérèse Malveaux had a daughter a few years after that, an absolute little horror, Catherine, to whom she told the tale of Amalie and Bitter Creek, and that is who you have buried in your churchyard. It will not be very long before reporters find this out. With computers, there's no privacy left, and anyone can find out just about anything. . . ."

"Christ," said Du Pré.

"So," said DuHoux, "Thérèse told Amalie's story to Catherine, who after some jail time—a five-year prison sentence for forgery—decided to start anew as someone she had never met. . . ."

Du Pré laughed.

DuHoux looked at him.

"People," said Du Pré, "ver' strange world with them in it."

"But," said DuHoux, "little Suzette doesn't know this. Granmaman was a bad girl, just like Suzette, and I have half a feeling the old bat knew it would come to this. . . ."

"It does not matter," said Du Pré.

"I suppose not," said DuHoux. "Just giving you a heads-up. . . ."

"You are writing a book," said Du Pré.

"I am," said DuHoux, "and I would really love to talk to the riddler, the medicine person Benetsee. . . ."

"Good luck," said Du Pré. "Shoot him, you get a chance. . . ."

"I was hoping," said DuHoux, "you might make an introduction. . . ."

Du Pré laughed. He took a pen from his pocket and he found a cocktail napkin. He sketched out a map.

"You go there," he said, "from Toussaint. Take wine and tobacco. Old fart will know you are there. Him want to speak, he will come. . . ."

DuHoux took the napkin. "Thank you," he said.

"I got extra guns," said Du Pré.

"You really love the man, don't you," said DuHoux.

A shadow flickered; someone had come up behind them.

Du Pré turned.

Rudabaugh was standing there, massive, red, a toothpick in his mouth. He chewed it a bit. "Mister Doo Pray," he said, "if you are done here, I would like a word with you, perhaps outside, where it's private. . . ."

Du Pré stood up.

Eleanor came out of the kitchen. She looked at Rudabaugh.

"He's out, Ellie," said the sheriff. "He comes round, you call right *then*."

She nodded.

Rudabaugh jerked his head toward the door and he moved with his heavy grace toward it. Du Pré nodded to DuHoux and he got up and followed. Rudabaugh's cruiser was parked next to Du Pré's.

The huge sheriff opened the driver's door and he got in, and Du Pré went round to the passenger door and he got in, too.

"Been talking to a few folks about you," said Rudabaugh. "All of them, after the customary complaints about your bad habits and lousy character, do seem to have a high opinion of yer brains and character and all, which I expected. Sheriff Klein, who sounds like a nice feller, says you kin figure about anything out. He calls you first thing he has something needs figurin' out. . . ."

Du Pré sat, waiting.

"It's late and maybe you would be good enough to get in yer car and foller me. I got something I would like you to take a look at. . . ." said Rudabaugh.

"OK," said Du Pré. He got out of the sheriff's car and into his own.

Rudabaugh backed and turned and drove out to the

blacktop. Du Pré followed. Rudabaugh drove toward the site where Chappie and Patchen were camped and Du Pré tensed, but Rudabaugh passed the gate and drove on another mile and a half.

Du Pré could see flashing lights off to the left, out of sight over a low hill.

Rudabaugh drove in and Du Pré followed.

There was a sheriff's cruiser parked in front of an old two-story ranch house, the standard Sears Roebuck ranch house from the twenties.

Rudabaugh parked.

He got out and he waited for Du Pré.

Red lights showed out on the county road.

An ambulance turned in and came on toward them.

A deputy stood by the front door of the house.

Rudabaugh nodded and the man stepped back.

"Thank you, Tom," he said as he passed.

Du Pré followed.

Rudabaugh went through the living room to the kitchen.

Jackson Pardoe was lying on the floor, next to the pantry. A telephone lay on the floor beside him. A faint blood trickle ran from his ear down his cheek.

Footsteps sounded, coming through the front door. A man with a big nylon bag came in. He looked at Pardoe.

"Hi, Doc," said Rudabaugh.

The coroner put on thin rubber gloves. He took some cases, small ones, out of his bag. "He's dead," said the coroner, "if you can't stand the suspense."

"What'd he die of?" said Rudabaugh.

"Something fatal," said the coroner. "Don't see any holes right off. Blood could be from the fall, or not. Lessee here . . ." And he reached under Pardoe's body and he rolled him. Pardoe was stiff.

Nothing. No blood underneath.

The coroner stood up.

"You want to keep lookin' for somethin' ain't there?" he said. "Or shall I call in the boys and get him sent off fer an autopsy?"

"Fine," said Rudabaugh.

The coroner went out and he came back with two helpers and a rolling stretcher. They got Pardoe's body on it and they wheeled him out. His left arm stuck forward, his palm out.

"Could be a massive coronary," said the coroner.

"Don't think so," said Rudabaugh. "Called 911."

"Oh," said the coroner.

"Didn't say anything," said Rudabaugh, "but we knew where the call come from."

"Well," said the coroner, "we'll just have to wait on the autopsy."

He went out.

Du Pré looked at Rudabaugh.

"If he had him a heart attack," said Rudabaugh, "how'd he manage to dial 911?"

Du Pré shrugged.

Rudabaugh crooked a finger.

He led Du Pré up the stairs.

One room was a bedroom, in bachelor disarray. The other Pardoe had used as an office.

The office had been ransacked. Drawers were on the floor, papers had been kicked around, books pulled from the shelves. A computer sat, a weird geometric form waving on its screen. "Like I said," said Rudabaugh, "I don't think it was a heart attack."

· Chapter 26 ·

"SO," SAID RUDABAUGH, "seems that pore ol' Jackson is dead and as he was not dead 'fore all this blew up about that massacre, I suspect that had somethin' to do with it. . . ."

Du Pré nodded. He was walking around the parking gravels. The mercury lamp was bright and threw any shadow into high relief.

The tracks were jumbled, vehicles, the narrow wiggling lines left by the rolling stretcher.

"Not knowin' what they will find when they cut ol' Jackson up yet," said Rudabaugh, "I 'spect he was poisoned, and poison is somethin' a woman who is squeamish about blowin' someone's head off uses. . . ."

Du Pré nodded. "State people will help," he said.

"Could come to that," said Rudabaugh. "Doubt I will need them. Thing about livin' on the ass end of nowhere is there ain't that many people to sort through. We got the ones don't like what you are stirrin' up down there, few of them. Bonner Macatee would come to about anyone's mind, but thing about Bonner is he's a hothead and this ain't hotheaded. . . ."

Du Pré nodded. "You look the kitchen?" he said.

"Did that," said Rudabaugh. "Everything nice and clean and put away. Jackson didn't drink much. Partial to scotch, which hereabouts is a blot on yer drinkin' character. Bertie down to the post office wondered about Jackson, as he subscribed to the *New Yorker* and other magazines didn't have useful articles on wormin' calves or how to sell mint jelly you made in yer spare time. . . ."

Du Pré nodded.

A sheriff's cruiser came up the road, sedately. "That'll be Ellie," said Rudabaugh. "She was the only livin' kin Jackson had round here anyway. . . ."

The car pulled up and the deputy got out and opened the passenger door and Ellie Macatee got out. Her face was composed and she stood very straight.

"Where is he?" she said.

"Been took off," said Rudabaugh, "might do to come sit. . . ."

Ellie nodded, and she walked up to the porch. She sat on the worn floor, her long legs folded, her boots in the flower bed. Rudabaugh sat down next to her.

"If he had a heart attack, "said Ellie, "why is *he* here?" She looked at Du Pré.

"Might have been one, might have been somethin' else," said Rudabaugh. "They're takin' him to Great Falls, see . . . ."

"Autopsy?" said Ellie.

"Got to," said Rudabaugh.

"If somebody killed him," she said, "it wasn't Bonner. That dumb son of a bitch might throw a punch. But . . ."

"Didn't think it was him," said Rudabaugh. "Somebody tore up his office, though, so I do wonder what they might have been lookin' for, as you might expect. . . ."

Ellie nodded. She looked at Du Pré. "My father is dead," she said, her voice flat, "because you bastards came here and raked up an old crime. It was a crime. But half the county are people descended from the folks who did it. . . ."

Du Pré nodded.

"And they are all dead and now my father is too," said Ellie. "Goddamn the lot of you. . . ."

Rudabaugh nodded.

"Maybe," he said, looking at Du Pré, "I don't need you no more tonight. . . ."

Du Pré nodded. He walked to his old cruiser and he got in and he drove back to the gate that opened on the big pasture. He got out, opened the gate, and he went through and shut it and he drove on toward the camp near the little bitter creek.

Two wall tents were set up, and an electric generator fuffled off in the dark.

Chappie and Patchen were sitting at a small folding table playing chess.

"Somebody kill Jackson Pardoe," said Du Pré.

"Jesus," said Patchen, "why?"

Du Pré shrugged.

"That asshole?" said Chappie. "Mctee or what he is?"

Du Pré shook his head. "Not him."

"God," said Patchen, "you would think people would want to air this out and let it go. . . ."

Du Pré looked at the long table close to the cutbank. He took a flashlight and he walked to it and he shone it on what was piled there.

Hundreds of cartridges, shotgun, rifle, pistol, were in small plastic buckets.

"We found one thing other than shells," said Chappie. Du Pré turned and Chappie held out a small silver crucifix. It was black with tarnish, but the Christ was all there.

. . . like the one that Amalie had, only hers was worn . . .

"Where was this?" said Du Pré.

"Patchen found it," said Chappie.

They walked back to Patchen, still studying the chessboard.

"Where you find this?" said Du Pré.

"Down in the flat, over there," said Patchen. "It was just sitting on top of the ground. I thought it was a piece of bark at first."

"Show me," said Du Pré.

Patchen looked at him for a moment and then he got up and he went to a bank of lights on poles and he turned them on. The gasoline generator picked up when the drain on the electrical supply flipped a switch.

The flat by the creek was bright with arc lights. Patchen pointed to a grid, near the creek.

"You find it there," Du Pré said.

"Yes," said Patchen.

"On top the ground," said Du Pré.

"Mostly," said Patchen. "Just the base was in the soil, not far, quarter inch maybe. . . ."

Du Pré nodded. He yawned. They went back and Patchen cut the lights. "You don't find any bones or teeth?" said Du Pré.

"No," said Patchen.

"Just the shells," said Chappie. "They were all up here but a few we found down there. Hard digging there, it is rocky. . . ."

"I am going, Toussaint," said Du Pré. "Maybe bring back horse. . . ."

Patchen looked at him.

The country to the south was a jumble of rocks and hills, a low reef in the distance under the starlight.

"They are out there, you think," said Chappie.

Du Pré nodded. He turned.

"You be careful," he said. "Somebody is willing, kill to stop this."

Chappie and Patchen looked at each other. Chappie went over and shut off the lights.

Du Pré got in the SUV he had driven down in and he drove back to the gate. He got in his cruiser and he drove out and shut the gate behind him.

He drove east, north, then east.

He yawned, reached under the seat, had a snort, rolled a smoke. There was no traffic on the two-lane.

. . . long time gone and long time they have been buried . . . it is winter they don't dig no big hole . . . old mine, blow it down . . .

He got to Toussaint just as the light was rising in the east. He drove out to Bart's and he went to bed in one of the guest cabins.

. . . winter . . . bitter cold . . . sundogs . . .

He dreamed, dark dreams with strange shapes roiling in them. He heard a voice.

"Git outta here, you son of a bitch!" yelled Booger Tom.

Du Pré yawned. He looked at his watch.

He had slept for three hours. Not enough, but it would have to do. He got up and pulled on his boots and went out.

The old cowboy was shoving on the water buffalo. Eustace had his head through a window in Booger Tom's cabin. Finally the buffalo pulled his head out. His face was smeared with dough. "Ate my biscuit dough," said Booger Tom.

Du Pré laughed.

"It ain't funny, you half-breed son of a bitch," said the old cowboy.

"I need some horses, trailer," said Du Pré.

"How 'bout a water buffalo?" said Booger Tom.

· Chapter 27 ·

DU PRÉ PULLED THE TRAILER with the four horses in it under some cottonwoods, for the shade.

"Yer coddlin' the sonsabitches," said Booger Tom.

"If I had not, you would say I was mistreating them," said Du Pré.

"Worst thing kin happen to a man is his friends understandin' him," said Booger Tom.

"Lunch?" said Du Pré.

"They got food here?" said Booger Tom. "Looks like one of them yuppie places got all sorts of noodles and soybeans and nothin' to eat."

"They have food," said Du Pré.

They walked to the roadhouse, passing Rudabaugh's car. The huge sheriff was at a table, picking at the last of his french fries.

"Doo Pray," said Rudabaugh.

"Sheriff," said Du Pré, "this is Booger Tom."

Rudabaugh looked at the old cowboy. "I thought things like this was extinct," he said.

"Yer fat," said Booger Tom.

"Take it back," said Rudabaugh. "I hoped that things like this was extinct."

"You are old friends," said Du Pré. "You kiss, tell old lies, I am getting something to eat. . . ."

Booger Tom sat down with the sheriff.

"Doo Pray," said Booger Tom, "fetch me some food and a beer would be right nice."

Dark-haired Lily was behind the bar, and she smiled at Du Pré. "What'll it be?" she said.

"Ditch, beer, two cheeseburgers, fries," said Du Pré. "I apologize for my friend."

Lily laughed. "You go and see he behaves," she said. "I'll rustle up your food and drinks. . . ."

A woman Du Pré had not seen before came out of the kitchen, carrying some tableware.

"All of them need it, Jerry," said Lily, and she ducked into the kitchen.

Du Pré wandered back into the little museum and he stopped in front of the portrait of Elizabeth Rhodes Pardoe. The beautiful blond woman looked back levelly, across eight or more decades. Three of her paintings hung on the walls.

There was a display in the corner, half sheets of plywood painted white hinged on the wall end, so that one could leaf through them like a book.

Du Pré looked at photographs of haying, huge crews, horse-drawn rakes, cutters.

An old white-haired man standing by a crossbar that twelve mountain lions hung from, holding his rifle.

Schoolchildren posed on the steps of a small white schoolhouse.

Elizabeth Rhodes Pardoe stood behind them, lovely in a white high-necked blouse. She had the intaglio brooch on her left breast.

Du Pré flipped the next page. AN ARTIST OF LIGHT AND

LAND said the caption. Elizabeth Pardoe in a studio, standing with a palette in her left hand and a brush in her right. She was laughing.

A photograph of Elizabeth Pardoe outdoors, seated on a folding stool, a painter's box open beside her, standing on spindly wooden legs. She had a canvas on an easel before her and wore a hat with flowers set round the brim.

Standing with her husband, Ellis Pardoe.

ELLIS ARTHURS PARDOE 1882–1981 had been inked below his feet. ELIZABETH RHODES PARDOE 1888–1969 inked below hers. Two different hands.

Du Pré went back out and he saw Lily carrying platters to the table where Booger Tom and Sheriff Rudabaugh were sitting. Booger Tom was waving a finger at the sheriff, who was about four times as big. Du Pré sat down, picked up his cheeseburger, shook salt on it. "You know each other," said Du Pré. "Booger Tom, him want to move here, live. . . ."

"Doo Pray," said Booger Tom, "has no respect fer his elders."

"We run him out once," said Rudabaugh. "We kin do it again." He grinned at Booger Tom.

Du Pré ate, drank, went to the bar with his empty glass. He paid for the food and the drinks.

He waited for his change, put a five-dollar bill on the counter. "Elizabeth Pardoe painted," said Du Pré. "Are there more of her paintings?"

"Lots of them here and there," said Lily. "You know, we had her painter's kit, that box with the legs, back in the museum but some bastard stole it. . . ."

Du Pré nodded. "When?" he said.

"Couple weeks ago," said Lily. "Somebody jimmied the back door and came in, stole some money from the deposit bag—we don't have a safe—took a buffalo rifle from the wall and that kit."

Du Pré nodded. "Ellis Pardoe, he was killed in the First World War?" said Du Pré.

"Uh-huh," said Lily, "he was killed the second of November. Just nine days before it ended. . . ."

Du Pré nodded. "Thank you," he said.

He walked back to the table. Rudabaugh and Booger Tom were standing, waiting.

They all walked outside. "Sheriff," said Du Pré, "you know where I can find, report on that Lieutenant Albert, shot himself here, 1931? Suicide, would have a report."

"I s'pose so," said Rudabaugh. "Thing is, you got to use one of them com-pooters and my fingers is too big fer them little keys. . . ."

Booger Tom looked at Du Pré. "Rudy," said Booger Tom, "I knows you are all embarrassed at bein' so feebleminded, but do allow me to help. I know com-pooter. . . ."

"You?" said Rudabaugh. "You got useful?"

"Yup," said Booger Tom.

"It is important maybe," said Du Pré, "the Pardoe business, you know."

Rudabaugh looked at Du Pré.

"You are hangin' this miserable old goat on me, ain't you?" he said.

"Yes," said Du Pré.

"The voters knew you, how sorry you are," said Booger Tom, "I'd be the sheriff."

"That don't even bear thinkin' about," said Rudabaugh.

"If you can," said Du Pré, "maybe lock him up when you are done?" And he walked back to the truck.

He got in and started it and he drove out on the blacktop, heading for the Pardoe ranch.

The gate was open when he got there.

He drove in and looked round. An SUV was sitting by the fence.

There had been no cattle in the pasture, but the gate had always been closed before.

Du Pré drove on.

He crested the hill and saw the wall tents below, with Chappie and Patchen at work, the earphones on, the metal detectors sweeping back and forth across the ground.

Du Pré pulled down to the camp. Chappie saw him and waved. Du Pré opened the stock trailer and he slipped in and backed the horses out one by one.

They whuffled and snorted and walked down to the little creek to drink.

Chappie took off his earphones. "Will they be all right?" he yelled.

"Yes," said Du Pré.

There was no water near but the little creek, rising up and sinking down in the land in less than half a mile.

"I am going, see about something," said Du Pré. "I leave the trailer." He racheted down the stand and he unhitched it, unplugged the electrical cable. He drove back up to the gate and he got out, opened it, drove through and shut it again.

He drove to Jackson Pardoe's house. It had the usual yellow tape stretched across the door.

Du Pré walked round the house.

There was a much smaller house behind it, a neat clapboard building about twenty by fifteen feet.

He walked up to it, looked at the door.

It had a padlock on a hasp, but the lock was not snapped to. Du Pré looked at it. It gleamed with oil.

He unfastened the hasp, pushed the door open. The air was stale but did not stink of rodent. It had been swept fairly recently. The windows were covered with shutters.

Du Pré went outside and he opened the big shutters at the far end. He went back in.

There were racks of paintings set against the one blank wall.

Above a big table, between the two windows, was a painting of a boy, dressed in jeans and boots, holding a halter. The halter held a palomino horse.

Jackson Pardoe, aged twelve or so. No. Jackson Pardoe's father, probably.

Du Pré went to the painting, took it off the wall.

It had a paper backing.

Du Pré slit the paper. He reached his hand in. He pulled out a leather book, one with a strap and snap.

He put it in his pocket. He reached in again.

He pulled out four thick bundles of letters, each bundle tied with a pale violet ribbon.

. . . this was red once . . .

· Chapter 28 ·

DU PRÉ DROVE INTO THE COUNTY SEAT, a little dying western town.

WELCOME TO RYLAND said the sign.

The Sheriff's Department was in the old courthouse, a structure ten times larger than the county now needed. The post office sat across the street. Du Pré went in, got an express mail box, put the book and the letters in it, scribbled an address, and took it to the window.

A heavy woman with tightly curled gray hair came out of a back room.

The little plastic square on her uniform shirt read BERTIE.

"Seven eight-five," she said. "Hope you got change or a ten. I just got cleaned out, big money order."

Du Pré pulled out exact change, paid, took his receipt.

"You want a delivery guarantee?" said Bertie.

Du Pré shook his head. "Thank you."

He walked out and across the street to the Sheriff's Office.

Booger Tom and Rudabaugh were in the office, pitching darts at a picture of Osama Bin Laden.

"Doo Pray," said Rudabaugh, "I was about to trump up a charge and throw this old scoundrel in the hoosegow."

"He's pissed 'cause I won ten bucks off him playin' darts," said Booger Tom.

"He cheats," said Rudabaugh.

"I suppose," said Booger Tom, "you want that report. Well, I done found it easy enough, even with him jigglin' my elbow. . . ."

"You *are* takin' him away?" said Rudabaugh.

Du Pré nodded.

Booger Tom picked up a small pile of papers. Pale facsimiles of old documents.

Du Pré looked through them.

"Coroner's report said he shot himself right down there where they say the massacre was," said Booger Tom. "His feet was up on the bank and he was facedown in the water, one shot to the right temple. Didn't find a note. Gun was a thirty-eight, not an army issue."

"Musta about et him up," said Rudabaugh.

Du Pré folded the papers and put them in his shirt pocket.

Rudabaugh tossed a final dart. He took out his wallet and he fished a twenty-dollar bill out of it and he handed it to Booger Tom. The radio began to squawk and Rudabaugh went into the back room.

"Tomorrow," said Du Pré, "maybe I go and ride south some there. . . ."

"OK," said Booger Tom, "then what am I here for?"

Du Pré laughed. "I am worried, Chappie and Patchen," he said.

"OK," said Booger Tom. Rudabaugh came out of the office, clapping his Stetson on his head.

"Gotta go," he said. "Lemme know when you figger how old Pardoe done died. Still don't have the coroner's report."

"I let you know," said Du Pré.

He and Booger Tom walked out to the pickup. "There are bunks, the camp," said Du Pré.

"Hi-falutin'," said Booger Tom. "I sleep on cactus mostly, less I can find some snow. . . ."

Du Pré drove back to the Pardoe ranch. Booger Tom got out grumbling and he took care of the gate.

Chappie and Patchen were in camp but not in the tents when Du Pré and Booger Tom got there. Du Pré looked in one of the wall tents and then the other, and when he stood back from the second tent, he heard a low whistle.

"We are just doing guard," said Patchen. "We got a lot of practice in Iraq."

"You see or hear anything?" said Booger Tom.

"Just the critters," said Chappie, "I can only hear out of my left ear anyway . . . but just the mice and the weasels."

"Weasels?" said Booger Tom.

"Couple went dancing through camp," said Chappie. "Seemed to be in love. . . ."

"Oh, fer Chrissakes." said Booger Tom.

Du Pré went into the big wall tent and he got a wide-beam light and he went back out and down by the creek. He paused between two rocks and he set the light on one of them. He took out the coroner's report and his reading glasses.

The writing was faint and hard to decipher.

Du Pré looked at it intently. He shone the light behind the paper and the pale gray photocopy ink leaped out.

"Find anything interestin'?" said Booger Tom.

"I am looking," said Du Pré.

"One of the things I have always admired about you, Du Pré," said Booger Tom, "is how you kin say things without sayin' anything. You are right practiced at it. . . ."

Du Pré laughed. "General Albert," he said, "he was a general then, twenty years after the massacre. He is found about there . . ." And Du Pré pointed to the little creek, near where the willows began "He is shot once, the right temple. The pistol is in the water and so is he, facedown, feet up. . . ."

"Who found him?" said Booger Tom.

"Mrs. Elizabeth Pardoe," said Du Pré.

Booger Tom grunted.

"Not her husband?" said Booger Tom.

"Died 1918, week before the war ended," said Du Pré.

Booger Tom nodded.

"Sheriff Dunning came with deputies LeFabre and Goss. They noted where the body was, lifted it to the back of a mule, and went out to the main ranch house . . . where the body was transferred to a truck. . . ."

"So he come back here, all guilty," said Booger Tom.

Du Pré nodded.

"Et him up," said Booger Tom.

"He had four hundred and twenty-seven dollars and sixty-seven cents in his pockets in coins and bills . . ." said Du Pré. "A wallet, a few cards—not his—a pocketknife with an ivory handle, his clothing was a suit from Brooks Brothers, New York, shoes by Lester and Frye, black silk socks, small clothes, a fountain pen, an address book, a pocket diary recovered but ruined by the water. . . ."

Booger Tom held out his hand. Du Pré rolled a smoke for him and one for himself.

"The coroner's jury ruled the death a suicide. The body was embalmed and sent east with General Albert's possessions. . . ." said Du Pré.

"Who to?" said Booger Tom.

"Next of kin, Mrs. Letitia Albert, Manassas, Virginia," said Du Pré.

"Wife?" said Booger Tom.

"Maybe," said Du Pré. "And there is a statement from Elizabeth Pardoe, she give to the coroner's jury."

"They have them things here?" said Booger Tom.

"Ranchers here are mostly English early on," said Du Pré, "so yes, I guess so. . . ."

"And she said?" said Booger Tom.

"She say that Albert is her husband's commander, the

Great War, and that he had been here before that. She did not say why. She said he came to the ranch 'having taken drink' and that he borrowed a horse and rode off the day before she found his body. . . ." Booger Tom blew out some smoke. "The next morning the horse was back, still saddled, but not Albert. Mrs. Pardoe had gone to town and did not discover the horse until she returned about noon. She immediately set out looking for Albert, found him shortly in the place described. . . ."

Booger Tom laughed.

Du Pré looked at the last sheet of paper.

"Anything else?" said Booger Tom.

"Jury verdict, suicide, foul play not suspected," said Du Pré.

"Bunch of crap," said Booger Tom. "She killed him, what I think."

Du Pré folded the papers and he put them in his pocket. He flipped the switch on the flashlight.

It seemed dark for a moment, and then his eyes got used to the dark.

A nightjar flitted past, eating insects on the wing.

Something thrashed in the willows, gasped, died.

"So what you think, Du Pré?" said Booger Tom.

"Tomorrow we go and look, see if we can find that place Elizabeth Pardoe painted. Little cleft canyon, little cabin. Cabin was in bad shape, roof caved in, long time ago. . . ."

Booger Tom nodded. "That's where you figure the Métis was dumped?" he said.

"Yes," said Du Pré.

"Any of this make sense to you?" said Booger Tom.

"Not yet," said Du Pré, "maybe soon, it is still cloudy."

"Murky is what you mean," said Booger Tom.

Du Pré laughed.

"Hold it down," yelled Chappie. "Ya sound like a pair of schoolgirls."

Booger Tom made a loud farting noise. "If you is all we

got protectin' us," he yelled back, "I think I will go toes up now. . . ."

"Peace is our profession," said Chappie.

"I am tired," said Du Pré.

· Chapter 29 ·

DU PRÉ STOOD A HUNDRED FEET from the tents and pissed, and the cold air made it steam as he yawned.

The horses whuffled and stirred. They were shadows gaining mass as the sun rose in the east. There was a faint rim of pink on the land to the east.

He walked back to the camp.

Booger Tom was cooking eggs and sausage on a propane stove. He shoveled a mess of eggs and two patties of sausage on a steel plate and he handed it to Du Pré.

Du Pré buttered some toast kept warm in a small oven set over one of the burners on the stove.

They ate sitting at the folding camp table. The coffee was strong and thick.

Chappie came out of the wall tent yawning. He had a rifle in his hand. He moved off toward a high spot. As he got there, Patchen came in from a different direction.

"Plenty of food," said Booger Tom, pointing to the stove. Patchen filled a plate, ate quickly, drank some coffee, went into the tent.

"We coulda helped 'em," said Booger Tom.

"They sleep some today," said Du Pré. "We are old and we may have long ride, you know."

"I'm *old*," said Booger Tom. "Yer in early middle age."

. . . the old bastard must be eighty, Du Pré thought, looks sixty . . . think ill of the human race, makes you young . . .

"Ever' time I look at them two, missing parts on account of that farina-faced little moron we had in the White House, I get pissed off. . . ." said Booger Tom. "Best soldiers in the world and he makes 'em rubber ducks in a shootin' gallery."

Du Pré nodded.

"Bart should be here any minute with that mackerel-snappin' fool," said Booger Tom.

"He will come," said Du Pré. "You have not converted yet."

"Not likely," said Booger Tom. "And he ain't never brought it up."

"You are almost dead," said Du Pré. "You could cover your bets."

They heard a truck, saw headlights gleam on top of the hill. Two mule deer bounded through the beams of light.

The big SUV pulled into the camp.

A door opened and Father Van Den Heuvel fell out. He got up quickly, and he reached in for something. He pulled out a duffel bag. Walking over to Du Pré and Booger Tom, the priest dropped the bag and tripped over it.

"That does it," said Booger Tom, "I am gonna shoot him. Now. It ain't *safe*. . . ."

Father Van Den Heuvel stood up, picked up the bag. "Watch your mouth," he said. "I have powerful friends."

Bart stuck his head out of the driver's window.

"Is it safe to get out yet?" he said. "Could you get him a chair and keep him there?"

Father Van Den Heuvel made an unpriestly gesture in the direction of everybody.

Bart got out and he approached cautiously.

"Oh, quit," said Father Van Den Heuvel. "It's early and we've been surviving on bad coffee. I want good coffee. And sympathy. I think I sprained my ankle. I am in *pain*. . . ."

Booger Tom looked at Du Pré, his eyes narrowed. "Why we got this hopeless idiot here?" he said. "And we plan to put him on a horse? Let him go ridin'? With us? I'll spend the day ridin' after his horse and puttin' on splints and plasters. . . ."

Bart unfolded a camp chair. "Your friend is flying here," he said to Du Pré, "in his own plane. He'll be here late this afternoon. . . ."

Du Pré nodded. He got up and so did Booger Tom and they went to the horses and slipped halters on three. Booger Tom led a fat old brown horse over to the box trailer, pulled out a saddle and tack and a blanket, and he put them on. He led the horse to Father Van Den Heuvel. Father Van Den Heuvel took the reins.

"Good morning, Duncan," he said. He rubbed the horse's nose and he fished something out of his pocket and let the horse nibble it from his palm.

Du Pré and Booger Tom saddled the other two; Du Pré put bottles of water and some salami and cheese and bread in his saddlebags. The light was rising fast now.

Father Van Den Heuvel put on his wide-brimmed black hat. He lifted his left foot and stuck it at the stirrup.

He missed.

Du Pré sighed. He went to the horse and priest. He brought along a short stepladder.

With one hand on the saddle horn, standing precariously balanced on the top of the stepladder, Father Van Den Heuvel managed to get on.

Duncan stood, imperturbable.

"Horses usually try to kill me," said the priest.

"We drugged him up good 'fore you got here," said Booger

Tom. He was sitting easy in the saddle, his horse dancing a little, eager to run.

Du Pré mounted his horse.

"All right," said the big priest, pulling a folded sheet of paper from his pocket, "the mother rock here is limestone, but there was an igneous incursion thirty million years ago. . . ."

"It say that in the Bible?" said Booger Tom.

"The incursion went mainly up and under an area about ten miles away, but pipes of material splayed out from it. There is one six miles from here and from the contours on the map, that may be the place we are looking for," said the priest. He folded the paper.

"Which way it might be I haven't the foggiest," he added.

"South is that way," said Booger Tom.

"If one has faith," said Father Van Den Heuvel, "one has revelations. One hears voices. . . ."

"Is it south on the goddamned map?" said Booger Tom.

"Definitely," said Father Van Den Heuvel. "Lead on. Do go out in front a few hundred feet. . . ."

"Christ," said Booger Tom, riding past the priest and Du Pré.

The old cowboy's horse broke into a run for the hell of it and Booger Tom let him go.

He ran the horse in a wide circle, up a hill at speed and along the crest and then over it and out of sight.

"I am glad he didn't give me that horse," said Father Van Den Heuvel.

Du Pré laughed.

He rode ahead and his horse danced a little, and Du Pré reined him toward the short drop at the far end of the flat. The horse stepped down into the floodplain and then he jumped the creek easily.

Old Duncan did the same, more slowly, and when he got to the creek he stepped across.

Du Pré took the trail that headed south.

Father Van Den Heuvel rode behind.

"Aha!" he said. "See that saddle over there . . . ?"

Du Pré turned.

"That would have had an ice dam across it," said the priest. "I have been looking at this. This was a lake, and then there must have been another dam back that way, which held longer. That is the old river channel there. . . ." He pointed straight ahead.

"Yahoo!" yelled Booger Tom behind them.

He rode past.

His horse moved, Booger Tom did not. He was just sitting on the running animal, loose and easy.

"I wish I could do that," said Father Van Den Heuvel.

"So do I," said Du Pré.

"You ride well," said the priest.

"I am OK," said Du Pré, "but I am not like him. . . ."

They rode along in silence.

The rains had stopped for a time and the grass was brown and withered, save along the little watercourse. The banks were still green, but the water would sink deeper and those grasses would die too.

Booger Tom turned around and rode back, his horse calmer.

"We are gonna spend all day out here with this fool?" he said.

"Bless you, my son," said Father Van Den Heuvel.

Du Pré handed a piece of paper to the priest.

The three stopped.

"That is what she painted, over and over," said Du Pré, "that cabin, that little cleft canyon. . . ."

Father Van Den Heuvel nodded.

"The way it is eroded," he said, "I suspect the incursion is the left side, the mother rock the right. It is much more worn down there. . . ."

"They could get a wagon to it," said Du Pré.

. . . filled with the dead . . .

Booger Tom stood up in his stirrups.

He peered at the land ahead, cut and carved by water and ice and wind and time.

"So we are lookin' for an old wagon road," he said.

"Yah," said Du Pré.

He rode to the priest.

Father Van Den Heuvel handed him the sketch of the cabin and the canyon.

"Me and old Ranger here will go up on a look-see," he said. "The danged horse is gettin' dancy again. . . ."

And he was gone.

Du Pré and Father Van Den Heuvel slowly plodded on.

· Chapter 30 ·

THEY ATE LUNCH IN THE SHADE of a cliff, above a wide river channel that carried a great deal of water long ago and now carried only the wind.

They ate quickly and remounted.

Horseflies buzzed about, thwacked when they ran into men and horses.

"This could go on a ways," said Booger Tom, "and so far you could get a wagon through it, had a four team on it, easy."

"When you started out as a cowboy," said Father Van Den Heuvel, "had the wheel been invented?"

"Saw the first one," said Booger Tom. "Didn't think much of it, tell you the truth. Speeded things up. Most of our troubles today come of speedin' things up. . . ."

Du Pré laughed.

They went on.

The sun was very hot and a stiff wind was rising. It came from the east.

. . . be heavy rain before morning . . . be very wet . . .

"Gonna rain before mornin'," said Booger Tom, "and I don't want to be down in this when it does. . . ."

Du Pré laughed.

The trail left the riverbed and went through a cut in the rock, not deep, only ten feet or so to the top of the yellow-gray limestone.

Father Van Den Heuvel looked at the rock.

He pointed to a faint vertical line. "Drill hole," he said. "They blew rock out of this, so this must be the trail."

"Wide enough for a big freight wagon," said Booger Tom.

They rode on.

They saw a small pile of boards weathered to gray, so sun eaten there were gaps an inch wide in some places.

"Old wagon box," said Booger Tom. "Woulda taken the metal parts and the frame and wheels. . . ."

"Moving ore?" said Du Pré.

"Probably," said Booger Tom. "Rough rock would eat the boxes pretty quick, all the heaving on this road. . . ."

"This," said Father Van Den Heuvel, "is not a road."

They went on.

The narrow track went straight to the side of a huge butte that rose up sheer from the land. Father Van Den Heuvel stopped and he looked at the butte. He took out a pair of binoculars. He studied the rocks. Off to the right there was a reef of rock that was triangular, one broken end upthrust. "That is the incursion," he said.

"Carries metals," said Booger Tom. "Don't they, I mean . . . ?"

"Sometimes," said Father Van Den Heuvel, "not always, but often enough so any miner would be encouraged."

They rode on.

Du Pré unbuttoned his shirt. He was sweating and now the wind was hot too.

"Big rain tomorrow," said Booger Tom. "Low pressure's enough to suck stuff up from Colorado, it's so danged low. . . ."

They went through another cut in the mother rock, and then the country opened up.

They rounded a knee thrust out from the reef.

A narrow little canyon had eroded into the rock, darker than the limestone mother rock, which had worn away on the right. Booger Tom trotted on ahead. He reined up.

"There's where the cabin was," he said, pointing to the ground ahead.

Du Pré and Father Van Den Heuvel came to where the old cowboy was. "And there's the mine," said Father Van Den Heuvel. He pointed to a flat place covered by a jumble of rocks, blocky and broken, about thirty feet deep at the top. The skirt reached out fifty feet from the rock wall.

Du Pré crossed himself. So did Father Van Den Heuvel. "You'd have to get heavy equipment in here, to move this," said the priest. "This was deliberately blown down over the mine entrance." Du Pré nodded.

"So," said Father Van Den Heuvel, "you think those poor people were buried in the mine?"

Du Pré nodded.

The big priest got down and he walked to the first big rock. He knelt and he began to pray.

Booger Tom took off his hat.

So did Du Pré.

The priest finished and he stood up and put on his big black hat.

"What would they have been minin' here?" said Booger Tom.

Father Van Den Heuvel shrugged.

"They would have been looking for copper, silver, gold," he said. "In mining, it has been said, you never know if you are ten feet from a million dollars or a million feet from ten dollars. Perhaps the veins were poor but got just a little richer. So they were encouraged. This was hard-rock mining. They had to blast and dig. . . ."

Du Pré looked up at the rock face.

"There would have been some fractures in the rock," said

Father Van Den Heuvel. "They could have packed one with powder and tamped that with mud. Enough powder, the face would have broken away. . . ."

Du Pré nodded.

"Look up there," said Booger Tom, pointing. "You see them drill holes?"

Father Van Den Heuvel squinted.

The three of them clambered from rock to rock, up to a long ledge of dark gray stone that ran two hundred feet or so across.

Father Van Den Heuvel pulled a small magnifying glass from his pocket and he slid it from the leather case and he looked at the vertical drill holes. He looked at the top of the ledge. The light was strong and the vertical holes were hard to see.

"They would drill holes every so often," said Father Van Den Heuvel, "and pack perhaps every fourth one with explosives. The holes would weaken the rock and the explosion would sheer the rock away." Father Van Den Heuvel looked at the rock he stood on. He knelt and he peered down into a cleft between the stones. "If we could find a piece of rock that had a hole drilled in it," he said, "I . . ."

Du Pré and Booger Tom looked round. The rocks were all huge.

"I think this was done much more recently than 1910," said Father Van Den Heuvel. "This is competent rock. *Very* competent. The old mine probably went through a piece of the old mother rock caught in the incursion, where it was much softer. But to blast this down, you would need hydraulic drills, air drills, a lot of power. I doubt a few people using sledges and hand drills could do this. . . ."

Du Pré nodded.

"Somebody spent a lot of money to do this," said Father Van Den Heuvel. They clambered back down and stood on the flat. "Damn big lot of work," said Father Van Den Heuvel.

Du Pré nodded.

"What's around the other side, I wonder," said the priest. They got back on their horses and they rode on and found that the track widened greatly and showed signs of trucks rather than wagons.

A road snaked across the land toward the south for a bit and then it headed west.

"This isn't on the map," said Father Van Den Heuvel. He peered at the road. He urged his old horse forward. There was a small mound of square-shaped rocks set beside the road a hundred yards away. He rode to it, waved his hat.

Du Pré and Booger Tom looked at each other. They put their horses to a walk and came to the place the priest was standing. He nodded toward the stones.

A metal sign was fixed to one, corroded but still readable. Much of the original black and yellow paint still stuck to the metal. A series of numbers was stamped in the metal at the bottom of the sign, most of which had been taken up by the symbol for radioactive material. The danger sign, the three-bladed fan.

"I'll be damned," said Booger Tom. "They used that damned mine for one of them dumps . . ."

"So the blasting was done after the Second World War," said Father Van Den Heuvel.

"I didn't know there was any of them out here," said Booger Tom.

Du Pré laughed. "If that sign for real," he said.

· Chapter 31 ·

"THEY SHOULD BE ON TV," said Patchen.

"Quite a performance," said Chappie.

Du Pré nodded.

They all laughed.

Father Van Den Huevel's arm waved out the truck window. The horse trailer shimmied a little, one of the horses had moved.

"I am hungry," said Patchen, "for actual food, brought to me by somebody, cooked by somebody else, and the dishes washed by somebody else, too. . . ."

"Me, I would like that, too," said Chappie.

Du Pré laughed.

"We go the roadhouse then," he said.

"Who is this guy you're picking up, the one flying here?" said Patchen.

"Jacques La Salle," said Du Pré.

"Another of them Frenchy Indians," said Booger Tom. "Gonna play some music, Du Pré?"

"*Non*," said Du Pré, "him not play."

Patchen and Chappie got in the big green SUV. Du Pré pulled out his keys and he got in too.

"If your friend's going to stay," said Patchen, "we should take two rigs, since if he's late, we might want to be able to split up."

"OK," said Du Pré.

Chappie and Patchen got out and went to another SUV. Du Pré drove to the gate, got out and opened it, let them through, drove his SUV to the road, and shut the gate.

Chappie and Patchen were long gone, and there was a plume of dust where they had been. Du Pré laughed.

. . . I am in my car, I can pass them sure, but I am not . . .

He rolled a smoke, fished a flask out of his leather bag, had a drink. He lit the cigarette, started the engine, drove away.

He passed a couple of trucks headed west on the blacktop but no other cars, and when he crested the last hill before the hidden dell where the Pardoe Roadhouse was set, a sheriff's car passed going the other way. The driver waved and so did Du Pré.

There weren't many vehicles out in front of the roadhouse. A weeknight. Just a few pickups, ranchers who wanted a drink at the end of the day.

Du Pré went past the roadhouse to a big field, which had a windsock made of bright orange material hanging on a tall metal pole and a grass runway a thousand or so feet long. The grass had been grazed down, but there were no cattle in the pasture.

Du Pré sat in the SUV, the sun falling toward the west but still warm.

He looked at his watch, rolled a smoke, lit it, had a pull at his flask.

. . . it is ver' strange how things are in the world . . . I wonder who got the military, bury the radioactive waste there . . .

He saw the flash of metal; the little airplane was coming out of the west and hard to see with the sun behind, and then the plane began to descend.

The pilot passed over Du Pré, tilting the plane and waggling the wings, and then the plane turned and looped wide and slowed and came in for its landing. The ground was rough and the plane bounced a little, then slowed. A light machine, it would have to be tied down.

The wind was weaker now and the sky to the west had a thin black rim of cloud rising.

The plane slowed and stopped and the propeller did a few more turns and then bounced back.

The door slid open.

A white-haired man with a long face, dark skinned and big nosed, got out of the cockpit, dropping lightly to the ground.

He walked toward Du Pré with his right hand out.

"Mister Du Pré," he said, "good to see you after these forty years or so. . . ."

"General," said Du Pré. They shook hands.

"I retired," said the man, "and am glad of it."

He and Du Pré pushed the plane to a metal hardstand hidden in the grass and they tied it down with nylon cables.

The retired general got a heavy Filson bag from the plane, a soft hat, a briefcase.

Du Pré opened the rear door of the SUV and the older man loaded his luggage in. "I could have brought a sleeping bag," he said.

"We have plenty," said Du Pré. He rolled a smoke.

"Thank you for sending me the journal and the letters," said the white-haired man. "So after all these years, you remembered our conversation, long ago in a German bar when we were younger. And we were soldiers. I put you up for captain, you know, but you wouldn't stay in no matter how much schnapps I poured down you. . . ."

"I thought it was the right thing to do," said Du Pré.

They laughed.

The white-haired man took out a small cigar from a tin box and he lit it.

"And now someone else has been killed over this ancient crime," said the white-haired man.

"Yes, sir," said Du Pré.

"We are both out of the army, Du Pré," said the white-haired man. "Call me Jack or La Salle."

Du Pré nodded.

"Jackson Pardoe," said Du Pré, "maybe he is poisoned, maybe he just kills himself, I do not know. . . ."

La Salle nodded.

"There was a bit on the news last night," said La Salle. "It seems that Suzette Murphy successfully proved that her grandmother was lying about being the girl, Amalie. She wasn't at the massacre. She took the girl's identity later. . . ."

Du Pré nodded.

"Made some sense," said La Salle. "Gave her a clean slate to start over with. She never got in trouble again. . . ."

"She believed she was there," said Du Pré.

"Ah, yes," said La Salle.

They got in the SUV and Du Pré drove back to the roadhouse. They went in.

A half-dozen drinkers looked at them, turned away. Chappie and Patchen were sitting at a table set for four. They had a pitcher of beer. Chappie had a glass of whiskey, too.

Patchen and Chappie looked up as Du Pré and La Salle approached the table.

Patchen stood up.

"General La Salle," he said.

Chappie scrambled to his feet.

"Sit down, please," said La Salle. "I'm retired, and so are you. . . ." He looked at Patchen's artificial hand, Chappie's scarred face, false eye.

"I didn't know you meant . . . Jack La Salle," said Patchen.

They all sat. The television murmured over the bar.

Lily came out of the kitchen, saw them, mixed a ditch for Du Pré, and brought it with her.

"And you?" she said, looking at La Salle.

"A ditch," said La Salle. Lily went off and soon came back

with the drink. The four men ordered burgers and fries and salads. The ditches did not last long and Du Pré got up, went to the bar, and set down the empty glasses.

A rancher turned and looked at him.

"The danged woman lied," he said. "She lied 'bout what happened, wasn't the person said she was. She lied. . . ." Du Pré nodded.

"So why don't you pack up and git," he said. He looked angry.

"Bill, calm down," said the man next to him.

Du Pré looked at the TV. A pretty woman holding a bottle of something.

Lily appeared, fixed two more drinks. Du Pré carried them back to the table.

Chappie and Patchen were looking at La Salle, who was telling a story. "They got rid of anyone who knew anything about Iraq," he said, "or anyone who said it was going to be terribly difficult."

"We never had enough men," said Chappie sadly. Patchen nodded.

"They are a bunch of fools," said La Salle, "and criminals. They belong in a batch of cells, not where they are. . . ."

"Soldiers don't get asked," said Patchen sadly.

"They never are," said La Salle.

"I want justice for those poor people in that mine," said Patchen.

"Justice," said La Salle.

Du Pré sighed. He sipped his drink.

The people drinking at the bar all laughed, too loudly.

"We can only do our best," said La Salle. He got up then and headed toward the bathrooms.

"Jack La Salle," said Patchen, "how do you know him?"

"He was my commanding officer, Germany," said Du Pré.

Patchen nodded.

"He was not a general then," said Du Pré.

· Chapter 32 ·

"SO SHE WAS A FRAUD. . . ." said Chappie. He looked baffled.

"Yes," said Du Pré, "Amalie was not Amalie, but that does not matter."

Chappie looked at him.

They were sitting at the table.

Patchen and La Salle were up at the bar, talking to three cowmen who had just come in.

"She heard the voices of the Bitter Creek people," said Du Pré. "She heard them, carried them. The real Amalie died, tuberculosis. In the sweat lodge, you heard many voices . . ."

Chappie nodded.

"They want to go on," said Du Pré, "can't. . . ."

"What matters, we help them, "said Chappie.

The door opened and the giant sheriff Rudabaugh came in. He wore his usual half smile. He was wet on his hat and shoulders.

"Pissin' rain," he boomed, "case any of you forgot what rain's like in this part of the world, it's happenin' right outside. . . ."

The people at the bar and Du Pré and Chappie and Patchen and La Salle went outside onto the covered porch.

Rain was sluicing down, so heavy headlights shimmered and faded through the water. The skies rolled with thunder, lightning flashed so close all was thrown in high relief for a brief moment. Puddles formed, danced with rain.

"It's rain, Joe," said one of the ranchers, "M' grandad tol' me what it was like and there it is. . . ."

"There goes my first cuttin' of hay," said another man.

"You kin raise catfish," said the first rancher.

They all laughed.

The air smelled clean and wet.

Du Pré walked down to the end of the porch and he looked out toward some Siberian elms that lined a little irrigation channel on the far side of the parking area.

. . . rain . . . glad we are not in that river bottom . . . ghost river turns to water . . .

It was getting colder rapidly.

Du Pré shivered and he walked back inside.

Rudabaugh was standing at the bar, talking to Lily, who was laughing. He laughed, too, and Lily went back into the kitchen and Du Pré walked up.

"Nice rain," said Rudabaugh.

"You hear anything about Pardoe?" said Du Pré.

"Poisoned," said Rudabaugh, "sure as hell. Thing was, it warn't rat poison or some stuff you could get by mail. . . . Warn't nothing any person would much think of, 'less you was a government trapper in the fifties. Last time I heard of it. . . ."

Du Pré looked at the sheriff.

"What you thinkin', Du Pré?" asked Rudabaugh.

Du Pré shook his head.

"Thallium's what killed ol' Pardoe," said Rudabaugh. "Got used killin' coyotes and the like back when, but the trappers up and refused to use the stuff, it did such terrible things. Took a while. . . ."

Du Pré nodded. "I have read about it," he said.

"Most folks wouldn't know what it was," said Rudabaugh. "Thing was, Pardoes've been there for a good long time, and for a while there in the fifties, Jackson's father was a government trapper—ol' Verne—but by then there wasn't much to do. . . ."

"Killed himself," said Du Pré.

"Thallium is so danged miserable and slow, takes a couple days, you'd think a feller got it slipped to him would suspect something was wrong. Your arms and legs feel like they are on fire, yer hair all falls out—his had just started—and you shit water, every drop you drink. Feller wasn't expectin' that, you'd think they might just trot off the emergency room and allow as how they didn't feel quite right . . ." said Rudabaugh.

Du Pré shook his head.

"Yeah," said Rudabaugh. "Now my eyes deceive me, or was that General Jack La Salle out there?"

Du Pré nodded.

Rudabaugh looked at him. "He here for the Bitter Creek bidness or are you takin' him *fly fishin'*?" said Rudabaugh. "Seems that's what folks come here for."

"We hunt, gophers," said Du Pré.

"Seen him on the TV," said Rudabaugh. "He don't think much of our little war in Iraq there. . . ."

"He was my commanding officer, I am in the army in Germany," said Du Pré.

Rudabaugh nodded. "Kept in touch with you," he said.

Du Pré laughed. "*Non*," he said, "but he come to visit."

Rudabaugh looked at Du Pré. "Old woman started this mess was a fake, suppose you know that," he said.

Du Pré shrugged.

"You ain't playin' straight with me, Du Pré," said Rudabaugh.

"I cannot say now," said Du Pré. "La Salle, he could say but I cannot."

"Nice boots," said Rudabaugh. He bent over, looking carefully.

"Old boots," said Du Pré.

Rudabaugh grinned.

Eleanor Pardoe Macatee came in through the kitchen, dripping, wearing a long riding coat.

She had on a Stetson, broad brimmed, and it ran water down the back of the waxed cotton.

"Howdy, Miss Ellie," said Rudabaugh.

Eleanor smiled, but her eyes looked faint and faded. She put the hat on a rack and she unbuttoned the coat and hung it from a peg on the wall. Her boots were soaked, and they squeaked when she walked. "Hi, Rudy," she said softly. She went back in the kitchen.

"C'mere," said Rudabaugh. He led Du Pré to the little museum off the dining room. Water sluiced down the windows, a skein of golden worms from the light in the parking area.

Rudabaugh flicked on lights.

Du Pré looked at the portrait of Elizabeth Rhodes Pardoe.

Rudabaugh came over.

He nodded to the end of the row of photographs. To one of a tall white-haired man, pale eyed, dressed in a Prince Albert frock coat, holding a cane with a gold knob.

"That's Hoeft," said Rudabaugh. "What I understand, he would have led the posse. He was said to have hung forty-seven cattle thieves by himself, one time owned a quarter of a million acres. . . ."

Du Pré looked at the photograph.

The long-dead man stared fiercely back, erect, cold eyed, contemptuous.

"Here's Macatee," said Rudabaugh.

Du Pré bent to look.

A younger man, insecure enough so he wore both a fancy embroidered waistcoat and a pair of ivory-handled pistols. But his gaze was very level.

"Pinnock. Montgomery," said Rudabaugh.

Du Pré stood up straight.

"All their descendants are still here," said Rudabaugh. "Lily is a great-granddaughter of old man Hoeft, Macatee is still a Macatee. That hothead is behavin' hisself because he don't, Judge Bennett will throw him in for sixty days, and Judge Bennett means what he says, unlike most of them judges. . . ."

Rudabaugh looked at Du Pré.

"Hoeft was a feller," said the sheriff, "got his land together killin' nesters, or scarin' them so bad they give over their homesteads to him. He sorta specialized in ambush whackin'. Used one of them Sharps Creedmore rifles. Forty-five-ninety. Wait for days in the rain. . . ."

It was raining harder now.

"You owe me an answer," said Rudabaugh.

Du Pré shrugged.

The thunder rolled again and the lightning flashed.

There was a commotion out in the dining room.

Rudabaugh looked at Du Pré. They moved out of the museum.

Chappie was leaning against the pool table.

Du Pré ran to him.

"Patchen's dead," he said. "Shot. I brought him to the porch but it's no good. . . ."

Du Pré went out the front door.

La Salle was giving Patchen chest compressions. He paused, put his ear to Patchen's chest.

He stood up and shook his head.

"Goddamn," said Rudabaugh.

"Yes," said La Salle.

· Chapter 33 ·

A HUGE BOLT OF LIGHTNING washed the porch with light.

Du Pré glanced at the parking lot.

Rain spackled the puddles; they danced and it got dark again. The mercury-vapor lamp on the pole dimmed and went out. So did the lights. Rain thrummed.

Du Pré hunkered down and he dashed for the SUV. He opened the door and he got a flashlight. He grabbed the briefcase that La Salle had brought on the plane and he carried both back to the porch. He flicked the flashlight on.

Patchen lay on his back.

His face was wet; the cheap plastic poncho he had shrugged on was rumpled and stretched.

La Salle tugged the flashlight away. He knelt and he played the light over Patchen's head. He took a pocketknife and slit the cheap plastic poncho. Patchen's blue chambray shirt was wet.

. . . damn things never work, keep off the rain but you sweat yourself soaking . . .

La Salle opened Patchen's shirt. "Help me turn him over," he said.

Du Pré bent to help. They rolled Patchen over.

"There," said La Salle. He pointed to a thin trickle of blood at the base of Patchen's skull.

Headlights shone out on the road, and a pickup turned in, going fast. It pulled up, its lights on the porch. The door opened.

Bonner Macatee got out. He left the engine running and the lights on.

"Goddamnit, Rudy," yelled Macatee, "where is Ellie?"

"I'm here, Bonner," said Eleanor, coming into the doorway.

"He don't go, I will arrest his ass," said Rudabaugh, "though I do have other things on my mind at the moment. . . ."

"It's all right," said Eleanor.

Jack La Salle stood up. He went inside and he pulled a checked tablecloth from a table and he came back and he covered Patchen.

Bonner Macatee stepped up on the porch out of the rain. He looked at Du Pré and then he looked at Jack La Salle. "What is goin' on?" he said. "Jackson Pardoe is dead. Now this feller is dead. What is goin' on?"

La Salle looked at Rudabaugh.

The huge sheriff shook his head.

"You come on home, Ellie," said Macatee, "it's dangerous here."

"It's dangerous there, Bonner," said Eleanor. "I can't do it anymore. I don't want anything from you. Go on home. . . ."

Du Pré sighed.

Macatee got back in the truck, backed up, drove off, the truck lurching when he got up on the road.

"He said he was going to go and rest in the car," said Chappie. "So I didn't worry when he didn't come back right away."

"Where was he?" said Rudabaugh.

"On the ground," said Chappie, "on the other side of the car we drove here in."

"Point it out to me," said Rudabaugh.

Chappie walked to the end of the porch and pointed back along the building's side.

His SUV was parked at the back.

Du Pré's was out in the lot, a hundred feet away.

Rudabaugh nodded.

The lights flickered and then they rose to full power.

The air was thick with the smell of ozone and rain.

Rudabaugh went inside, stood at the bar, the toothpick rolling around his mouth.

Jack La Salle joined him, and so did Du Pré.

Eleanor Pardoe Macatee sat on a stool, her head in her hands.

Lily came out of the kitchen, smiling.

She went to Eleanor and patted her hand.

Eleanor looked up. She drew in her breath. Her face went white.

"You don't think I . . . ?" she said, looking at Rudabaugh.

Rudabaugh looked at her.

"It was rainin' when you come?" he said.

"Yes," said Eleanor. "Lily called me and said she needed some help. It's usually slow on Tuesday evenings. I knew the rain was coming so I put the riding coat and the hat in the truck cab, and by the time I got here, it was pouring. I don't park near the front door, of course; we leave those spaces for customers. There isn't any parking right in the back, just room for the dumpsters. I parked way back where I usually park. . . ."

"Then you run to the back door," said Rudabaugh.

"Walked," said Eleanor, "slowly, with my collar up and my head down. I could see the light over the back door but nothing else. . . ."

Rudabaugh nodded.

Lily went on patting Eleanor's hand.

Du Pré rolled a smoke.

Jack La Salle was sitting at a table with Chappie, talking softly. The ranchers were all gone.

Rudabaugh sighed. "Doo Pray," he said, "could you do me a favor?"

Du Pré put out the cigarette.

Rudabaugh went round the bar. Lily smiled at him.

Eleanor looked stunned and frightened.

Rudabaugh stopped. He glanced through the cutaway to the kitchen. "Back there on the stove there is a stockpot," Rudabaugh said to Du Pré. "I wonder you could see if there is a gun in the bottom of it."

Lily shrieked and she clawed at Rudabaugh's eyes. The huge man grabbed her wrists. She kicked at him, but he lifted her up so she had no purchase.

Du Pré sighed.

He went in, got a long-handled strainer.

He shoved it down in the boiling liquid, scraped the gun to the side of the pot, pushed the strainer under it and lifted it out. He carried it to the sink, dumped it in, turned on the hot water, and washed the grease and bits of meat away. He turned the water to cold, chilling the gun down, and lifted it out.

Du Pré found a white paper sack. He put the gun in it, folded the top, walked back out with it into the dining room.

Rudabaugh had turned Lily around and put handcuffs on her. "Yew got a right to ree-main silent," he said, "and the rest of that crap. Knowin' you as I do, you will keep quiet anyways, till you get you a lawyer."

"You fat prick," spat Lily.

"Language," said Rudabaugh. "You gonna walk on your own? And be nice. I kin always lock ya in the trunk."

"Fuck you," said Lily.

"Yer chariot awaits," said Rudabaugh. He picked her up under one arm and walked out.

"Lily?" said Eleanor.

Du Pré nodded.

"Mother of God," said Eleanor. "Lily."

"Yes," said Du Pré.

Eleanor Pardoe Macatee put her face in her hands and she cried softly. "Is this ever going to be over?" she said. She grabbed a handful of bar napkins and she wiped her eyes and nose. She got up and went to the ladies' room. Water ran.

Rudabaugh returned from the parking lot.

"County ambulance is on the way," he said, "pick up poor Patchen there. Nice young feller, gets hell blown out of him to Iraq, gets killed here in the matter of something danged near a century old. . . ."

Du Pré nodded.

Rudabaugh looked at him.

"I knowed both them girls since they was sprouts," he said. "Had to be one or the other. . . ."

Du Pré looked at him.

"Eleanor was a sweet kid," said Rudabaugh. "And Lily had this nice smile. Lily got to be fourteen, maybe, she started losin' animals. Cats. A dog. . . ."

Du Pré nodded.

"Went away for a while," said Rudabaugh. "Dunno where. Anyway, on this particular evening, I went with the cats and dogs. Lily's smart. So if she done it, she'd get rid of the gun, hide it in plain sight but someplace you was not likely to stick yer hand in. . . ."

Eleanor Pardoe Macatee came back from the washroom, her face composed, her eyes a little puffy.

Rudabaugh put his hand on her shoulder.

She looked up at his face.

"Ellie," he said, "over there at that table is General Jack La Salle who I would bet a nice shiny quarter wants to tell you he is your long-lost cousin. . . ."

"What?" said Eleanor.

"Like I said," said Rudabaugh, "a shiny quarter." One

arced through the air and the sheriff put out his huge hand and it disappeared.

"Cousin Eleanor," said La Salle.

He motioned to the table.

· Chapter 34 ·

DU PRÉ WATCHED THE AMBULANCE GO, no lights, no siren. The rain was beginning to lessen, though it was still strong.

He put the CLOSED sign in the window and he flipped the lock.

Chappie was sitting alone, a bottle of whiskey in front of him. But it was still full. His glass was empty.

Eleanor Pardoe Macatee sat at the table with Jack La Salle.

She was looking into some far country.

La Salle got up and he walked over to Chappie.

"Soldier," he said, his voice steely, "there is a good deal left to do. . . ."

Chappie scrambled up to attention.

"Come on," said La Salle, "Du Pré has figured it out but you probably have not. . . ."

He pointed to a chair at the table with Eleanor. Du Pré went to the bar, poured some brandy in a glass, brought it to the table, set it in front of Eleanor.

"You might drink that," said La Salle. "You're shivering."

She nodded, lifted the glass, drank.

"Ellis Pardoe was killed a week before the Armistice,"

said La Salle, "and afterward his commander, Brigadier General Albert, came here to offer condolences to the widow. It was a strange fate that sent him back to the very place he had seen worse than anything he'd encountered on the Western Front, and to the widow of the very man who had taken that massacre's sole survivor to safety. But he came and he and Elizabeth had much to talk of. . . ."

Eleanor nodded.

"And ultimately there was a child. Albert was married, of course, loved his wife, too. They had four children. So Elizabeth left Montana and she stayed in Seattle until the baby was born and gave the child up for adoption. To the La Salles. They never mentioned it to my grandfather. When Albert's wife died, he wanted Elizabeth to marry him. He wanted to recover their son. But she wouldn't do it. She wrote him, he wrote her. She said they shared too much sorrow, too much ill fate, she had other children, it might hurt them. So Albert finally came back here again and shot himself. Selfish bastard. She was right not to marry him," said LaSalle.

Du Pré fetched more brandy for Eleanor.

"It was Elizabeth who found him. He probably had her letters and the journal he kept when he was in Montana in 1910. She took them, hid them with her letters from him. . . ."

"Jesus," said Eleanor.

"Time went on, the old families did their best to bury what their founders had done that January day in 1910. And then Du Pré shows up. Jackson Pardoe was a good man. He was pulled several ways. . . ."

Eleanor laughed, just a little. "Mama always said Papa could find four answers to a yes or no question. . . ." she said.

"In the journal," said La Salle, "Albert tells the story of what happened, how he and his six black troopers took off after the Mètis, how they were housed and fed along the way, how the Mètis killed one or two steers missed in the roundup, and finally how they got the attention of Hoeft, who wanted them dead, who gathered the posse, who offered money, and who was really the one man—and there is always one—without whose stupidity and viciousness not one thing would have happened. But he was powerful, and so when the troopers got near his posse, he had the soldiers disarmed. His mob killed the Mètis, all but the girl, and the soldier's rifles were used. . . ."

Eleanor nodded.

"Hoeft heard rumors that Ellis Pardoe and Elizabeth had got a girl to safety, but they denied it. He knew the bodies would be found, so he paid to have them hauled to an old mine. That would have been not long after the killing. It is easier to travel in winter in this country than spring. . . ." said La Salle.

"So my grandfather . . ." said Eleanor.

"Never knew what really happened, I suspect," said La Salle.

"And my father . . . ?" said Eleanor.

"Hard to tell," said La Salle. "Elizabeth Rhodes Pardoe died in 1969; she and her son Jackson were close. Not all the letters were to or from Albert. . . ."

"What could she have wanted?" said Eleanor. "My God. . . ."

"She wanted the truth to come out," said La Salle, "but after all the people were dead, so there would be history rather than shame. . . ."

Eleanor shook her head. She looked at La Salle. "So this old woman, who turns out to be a fraud anyway, tells Du Pré that these people were killed down on little Bitter Creek," said Eleanor, "and he comes here and finds nothing. The old fraud dies. . . ."

La Salle nodded.

Du Pré rolled a cigarette.

"I never met my grandmother," said Eleanor. "She died a dozen years before I was born. But I look so much like her, people who come here and look at the photograph in the museum tell me I must have posed for it dressed up in antique clothing. I wonder whether they'll be certain now that the photograph's a fraud, as well. . . ."

"It is a stunning resemblance," said La Salle.

"But I don't think it was just modest propriety that kept Elizabeth silent," said Eleanor. La Salle looked at her.

"I think she was just plain afraid," said Eleanor. "Hoeft lived to be a very old man. Died in '49 or '50. I know something about being afraid. And maybe one of the good things to come from this is that I can finally divorce Bonner Macatee."

La Salle leaned forward.

"Do you know who killed your father?" he said.

"Could he have done it himself?" said Eleanor.

La Salle leaned back.

"He had dreams, sometimes," she said. "He took things deeply to heart. It would come and it would go. But if he knew about all this for so long, and it was finally going to come to light . . . ?"

"Thallium is an awfully hard death," said La Salle.

She shook her head.

"It makes no sense. *None* of this makes sense," she said.

La Salle waited.

"And Lily?" said Eleanor. "I've known Lily all my life. I'm twenty-eight, she's thirty-two. She could be moody sometimes, bitchy even. But since she got this place she seemed to settle down. . . ."

"Didn't marry?" said La Salle.

"No. She was the prettiest girl around, no shortage of men who wanted her. But she never did." Eleanor paused. "I want to read the letters and see the journal."

"Of course," said La Salle.

Eleanor shook her head as though she was clearing it and looked at La Salle.

"What does thallium do, exactly, and in what dose?" she said.

He leaned forward again. "I don't really know," he said.

She nodded, then looked around the roadhouse.

"I wonder who will end up with this?" she said.

Du Pré smoked.

He went back to the kitchen, found some good roast beef, made himself a sandwich with lots of mustard.

The voices in the dining room went on murmuring.

He stepped out the back door.

The rain had stopped, thin veils of cloud sat high. A half-moon hung in the sky.

A pickup truck pulled in, drove slowly past the front of the building, drove away.

Du Pré went back inside.

The voices went on murmuring.

He went to the bar, made himself a ditch, drank it and made another.

Chappie had leaned over the table, his face in his hands.

Eleanor was nodding.

". . . I think the next thing to do is get the bones out of the mine. . . ." said La Salle.

"This isn't going to be over until we do that," said Eleanor.

"That's right," said La Salle.

Eleanor shook her head again. "Have you ever had one of those thoughts you can't quite get hold of?" she said.

"Most of mine are like that," said La Salle.

Eleanor smiled a little. She sipped some more brandy.

La Salle yawned. It was late.

"My grandmother was afraid," said Eleanor. "I know she was afraid. And one other thing . . ."

La Salle looked at her.

"Do we know how Ellis Pardoe died, exactly?" she said.

· Chapter 35 ·

"YOU ARE SURE YOU CAN DRIVE all that way?" said Du Pré.

He and La Salle were standing by the SUV, which was running. It had turned cold and the SUV's heater was roaring.

"Yes sir," said Chappie.

Eleanor sat in the passenger seat.

"Thank you," she said.

Du Pré nodded.

"You'll be safe there," said La Salle.

"What about you two?" said Eleanor.

La Salle looked at Du Pré.

"There are some people," said La Salle, "who live through just about anything. Du Pré and me, well. . . ."

Du Pré rapped on the door, and Chappie nodded and pulled away.

There were no lights from cars, nothing.

"We stay at the camp?" said La Salle.

Du Pré shook his head.

"We follow them," he said. "The camp has no one in it. . . ."

They got in the other SUV. Du Pré reached into his bag,

pulled out one of the two Sig Sauer combat pistols he carried in it, and two extra magazines.

"Mine's in my bag," said La Salle.

Du Pré started the SUV. They caught up to Chappie's in a few minutes. Du Pré hung back a half mile.

"Not that many ways to get to Toussaint," said Du Pré.

"We could fly," said La Salle. "Of course, it is hard to do much in my little kite. . . ."

They laughed.

"So," said La Salle, "I lost track of you after your tour was up. I know I gave you the standard pitch about the army as a good way of life. . . ."

"Food was terrible," said Du Pré.

"Hours, too," said La Salle.

"I come back, go home, get married, wife, she die when the girls are ver' young . . ." said Du Pré.

"I'm sorry," said La Salle.

"I wanted to smash God's face in," said Du Pré, "but I had my little girls. Then I meet Madelaine, we have been together many years. . . ."

He rolled a cigarette. La Salle took out a small cigar. They put the windows down.

It was cold and smelled of rain.

"Both of my sons are in Iraq," said La Salle, "and so far, so good. I retired after telling the congressional committee that it would take a million men and twenty years to refashion Iraq—if it could be done, and it could not. . . ."

Du Pré nodded.

"That didn't help my sons' careers," said La Salle, "and both are going to resign their commissions as soon as they are rotated home. Won't leave their men. This bunch of morons is destroying the entire military structure. . . ."

"They are that bad?" said Du Pré.

"That bad," said La Salle.

They crested a hill and saw Chappie's taillights. He tapped

the brakes and the lights flashed a little. "Spotted us," said La Salle. "Good man."

They rode in silence the rest of the way to Toussaint. La Salle slept a little.

Du Pré drove out to Bart's ranch and he took La Salle to the guest cabin next to Booger Tom's.

Eustace the water buffalo was lying in the flower bed out in front of Booger Tom's cabin. He was chewing his cud.

La Salle nodded, yawned.

"I am about your size," said Du Pré. "I will get clean clothes for you, put them in the door here. . . ."

He went to the cabin he used when he was at the ranch, got the clothing, took it back to La Salle. Who was already snoring.

Du Pré showered and fell into bed.

Du Pré woke to the sound of Booger Tom cussing.

"My goddamned *posies*, you cud-chewin' bastard!" the old cowboy yelled. "Git yer fat ass up and out of there. . . ."

Du Pré made coffee, listened to Booger Tom and Eustace.

By the time he took a cup outside, they were gone. Booger Tom was on a horse, Eustace trotting along behind. They were headed toward a big pasture full of the other water buffalo.

La Salle came out of the other cabin. Du Pré fetched him a cup of coffee. Pidgeon came out of the main house.

"Breakfast!" she said. Du Pré waved.

"My God," said La Salle, "that is one of the most beautiful women I have ever seen in my life. . . ."

"Yes," said Du Pré. "She is married to Bart, owns this ranch, no one knows why, and we all hate him."

"I understand," said La Salle.

"We get Bart, his heavy equipment," said Du Pré, "maybe Father Van Den Heuvel. He is a priest but also geologist. . . ."

"Sounds good," said La Salle. They carried their coffee to

the main house. Du Pré opened the door and they went in. Pidgeon was setting plates on the table.

"This is General La Salle," said Du Pré.

"Jack La Salle," said La Salle, "no longer a general. Thank God."

Pidgeon smiled.

Bart came in, a little shaving foam stuck to his neck; Pidgeon reached out and wiped it away, turned to the sink, the water ran.

"La Salle," said La Salle, holding out his hand. Bart shook it.

Pidgeon dished up eggs and ham and home fries. They ate, talked of nothing much.

Afterward, La Salle and Bart went outside and Du Pré helped clean up.

"General Jack La Salle?" said Pidgeon. "Guy's got more medals than a good pawnshop and he earned every one of them. How you know him?"

"This Bitter Creek," said Du Pré, "reaches many places. . . ."

Pidgeon nodded. "So what's next?" she said.

"The bones are in an old mine, I think," said Du Pré. "Been blasted so we need heavy equipment, move the rock. . . ."

Pidgeon nodded.

"Good," she said. "Bart needs something to do. I have to go east and he can't come this time. . . ."

"OK," said Du Pré, "you say hello, that Harvey. . . ."

"Will do," said Pidgeon. "Thing about having a profession in law enforcement is all the fun. . . ."

She wiped her hands and went off, whistling. Du Pré went outside.

La Salle and Bart had a pair of binoculars. La Salle had them to his eyes.

"He hazes him to the gate and then the bastard dodges him," said La Salle.

Bart looked at Du Pré. "Booger Tom's half-ton house pet," said Bart. "Old fart's gonna die of a stroke. . . ."

La Salle offered the binoculars to Du Pré. Du Pré put them to his eyes, found Booger Tom.

The old cowboy was riding his horse back and forth, trying to haze Eustace in with the other water buffalo. Eustace would dance this way and that, dodge back out at the last minute. The other water buffalo had come to watch and were enjoying all this very much.

"We need your heavy equipment," said Du Pré to Bart, handing the binoculars back to La Salle.

"Bitter Creek?" said Bart.

"Yah," said Du Pré. "I'll call Coff and have him come," said Bart. "We need Little Bill, too?"

"Yah," said Du Pré.

"He got away," said La Salle. "Now that water buffalo is headed this way and all the others have broken out."

Booger Tom was standing up in the stirrups, waving his hat and yelling, but too far away to hear, not that they needed to.

"All the years that old bastard tormented me," said Bart, "and now I get mine. . . . So we gonna stay in the camp?"

Du Pré nodded. "Set it up by the mine," he said.

Bart went off, punching numbers into his cell phone.

· Chapter 36 ·

RUDABAUGH PULLED OFF the county road at a wire gate. He lifted the loop off the post and set the gate off to the side, and then he drove on.

Bart turned off the road with the heavy tractor hauling his giant backhoe and he eased it through the opening, then drove on after Rudabaugh's SUV.

The rest followed: a huge bulldozer, the tractor-trailer with the dragline, and five other vehicles.

Du Pré and La Salle were last.

La Salle jumped out and he put the gate back up.

They drove on.

The road was fair and snaked through the low hills, coming up to the old mine from the southwest.

Rudabaugh stopped in a huge flat, a playa lake now dry and grassy.

. . . find old campfires where the shore was . . ., Du Pré thought, old bones and tools, stone points, bones cracked open for the marrow fat . . .

They set up camp, putting up the wall tents and the solar showers and the long trestle tables that were light enough for a man to lift with one hand, and strong enough for him to stand on.

Rudabaugh and La Salle and Du Pré and Bart walked on to the old mine, now hidden behind the mass of huge rocks.

Bart looked at the rubble. "Ugly," he said.

"Whole danged business is ugly," said Rudabaugh.

"Who owned that land we drove over?" said La Salle.

"Seattle land company," said Rudabaugh, "but I just got a search warrant. Judge owes me more'n one favor."

"What grounds?" said La Salle.

"Well," said Rudabaugh, "I tol' him I had it on good authority Jimmy Hoffa was buried in that there mine. He told me go screw myself. I told him there could be evidence pertainin' to Lily Hoeft's case and he scribbled on the dotted line. . . ."

La Salle nodded.

"Be nice get this all settled," said Rudabaugh. "Then folks here kin go back to shootin' each other while drunk, fightin' in the bars, and actin' like regular folks. Adultery, drunk drivin', you know . . ."

The men driving the huge tractor-trailer rigs backed and filled them into the end of the flat where they would be out of the way and easy to unload.

Rudabaugh looked round the land.

"Lotta blood here over time," he said. "Makes me want to go fishin'. No hook on the line, just set there and watch the water flow. . . . Well, you seem set. Phone up you need anything, and I sincerely hope that you don't."

He drove off, soon was just a plume of dust on the western horizon.

Chappie and Eleanor were setting up a big camp kitchen.

Du Pré and La Salle looked at each other, smiled, nodded, went on to Bart, who was watching Little Bill back the big backhoe off the trailer.

The huge machine lurched to the ground.

Bart heaved heavy chains into the bucket.

Little Bill waved and he drove off toward the old mine.

Bart followed with the bulldozer.

"So, Du Pré," said La Salle, "you think that the bones of the Métis will be in that mine?"

Du Pré shrugged.

"Maybe," he said. "No other place seems likely. I saw something when we were over there, the mine, come on. . . ."

They walked back.

Du Pré poked around in the sagebrush for a bit and then he bent and he picked up a hooked brown stick. He handed it to La Salle.

"Hayhook," said Du Pré. "There were others at Bitter Creek. It is winter, I think they use those, hook a body, drag it. Easier than grabbing something, and no one likes touching dead people. . . ."

La Salle nodded.

"So we should soon know," he said.

Du Pré spread his hands. "Don't know the mine," he said. "It has a vertical shaft, we will have to pump it out. . . ."

"You really want this," said La Salle.

"People die, I want to know why," said Du Pré. "The Métis, Pardoe, Patchen . . ."

"The dead hand of history," said La Salle, "can be a lethal thing. So we just wait. . . ."

Du Pré nodded.

He walked over to a watercourse, a deep cut worn by water thousands of years ago. He looked down.

The bank was caved in along the near side, had happened a long time ago.

Du Pré motioned to La Salle.

"What?" he said.

"This bank," said Du Pré, "it is funny, all slumped in like this. All happen at once it looks like, but it is pret' long time. . . ."

The deepest part of the cut was below them, filled with fine sand and gravel. A couple of hundred feet farther on, the bank was sheer and the stones on the bottom large and visible.

They heard a car horn honking, turned.

Father Van Den Heuvel's decrepit sedan flew over the rocky flat. A tire blew. The car lurched and came on, slowed, but not in time.

The front wheels dropped over the edge of the bank.

Du Pré ran to it. The car was still trying to move but was high centered.

Father Van Den Heuvel was slumped over the wheel.

"Good God," said La Salle.

Du Pré reached in and he turned off the ignition.

The priest moaned.

"He cannot be killed," said Du Pré, "knocked unconscious, but he cannot be killed."

They pulled the big man out of the car. He had a cut on his forehead that bled a lot.

Du Pré looked in the car, found some paper towels.

Father Van Den Heuvel sat up, holding the paper towel to his head.

"I hit the accelerator instead of the brake," he said.

"Yes," said Du Pré. He helped him to his feet.

"The sign, the radioactive warning, was real," said Father Van Den Heuvel. "It took a lot of trouble to find that out. It wasn't classified, just lost. . . ."

"So," said Du Pré.

Father Van Den Heuvel went to his car and he fished out his briefcase. He took out a handful of papers and he put them on the roof of the car. He unfolded them.

"This was a mine dug for copper," he said, "but the ore was not there. At first there was a little. They went in about two hundred feet farther and then it got absolutely sterile, no copper at all. But it was a good solid shaft in good stone without a lot of drainage. So in 1947, the army put a whole lot of very nasty isotopes in there, but they had a short half-life, months or even weeks, and the place was abandoned, unguarded, in 1959. The stuff is still in there but mostly converted . . ."

"No vertical shaft," said Du Pré.

"No," said Father Van Den Heuvel.

"And they found no bodies in there?" said La Salle.

"No," said the big priest. "This is the report that was made initially, and it says the place was clean. No rubble, nothing. The miners had even taken out the little rails they ran the ore carts on. . . ."

La Salle nodded.

"I feel dizzy," said Father Van Den Heuvel.

Du Pré sat him down on the trunk lid of the car.

"Put your head down," he said.

Father Van Den Heuvel did so.

He sat up straight again.

"But," he said, "the contractor who prepared the site had a bad time keeping his workers here. . . ."

Du Pré nodded.

"They heard things," said the big priest.

"And they would walk near the camp on hot days and it is cold," said Du Pré.

"Yes," said Father Van Den Heuvel.

"The guards didn't like it either," said the priest. "Finally they had to put army soldiers here. . . ."

Du Pré nodded.

"And a lot of them went AWOL," said the big priest.

He shook his head, rubbed his eyes. "So the bodies aren't here," he said.

"Yes, they are," said Du Pré.

Father Van Den Heuvel looked at him.

"They are under your car, there," said Du Pré, pointing down.

· Chapter 37 ·

BART SAT AT THE CONTROLS of the backhoe. The feet had been set out, the cylinders extended, the steel shoes sat hard on the ground.

The big-toothed bucket dug back toward the bank.

Bart lifted the bucket, swung it behind him, dumped its load.

Du Pré waved. He was sitting on the edge of the flat, feet on the slumped rubble that filled the old channel.

Bart dug as far as he could reach the bucket, a level down.

Du Pré looked at him, stuck his thumb up.

Bart set the bucket's teeth against the fill two feet below the first bite.

He dug and dug, cleared another two feet.

. . . this where a wagon could be pulled up easiest . . . Du Pré thought.

A young man in shorts with a lot of pockets on them, and a shirt with a sun cape sewed into the yoke, and a cap with a very long bill looked at the cleared place. He held up a hand. He stepped to the spot he was staring at, lifted up a piece of brownish rubble. "OK," he said, "metatarsal, definitely human. . . ."

He pulled a whisk broom from one of the pockets and he swept hard.

A whitish oval appeared.

"Skull," he said. "This is the place."

Bart pulled the bucket back, set the boom vertically, shut off the engine.

"You were right," said Bart.

The man with the broom whistled, swept.

"Two of them," he said, holding up two small brown pieces of bone, "means two people. Each of us has only one of those. . . ."

"How old are these?" said Bart,

"Century . . ." said the young man. "I'd have to run some lab work to be sure, absolutely, but I'd say a century, no more than that. . . ."

"What will you need?" said Bart.

"As an academic," said the man, "I always need money. Hire a few of my grad students at some pitiful wage, set up a camp . . . I'd say six others and me. There isn't that much overburden here. It's a grave, not a camp. Pretty straightforward, actually. . . . Maybe, fifty thousand?"

"If the bones are reassembled," said Bart, "I mean, not all mixed up. . . ."

"Tagged and bagged," said the young professor. "Great teaching setup. I should get a couple of articles out of it, too. . . ."

Bart and Du Pré walked toward the hauler that the backhoe traveled on. Little Bill was sitting on the trailer, drinking coffee.

"You have time to stay and take the top off this for him?" said Bart.

"Sure," said Little Bill.

"Good," said Bart. "If I stay, the cost will go up every three hours. Give the bastards a check and they think you're good for an endowed chair if they whine enough. . . ."

He and Du Pré walked to the SUV.

"Chappie and the Macatee woman are off safe from her louse of a husband until she's divorced his ass," said Bart. "La Salle is in DC, so is my lovely wife, and I want to go and see her. . . ."

"Yah," said Du Pré.

"So I am going home," said Bart, "and then get on a plane. I have such interesting times with you, Du Pré. . . ."

Du Pré nodded.

"So we've found the Métis who were slaughtered. Lily Hoeft is in jail, for killing young Patchen. She may have poisoned Jackson Pardoe, too. Do we know why?" said Bart.

Du Pré shook his head.

"This all seemed to be straightforward," said Bart. "And now none of it is. . . ."

Du Pré laughed. "You got people in it, never is," he said.

"I'll drop you at your ancient cruiser," said Bart. "And if you ever need to burn another one to cover your tracks, remember I have two more. . . ."

"Yah," said Du Pré.

Bart shook his head. "It's all so strange. The woman who claimed to be the little girl who survived all this turns out to be a fraud. . . ."

"Yah," said Du Pré, "people do that, they become other people, they don't like themselves. . . ."

"I did that," said Bart. "Didn't like myself much. . . ."

"Not fraud, though," said Du Pré.

Bart snorted.

They got in and Bart drove up to the gate.

Rudabaugh was parked there, out on the road, waiting.

Du Pré opened the gate and Bart drove through, turned right, honked the horn, speeded up.

Du Pré started his cruiser, pulled it out, parked behind Rudabaugh, closed the gate. When he turned, the huge sheriff was standing there, chewing a toothpick.

"Got it all figured out yet?" he said. He was poker faced.

Du Pré shook his head.

Rudabaugh sat on the rear bumper of his sheriff's SUV. The springs sagged under his weight.

"They done took Lily Hoeft off to Warm Springs, where I expect she will be for some time. She was crazy enough before she started killin' people and now 'bout all she says is 'He was a great man! He was a great man!' She'd make a good Baptist, she changed the words to the song a little. . . ." said Rudabaugh. "I s'ppose I am grateful she didn't spike up the chow up at the roadhouse with thallium. Kill us all. Damnit, now I got no place to eat. . . ."

Du Pré nodded.

"Somebody will buy it, open it again," he said.

"But not by suppertime," said Rudabaugh. "I suppose I can live on beans for a few years. Mebbe I will just waste away. . . ."

He looked down at his big belly.

"But not fer a while," he said. "Now, Mister Du Pré, did you find them people?"

Du Pré nodded.

"Anthropologist, he will bring his students here, collect the bones," he said.

"Feller in the shorts with the pockets?" said Rudabaugh.

Du Pré nodded.

"Had another one here lookin' fer dinosaurs," said Rudabaugh. "We prayed a lot and damned if he didn't find none. Lucky that time, not this one. . . ."

Du Pré laughed.

"My granddad come here, 1920," said Rudabaugh. "It happened to be rainin' then more'n usual, lot of folks come, rains quit, they left. Old man Hoeft was alive, Grandad knew him, my pa worked for him. The story about them Indians gettin' slaughtered was around, but folks didn't mention it to Hoeft. . . ."

Du Pré nodded.

"But folks definitely knew about it," said Rudabaugh. "An' Elizabeth Rhodes Pardoe, I knew her, too. I was a kid. Lovely woman. Always seemed to have a small smile on her face. One of them women is beautiful when she is old, too. . . . She used to ride a horse out here, sidesaddle. She was a good rider. . . ."

"She lived over there," said Du Pré.

"She did," said Rudabaugh. "Lived alone mostly. Had a couple of hands, with her for years. Buffalo and Blackie, they was called. They'd git drunked up and land in the sidebar hotel and she'd come in Monday and put up the fines. Them boys always drunk up their pay 'fore they got arrested so they wouldn't have to waste it on the court, you see. . . ."

Du Pré nodded.

"Old Man Hoeft," said Rudabaugh, "he was one of them come early and held on, and one time I heard it said he owned damn near this whole county and half the next one over. Those old boys was another sort of critter. . . ."

Du Pré nodded.

"He had three wives," said Rudabaugh, "old Hoeft. First one he had a family, she died birthin' a baby. Married again and had him another family. . . ."

Du Pré looked at him.

"Hoeft had bad luck with his kids, "said Rudabaugh, "and wives. They tended to die young. Last wife he married when he was about seventy and she was twenty-five. Had two more kids, one boy, one girl. . . ."

"Girl was Lily Hoeft's great-aunt," said Rudabaugh.

Du Pré nodded.

Rudabaugh got up. He went to the front of his SUV and he opened the door. He pulled out a brown paper sack and took from it a photograph of a young woman.

He handed it and the sack to Du Pré.

"Hoeft's youngest daughter lives in Seattle," said Rudabaugh. “Address’s there, I writ it on the bag. . . . Hoeft’s third wife and him was only married about eight, ten years, the old bastard died. Last wife left with the kids. The boy come back, ranched some, but the girl never did. . . .”

Du Pré nodded.

“I don’t got the time myself,” said Rudabaugh, “and I don’t like Seattle. It’s wet, and I am afraid of rust. . . .”

· Chapter 38 ·

DU PRÉ AND LA SALLE and Chappie and Eleanor stood back away from the family and friends at the gravesite. The grass under their feet was thick and freshly cut.

The minister blessed the handful of earth he held and then he sprinkled it on the coffin, set down in the hole. They all murmured the rest of the service. La Salle and Chappie were in dress uniforms. Du Pré and Eleanor wore dark clothes.

A tall woman, wearing black and a gauzy veil walked past them. She stopped and turned. "You must be John's friends from Montana," she said. "We are having some people over, please come, just follow us. . . ." She walked away, erect, majestic.

Du Pré and the others walked to a rented sedan painted with an odd finish that changed colors depending on how the light hit it. They all got in, La Salle at the wheel.

It was hot and very humid.

. . . it is so green here . . . Du Pré thought . . . the forests are so thick . . .

La Salle waited for the short line of black limousines to pass, followed by those cars behind with their headlights on, and then he pulled in behind them.

It was not very far to the house, a two-story Georgian set well back from the street. The driveway was full, so La Salle parked out on the street and they walked up the drive.

A young woman, perhaps fifteen, opened the door for them. She looked lost. "Come in," she said, and then tears welled in her eyes.

"Cat," said a young man, who looked like her older brother. "Come on, it will get better. . . ." And he hugged her. He smiled and nodded toward the back of the house.

In the great room, a table held food, another drinks, and men and women were pouring one another glasses of wine or mixing cocktails. The tall woman who had invited them had shed her hat and veil. She walked up to the four, standing out of the way. "Barbara Patchen," she said. "John's mother. . . ."

La Salle took her hand.

"Jack La Salle," he said. "And this is Chapman Placquemines, Eleanor Pardoe, and Gabriel Du Pré. . . ."

"Please," said Barbara Patchen, "have something to drink. I must see to the others, but I'm so glad you came. Perhaps we could talk later. . . ."

"Of course," said La Salle.

Du Pré looked out the window. There was a tent set up in the backyard, some tables. He jerked his head that way and the four of them went out the French doors, open behind them.

More people were coming through the front door.

There was another bar in the tent, and they got drinks, found a table set under a flowering tree. Hummingbirds danced in the air, dipped long beaks into the blossoms.

The girl who had been at the front door came down the steps from the patio, looked at them, cast her eyes down but came on.

She stopped in front of Chappie.

"What was my brother doing in Montana?" she said. "I don't understand."

Chappie stood up, but couldn't find any words.

"He was trying to do the right thing for some people," said La Salle. "He was trying very hard."

Chappie got a chair for the girl.

She sat down.

"I mean, he was wounded so badly in Iraq," she said. "Why . . . ?" And her eyes filled again.

Eleanor Pardoe moved her chair close to the girl. She put her arm around her and pulled her face to her shoulder.

The girl cried, softly.

"I'm sorry," she said, after a moment.

"It's all right," said Eleanor, "it's all right. . . ."

"He came there to help me," said Chappie, finally, "and then we were trying to do this other thing. . . ."

"What *other thing*?" the girl said. "Don't treat me like an idiot."

"OK," said Chappie, "I will tell you the whole story, but maybe we ought to go over there by ourselves."

He waited while she rose, carried two chairs off.

He set them under some flowering lilacs, heavy with blooms.

"I can't help feeling," said Eleanor, "that he died of my family's curse. . . ."

"Not your family's," said La Salle.

"If you stay in a place like that," said Eleanor, "maybe you deserve what you get. Look at me. I married that asshole. . . ." She caught herself, flushed.

"You don't have to go back there," said La Salle.

"I wish there was something I could do here," said Eleanor. "I feel like washing dishes. . . ." Then she laughed, mostly at herself.

Barbara Patchen came toward them then, carrying her grief tightly.

Du Pré rose and set down the chair he had for her. She nodded to him, sat.

"It's good of you to come, General," she said.

"He was a good man," said La Salle.

"His brother," said Barbara Patchen, "is on his way to Iraq. We are a military family, General. . . ."

Du Pré wandered away.

La Salle and Barbara Patchen put their heads close together.

. . . I wish that I was home . . . Du Pré thought. . . . I wish we could go now . . .

He went into the house, found a bathroom, used it, went back out. There were a few people in a side room, a music room, which had a tall vaulted ceiling. There was a grand piano, some electronic equipment, a cello sitting in a stand.

Eleanor came into the room, saw Du Pré, came over, found a place on a couch. "You are the one who always figures things out," she said. "Have you yet?"

Du Pré shook his head.

"I had always thought Elizabeth Pardoe was a saint," said Eleanor, "and then I find she had an out-of-wedlock child. I like her better, I think. Saints are hard people to like. . . ."

Du Pré laughed. "Yes," he said, "I know one, he is very hard to like. . . ."

Eleanor looked at him.

"Old man I know," he said. "Medicine person, and so he is a joker, a coyote. . . ."

"Coyotes," said Eleanor. "I grew up with 'em. I've shot a bunch. I can't help but like them, though. . . ."

"Ver' smart, ver' tough, ver' funny," said Du Pré.

"Don't ask for much from anybody," said Eleanor.

"Take what they want," said Du Pré.

Eleanor looked down at her glass. It was empty.

"I get us some more," said Du Pré.

She nodded, hugged herself.

Du Pré made his way to the bar, looked out the window.

Chappie and Patchen's sister were talking, and so were La Salle and Barbara Patchen.

Du Pré waited until the people ahead of him mixed their drinks and went on, then he did the same.

He walked back to the music room.

"Could I have a cigarette?" said Eleanor.

Du Pré nodded. They went outside; he took his pouch from his coat pocket and he rolled a smoke for her and one for himself. He lit them both with a butane lighter.

He handed hers to her.

They smoked.

Only one or two other people were smoking, though there were two dozen people in the yard.

Eleanor sipped her drink.

"So," she said, "let me see if I have the story down. A band of Métis are running for the border, and when the army finds out they're running, they send six troopers and a lieutenant after them. So they weren't expecting trouble. . . ."

Du Pré nodded.

"The Métis are hungry, they shoot a steer and butcher it out and eat it. . . ." said Eleanor.

Du Pré nodded.

"It was one of Hoeft's steers," she said, "so he blows up and gets a lot of people together and they kill all the Métis. . . ."

Du Pré nodded.

"No. It doesn't make any sense," said Eleanor. "It was January. Any steers out there would have been missed in the roundup. Hoeft would have had no way of *knowing* they killed and ate one of his damned cattle. . . ."

Du Pré looked at her.

"It doesn't make any sense," said Eleanor. She drank more of her drink.

Chappie and La Salle came in.

"We go now," said Du Pré.

Eleanor stood up.

"It doesn't make any sense," she said. She shook her head.

They went out to the rental sedan.

· Chapter 39 ·

"I WONDER EACH TIME I FLY in this crate if I made the right choice," said La Salle. "The whole game is having the number of takeoffs equal the number of landings."

"Will one way or the other," said Du Pré.

They were flying at twelve thousand feet, covering the distance between Washington, DC, and Montana steadily. Below them, the Ohio River wound through a lush landscape.

"I can touch down and you can get a commercial flight back," said La Salle.

"I have mustache, I am dark," said Du Pré. "I also have friends, would call the security people, say, he is not Du Pré, he is Mohammed. Fiddle case is full of anthrax. . . ."

"I have friends like that, too," said La Salle. "They make life interesting, in a life-threatening sort of way. . . ."

"If Chappie and that Eleanor get along," said Du Pré, "Madelaine will be ver' happy."

"They'll be fine," said La Salle. "Eleanor has decided they will be fine. If she has decided Chappie will do, what he thinks won't matter one small hill of shit. . . ." They laughed.

The little plane droned on.

"So," said La Salle, "Old War Department files open a bit more readily for a retired general than for a mere lieutenant."

"What you plan tell Eleanor, again?" said Du Pré.

"That the report of the death of Ellis Pardoe, the second of November, says Colonel Pardoe was killed by a sniper, a single shot that went through his head. . . ."

"Yah," said Du Pré.

"And there were several people in his brigade," said La Salle, "who could have killed him. There were two Hoefts. There was a Macatee. So I checked to see what the records showed as cause of death for other men in that sector. All shellfire. It was a quiet sector, otherwise. The brigade itself had been chewed up badly, the Germans across the trenches were starving. The war was almost over. Ellis Pardoe was the only casualty from sniper fire in the entire seven weeks they were there. . . ."

"So," said Du Pré. "But we cannot *know*. . . ."

"People are very mysterious," said La Salle. "The saintly Elizabeth Rhodes Pardoe . . ."

"She has an affair, your grandfather," said Du Pré.

"General Albert, who goes to console the widow, and so forth. He could perhaps have met her in 1910," said La Salle.

"Maybe," said Du Pré. "Also Eleanor, she says, it is silly to think that Hoeft got a posse to chase the Métis over a steer. Any steer there would have been missed, the fall roundup, Hoeft would not have known. . . ."

"Interesting," said La Salle.

"Ranch house there, studio, were build many years later, 1920s," said Du Pré. "The old house, miles away from Bitter Creek. They did not move there until they found water, underground, could pump enough. . . ."

"So it may have been something else," said La Salle.

"Report of Albert," said Du Pré, "he rides, says the Métis

got away. His journal, he says they are disarmed by Hoeft and his men, waiting for them, a narrow place. Hoeft's posse go on and kill the Métis."

"Yes," said La Salle.

They droned on in silence for a while, then La Salle turned north and set a course. He scratched a few numbers on a pad taped to his knee.

"We'll make it in good time," said La Salle.

They flew along, not speaking.

Du Pré looked down at the ground. He could see the little plane's shadow flit along, very fast.

. . . so that is how fast we are really going . . .

"There's Lake Michigan," said La Salle.

The ground looked blank through a haze.

Twenty minutes later, Du Pré could look down on the water. It was pale gray, and few boats were out on it.

"Storm clouds," said La Salle, nodding ahead.

Three clouds that looked like huge elongated anvils sat on the horizon like giant ships.

"We can go between those two," said La Salle, "at least I think that we can. If they close up we turn tail and head for clearer skies."

Du Pré nodded.

. . . if I die, I die . . . ever'body gets to do it, nothing exclusive about it . . .

The little plane droned on.

Du Pré saw a flash off to the left side of the line of flight.

"Metal, over there," he said.

La Salle looked. "Another light plane," he said, "quite a bit lower. Seems headed away. In ten minutes, we may find others, so keep an eye out for them. Most pilots are pretty good, but then so are most drivers. . . ."

Du Pré laughed.

They went on.

Six separate small aircraft flew ahead, all but one across their flight path, all higher than La Salle and Du Pré.

The huge anvil clouds moved, but very slowly. There was a gap twenty miles wide between them.

"May be wind," said La Salle, "and it may come on suddenly. . . ."

They droned on.

Suddenly, the little plane dropped a few hundred feet.

Du Prés stomach rose up under his scalp.

They were shoved violently from the left.

La Salle whistled.

He looked over at Du Pré and he grinned.

The air stayed calm for a moment, then they were lifted up a few hundred feet in seconds.

. . . stomach now hanging out my asshole . . . thought Du Pré.

He looked over at one of the huge malevolent clouds.

Lightning played inside it. The black heart of the cloud pulsed with pale light.

Then they were past the giant clouds, and ahead shafts of sunlight stabbed down through holes in the overcast.

La Salle whistled.

Du Pré fished a pouch of chewing tobacco out of his pocket and he tucked some behind his lower lip. He offered some to La Salle, who shook his head.

"You can drink whiskey, if you like," said La Salle. "I can't but you could. . . ."

Du Pré laughed. He reached into his bag, got his flask, had a swallow.

"Thank you," he said.

La Salle's head turned constantly.

Du Pré saw a flash off to his right. "Over there, seventy-five degrees," he said.

La Salle looked.

A plane was headed toward them and seemed to be about the same altitude.

"I'm going down," said La Salle. He flicked some levers, pointed the nose of the little plane down.

Du Pré looked at the other airplane. A jet, a small one. It passed overhead, heading south.

"Odd," said La Salle. "I had a transponder on, but they didn't acknowledge. . . ."

He shrugged.

They went on.

In another hour, they saw the patched forest and grasslands that marked the place where the Great Plains began.

Du Pré looked down. "That is the Red River," he said, "down there ahead."

"We should arrive in an hour," said La Salle, looking at some figures on his kneepad.

"That is Devil's Lake," said Du Pré, pointing down. The deep lake looked malevolent. The water was black.

"What have we found?" said La Salle. "Bits and pieces. I wonder if we'll ever know what happened on that January day so long ago."

"These things are not forgotten," said Du Pré. "There was a song. . . ."

"Ah, yes," said La Salle.

"It is over there," said Du Pré, pointing.

"Right you are," said La Salle, looking at a map.

He took the plane down.

They flew over the land at a thousand feet.

Du Pré pointed.

There was a runway in a grassy field, a bright orange sock on a pole.

An old van parked off near the county road.

They flew over the van.

Kim and Bassman waved.

"Your friends," said La Salle.

"Bassman smokes, lot of marijuana," said Du Pré.

"So do soldiers," said La Salle.

They laughed, and La Salle banked the plane and set it to land.

· Chapter 40 ·

THERE WERE TWO TRAILERS set in a small grove of Siberian elms, and tents and teepees here and there. A big awning over a cooking area and three huge fire pits.

Du Pré kissed Madelaine when he saw her. She came out of the crowd, moving quickly on her feet, a dancer in all she did.

There was music everywhere, little knots of people standing holding instruments or sitting on folding stools.

"So Du Pré," said Madelaine, "you have been running around, been lots of places. Do you know the story yet?"

Du Pré shook his head.

"Might not ever know it," he said. "It is not what I thought anyway."

A knot of Jacqueline's kids ran up, Marisa and Berne, Hervé, Nepthele, Marie and Barbara, all laughing.

Nepthele had a fiddle. One string was broken. He held out a packet to Du Pré, "Keeps breaking," he said.

Du Pré looked at the fiddle, took out his pocketknife. He touched the bridge.

"There," he said. "Little sharp place, you chipped it. You don' beat on Hervé with it. . . ."

Nepthele blushed.

"Use a rock," said Du Pré. He scraped a little with his knife, pulled out a new string, mounted and tightened it.

He pulled on the new string, finger and thumb in the center, stretching it. It was a flat note, he twisted the peg and brought it up. "Here," he said to Nepthele. "Go steal tunes, you can. . . ."

The boy trotted off.

"La Salle, he is a nice man," said Madelaine.

Du Pré nodded.

They stopped by a crowd of guitar players, young white kids with tattoos and earrings.

The kids were picking off, one doing a run and riff, the next trying to top it.

Du Pré listened for a while, nodding. They walked on.

"I am hungry," said Du Pré. They went to the kitchen tent and got some buffalo stew, frybread and chokecherry jam, coleslaw, apple pie.

They were just finishing when Michel DuHoux came up. He nodded to a chair.

"Sure," said Du Pré.

DuHoux sat, laced his fingers together, and pushed them outward. He yawned. "Reminds me of Cajun music a little," he said.

"Celtic," said Du Pré. "Gaelic, maybe better. . . ."

"I love the stuff," said DuHoux.

"Your book, how is it coming?" said Madelaine.

"Well," said DuHoux. "But I think I wish I hadn't got into it. . . ."

Du Pré nodded.

"It is all so very sad," said DuHoux.

"Old bastard!" someone screamed.

Du Pré looked toward the shriek.

Père Godin was running toward them.

He had his accordion up on his right shoulder.

He saw Du Pré, ran over, dumped the accordion on the table, looked back.

Suzette was coming, more slowly. She was fat, but she had a hefty stick.

"I see you sometime," said Père Godin.

He ran on.

Suzette passed them, puffing.

"Ever' time we come, one of these things," said Madelaine. "There is always somebody, try to kill Père Godin. . . ."

"Why does he come?" said DuHoux.

"Lots of women here he has not fucked yet," said Du Pré. "Père Godin, he is on a mission from God. . . ."

"Wonderful," said DuHoux.

"Bastard," shrieked Suzette.

Père Godin loped past again. "I am too old, this," he said as he went by.

Suzette puffed past. She had a friend with her now, who had a rolling pin in one hand.

"They wear out, start laughing soon," said Madelaine. "Poor Père Godin, him get caught one day."

DuHoux looked at Du Pré. "Did you find out anything interesting since I last saw you?"

"Some," said Du Pré.

"This is one of those stories," said DuHoux, "that I know I will never know completely. Not that you ever do. . . ."

"No," said Du Pré.

He looked up then and saw Benetsee standing at the edge of the crowd. The little old man grinned at Du Pré.

"There is Benetsee," said Du Pré. "That is him there. Here, I go get my gun, you kill him please. . . ."

DuHoux looked across to the crowd.

Benetsee grinned.

"That's him?" said DuHoux.

"Yes," said Madelaine.

Du Houx got up and he walked quickly toward the old man.

Benetsee stepped behind a couple of fiddlers.

"Poor DuHoux," said Madelaine. "Benetsee does not come to these things. . . ."

"No," said Du Pré.

Jack La Salle stepped past the last of the crowd that had screened him from view. He had a big plastic cup of something and a small cigar in his teeth.

He came toward them.

"I bring sleeping bags," said Madelaine. "I got one for you."

"Thank you much," said La Salle. "I should have brought one."

"Have to sleep on the ground," said Du Pré. "It helps if you are ver' drunk. . . ."

"I'll see what I can do about that," said La Salle, "and the ground will be fine. . . ."

"Pret' tough for a general," said Madelaine.

La Salle smiled a little.

"I was a POW for a while," he said. "After that I don't have much to complain about. . . ."

"Vietnam?" asked Du Pré.

"Yes," said La Salle. "I was just there recently. . . ."

"You go back?" said Madelaine.

La Salle nodded.

"I was invited," he said, "so I went. The war was a long time ago. Some of the people I fought with were there and some of the people that I fought against were as well."

"Do you like them?" said Madelaine. "The people you fought against?"

La Salle laughed.

"Some of them," he said. "Others I don't much care for. Like any bunch of people."

Père Godin trotted past again.

"Your wind is good," said Madelaine.

He nodded, panting a bit.

"I love this music," said La Salle.

"Ver' old," said Du Pré.

Bassman and Kim came out of a crowd of people who had formed to watch the Père Godin/Suzette match. They wandered over.

"Them women," said Bassman, "they say 'kill him' ever' time Suzette goes past. . . ."

"And the guys say 'keep movin' Godin,'" said Kim.

"Speaking of the oldest of all wars," said La Salle.

"We 'sposed to play," said Bassman. "Père Godin will not join us I think but there are other people, come, sit in. . . ."

Du Pré nodded.

He reached down for the old rawhide fiddle case Catfoot had made so long ago.

They got up and walked to the place where Bassman had set up his amplifier, soundboard, and speakers.

Du Pré drew the bow over the strings. He filled his bow with rosin. Bassman thumped his bass a few times.

A very large young man with a blue accordion sidled up to Du Pré. "I know your stuff," he said. "Practice with your music a lot. I keep pretty quiet, I join you?"

"You do a good job," rumbled Bassman, "you work with us. Accordion player we had, will be killed and scalped, tonight. . . ."

"Yeah," said the kid, "Him, I heard about. . . ."

Du Pré stood at the twin microphones.

"Du Pré!" someone yelled. "Do 'Baptiste's Lament.' . . ."

"'Drops of Brandy'!"

"'Boiling Cabbage'!"

"OK," said Du Pré.

He turned, looked at Bassman. "New one maybe," he said. Bassman nodded.

Du Pré riffed a few notes, warming his fingers. The melody twirled and rose like smoke.

Infinitely sad, patient, full of tears. Du Pré played for ten minutes. Bassman came in, but very softly. The accordion player didn't add even one note.

"Jesus," said the kid, "what was that?"

"'Bitter Creek,'" said Du Pré.

"Not one I know," said the kid.

"No," said Du Pré, "it is not. . . ."

· Chapter 41 ·

DU PRÉ EDGED THE SUV up close to the camp, four wall tents, a solar shower, a truck with a compressor and a huge refrigerator.

"Up there," said Madelaine, pointing.

They got out.

Halfway up the square butte a pale buttress of stone thrust out, the top a near-blade, so weathered it held jagged notches.

A pole had been stuck there, something black fluttered from it, dancing in the breezes.

It was cold, overcast, a north wind not strong but steady.

"I don't know what it is," said the professor. He wore pants with a lot of pockets on them.

"Raven wing," said Du Pré.

"Benetsee," said Madelaine.

"Two of my crew left early this morning," said the professor. "They were afraid of . . . something."

"They hear cries?" said Madelaine.

The professor nodded. "So did I," he said. "It was just the wind, though. It makes strange noises in the rocks. . . ."

Du Pré took his old leather jacket out of the SUV. He put it around Madelaine's shoulders.

"Live here my life," said Madelaine, "I don't bring a heavy jacket. I see it snow a lot, all months of the year. I don't bring a heavy jacket."

Du Pré laughed.

Madelaine kissed him on the cheek. They held hands, walked down to the bottom of the watercourse.

"The backhoe operator left two days ago," said the professor. "He said he'd be back for the machine. We needed it and tried to start it but we couldn't. . . ."

Du Pré nodded.

Three young people were using garden trowels to dig up yellow soil from deposits between large rocks.

"I think we got it all," said the professor. "Come over here and I'll show you what we have."

He led them to the largest wall tent. There were a dozen long tables there, covered in bones, small boxes of cloth scraps at each end.

"We have the remains of thirty-two individuals," said the professor. "Eighteen adults and fourteen children and adolescents. . . ."

Du Pré nodded.

"The bodies were dumped at the bottom of the watercourse," said the professor, "and the bank above caved in on them. All the skulls were crushed; few of the large bones are intact. . . ."

Du Pré picked up a plastic bag. There was a crucifix in it, on a blackened string of beads. He opened the bag.

"I must ask you not to. . . ." said the professor.

"Go away," said Du Pré, without turning toward the man.

The professor fidgeted, then left.

"He thinks these are his," said Madelaine.

Du Pré nodded.

Madelaine stood with her head bowed. Her lips moved.

Du Pré waited for her to finish praying.

"Bart will be here, little time," he said, "so then . . ."

"Poor people," said Madelaine, "murdered, bodies dumped here, long time gone. . . ."

Voices came on the wind, muffled by the tenting.

"But we aren't finished!"

"Enough!" came Bart's voice. Very loudly.

Rocks rattled as he slid down the bank.

He came into the morgue tent.

"So," said Bart, "it was going to be simple. Now, if I let them, they'd dig down to the damned mantle. . . ."

Du Pré laughed.

"Thirty-two," said Madelaine, "what Amalie said. . . ."

"Amalie who wasn't Amalie," said Bart.

"She was," said Madelaine. "Other one died, she remembered for her. . . ."

"There are miracles," said Bart.

The backhoe fired up, the big diesel popped and boomed. It ran hard for two minutes, then the noise dropped and the rain cap on the exhaust tapped.

The professor came into the tent.

"Could I have a word with you?" he said, looking at Bart.

"No," said Bart. "You did what I asked. Now kindly pack it up and leave. . . ."

"If you want the bones properly sorted," said the professor, "we will have to do DNA tests, and . . ."

"That takes time and is very expensive," said Bart. "And the answer is no. We are through here. . . ."

The professor slumped, walked out.

"My next unpleasantness," said Bart, "is to not pay him the final twenty grand. . . ."

Du Pré laughed.

A clattering began, a brief noise, a laugh.

Little Bill stuck his head in.

"Got 'em," he said. "Cleaned out two hardware stores to do it. I was about ready to go to Great Falls. . . ."

"We could've used heavy plastic bags," said Bart.

"Nope. Thirty-five plastic crates with lids," said Little Bill.

He brought in a stack, the sort of crates used to ship heavy stock to stores, and sent back to main warehouses.

They packed the bones into the crates, settling them in, then set the crates on the ground and fixed the covers tightly.

It did not take terribly long.

Bart went round to each table with a foxtail broom and a dustpan and he carefully swept up chips, dumping them into the last crate.

"Didn't need them all," he said.

Du Pré nodded.

Bart and Du Pré carried the boxes out of the tent.

Little Bill had moved the diesel backhoe close to the edge of the bank and lowered the broad front bucket.

Du Pré and Bart stacked crates, six on the first load, six on the next, five on the last.

Little Bill lifted the bucket, lowered it, stowing the boxes in one or another of the big green SUVs.

Madelaine had made her way to the top, she waited for Du Pré and Bart to go down the wash to the low place where they could scramble up.

"I am driving your car, Du Pré," she said.

Both SUVs were full of gray plastic boxes.

Madelaine and Du Pré got in one and Bart got in the other and they drove back up to the country road.

Rudabaugh's sheriff's cruiser was there, lights on, the huge man leaning against the front fender.

Du Pré and Bart stopped the SUVs behind Du Pré's old cruiser.

Madelaine got out and she went to the old car and she got in and started it, turned on the heater.

It was getting colder still.

Rudabaugh chewed his toothpick.

Du Pré walked up to him.

"All of 'em?" said Rudabaugh.

Du Pré nodded.

"Thirty-two," he said.

"I don't suppose," said Rudabaugh, "that asshole with the pockets has to stay much longer? He keeps diggin' he's gonna find something else and then he'll stay forever. I would admire, he *left*. . . ."

"Bart is through, they are supposed to leave," said Du Pré.

"Good," said Rudabaugh. "You make it to Seattle yet?"

"No," said Du Pré. "I meet La Salle there day after tomorrow."

Rudabaugh nodded.

"I find bein' a sheriff," he said, "is mostly listenin' to a lot of stories and not repeatin' any don't have to be said in court. That's a word of advice. . . ."

Du Pré laughed.

"So," said Rudabaugh, "you buryin' these folks?"

Du Pré nodded.

"Bury them together, the churchyard, Toussaint, there are lots of Métis there," he said.

"Camped up near that butte once a long time ago," said Rudabaugh. "I was lookin' for a feller had taken to that country. Heard strange things at night, the wind I guess. . . ."

Du Pré nodded.

"Well," said Rudabaugh, "you go to Seattle. . . ."

"Yes," said Du Pré, "I let you know what I find out. . . ."

"Appreciate it," said Rudabaugh, "though I am pretty sure I know already. . . ."

Du Pré nodded.

"And Eleanor took up with that Chappie feller?" said Rudabaugh.

Du Pré nodded.

"She should get outta here," said Rudabaugh. "This story is gonna chap some folks' asses and she would get most of the crap. . . ."

"She knows that," said Du Pré.

Rudabaugh held out his hand and he and Du Pré shook.

"I thank you," said Du Pré.

Rudabaugh nodded. "Have you a good trip," he said. "The one with the pockets ain't gone by tomorrow, I'll see to him. . . ."

· Chapter 42 ·

DU PRÉ STEPPED DOWN from the train, carrying his leather bag and his nylon suitcase. His hat began to fall, unsteady on his head. He set down the suitcase and caught his hat. "Sorry that the weather was so bad," said La Salle, coming to him. "I gather it's supposed to clear, which means we can fly back. . . ."

"In that tinfoil kite, yah?" said Du Pré.

"Hasn't fallen out of the sky yet," said La Salle. He led Du Pré out of the station to a parking garage, put his suitcase in the trunk of an old Land Rover. They got in.

"She said eleven," said La Salle, "so we can just make it." He pulled out and soon was on a wide street thick with cars.

He slowed and turned, went down a steep incline, drove along a winding lakefront road.

They came to a blinking yellow light, turned left, went up a hill.

"This was as hilly as San Francisco, once," said La Salle, "but they had those big hydraulic mining cannons when Seattle was being built, so they knocked most of the hills down. . . ."

The houses they passed were mostly bungalows set well

back from the street, thickly held by stands of rhododendrons and trellised roses.

La Salle leaned forward, saw a number, slowed, and turned into a driveway.

A white house with blue shutters.

Du Pré saw a curtain move a little as they walked to the front door.

La Salle was about to press the bell button when the door opened. A white-haired woman in a bright print dress stood there, smiled at them, stepped back, and gestured for them to enter.

"Mister La Salle," she said. "And this is Mister Du Pré?"

La Salle and Du Pré bowed a little.

"Come in," she said, "we'll go to the conservatory." The house was larger than it appeared, set so that the part that faced the street was one-story, but the back portion was spacious, two-storied, set into a hillside.

They went through an archway, to a room with one whole wall of windows looking out on a lake below.

Du Pré coughed. There was a smell of sickness in the house.

The woman poured tea into flowered cups, handed one to Du Pré and the other to La Salle.

She motioned to some wicker chairs set near a glass coffee table.

"Erma!" called someone, voice reedy, weak.

"Just a moment," said the woman. "My husband is failing and the nurse has gone out for a bit. . . ." And she went off, through another archway, this one hung with beads, long strings that rattled as she passed through them.

Du Pré got up, looked out at the lake below.

Small sailboats tacked, a windsurfer slid rapidly over the metallic-gray water.

The woman came back, poured tea for herself, joined them. Du Pré pulled out another wicker chair for her, she nodded as she sat.

"I was quite surprised to receive Mister La Salle's call," she said, "but he did convince me it was important. I left Montana when I was six, in 1935, and I have not ever returned. I remember only how dry and dusty it was. And how afraid I was. I was afraid of horses." She laughed.

"It was so long ago . . ." she said.

"Your mother was Henry Hoeft's last wife," said La Salle. "And you are his only surviving daughter."

"Yes," she said. "I'm afraid I don't remember him kindly, any more than I recall Montana kindly. Mother was so very much younger than he. He was an old man, he stank of whiskey and cigars, he was always angry, shouting, I suppose because he was deaf. . . ."

"But your mother left him," said La Salle. "Left him and took you and your brother away."

"Yes," said Erma, "they had a terrible argument. I remember the day. I don't know what caused it; they had never argued in front of Paul and me before. My mother looked terrible, her face was red, she was crying. . . ."

Du Pré opened his leather bag, pulled out a plain Kraft paper envelope.

He slid the photograph out.

"I remember this," said Erma. "It sat on the mantel. I remember that the house was so cold in winter, and I would stand there. The fireplace threw out good heat. I remember that. . . ."

Du Pré looked at the photograph.

Hoeft, not yet old, his hair streaked but still dark in places, sitting in a chair, a boy of twelve or thirteen standing beside him, in a high white collar, a tie, a Norfolk jacket.

"That day we had gone out to play, and Paul—he was two years younger than I—he was stung by a bee or a wasp. He cried and I took him back inside to get Mama to help. . . ."

She closed her eyes.

"I heard them shouting. The house was a ranch house, not

big, they were in the little parlor, and my mother screamed 'Murderer!' and then she screamed that again and again. . . ."

Du Pré waited.

"Mother had married him because she was a poor immigrant girl without prospects in life. There was an agency that matched girls of good character with men. The fact that Hoeft was much older did not matter much . . ." said Erma. "My mother didn't have much formal schooling, but she was hungry for learning, very hungry. She tried to be a good wife, but she took every moment she could find to read. . . ."

Du Pré nodded.

Erma looked at the photograph of the old man and the boy for a long time.

"I was very young," said Erma. "As I've said, I don't recall a lot, but one person I do remember was an old Indian woman. She would come to the back door and she and my mother would go for long walks on the hills near the house, and come back with plants. My mother would use them to make medicines. . . ."

Erma looked back on her life, was silent for a time.

"I suppose the old woman told my mother. That makes sense, doesn't it, that she would have?" she said.

Du Pré nodded.

"That day when they fought, the only time, my mother screamed *murderer* at my father and he was silent, shaking his head, shaking it like a dog with something in its ear, hard, as though he could make everything go away if he shook it hard enough. Finally, the old man grabbed my mother's wrists, shook her, and he shouted. I can still hear that voice . . ." said Erma.

Du Pré nodded.

"'They killed my Oscar,' he shouted. 'They killed my son.'"

Erma shook her head.

"My father left the house then, slammed out the door, and my mother packed a bag and she had the maid pack our trunks. A man came with a wagon and he took us to the rail station. It was summer, and pretty, I remember the bird songs. . . ."

Erma looked at her hands in her lap.

"That picture is of my father and Oscar," she said. "I know that because I remember my father pointing to it and saying 'That is my Oscar,' but he didn't tell me Oscar was dead. I wondered when he would come home. . . ."

Erma stopped.

"We came here, I know my father sent money, sent quite a bit, and on time. I never saw him again . . ." said Erma. "And my mother saw that Paul and I were well schooled. . . ."

Du Pré pulled another photograph from the envelope.

"Aunt Beth!" said Erma. "She would come from time to time. She wasn't really an aunt, I know, but she would come and stay for a few days. She was a friend of Mother's. . . ."

Du Pré put the envelope back in his bag.

"Erma!" called the weak voice.

"Where could that nurse have gone!" Erma looked as though she was about to cry.

"Thank you," said Du Pré, standing up.

"The photographs?" said Erma, pointing at them.

"You may have them," said Du Pré.

"Thank you," said Erma. "I have to see to my husband. . . ."

"We can find our way out," said Du Pré.

They went out, carefully shutting the door behind them.

It was raining, the fine coast mist.

They walked to the old Land Rover. Du Pré got in and so did La Salle.

"Didn't get much," said La Salle.

Du Pré nodded. "We can find out the rest, just find where Oscar Hoeft died. . . ."

"You think the Métis shot him?" said La Salle.

"*Non*," said Du Pré, "but Hoeft blamed them for his son's death. . . ."

"Why the troops were there in the first place," said La Salle.

"Yah," said Du Pré.

"Mother of God," said La Salle.

· Chapter 43 ·

DUHOUX NODDED TO DU PRÉ as he came into the saloon. He wore his black leather coat and his dark glasses. He got a beer and he came over to Du Pré's table.

Pallas had her eyes on her computer screen, a brightly lit and colored other universe.

"Sit down," said Du Pré.

Pallas gave a half smile, without looking away from the screen.

"I don't know what that thing is," said Du Pré. "Don't want to."

"Don't need to," said Pallas. "You got me."

"I found out some things," said DuHoux, pulling out a chair. "I suppose that you have, too . . . ?"

Du Pré nodded.

"So it all goes back to Henry Hoeft and his bad temper, his mean nature," said DuHoux. "He comes to Montana, while it's still a territory, makes his fortune by the usual ruthless means, becomes a powerful man. But his children are sickly or unlucky. All but Oscar, the apple of his father's eye . . ."

Du Pré nodded.

"Oscar is a boy, fourteen years old. He travels with his father and mother to Helena, as his mother is ill and Helena has the best hospital and the best doctors in Montana. They will find treatments for her, and perhaps they will do some Christmas shopping. Oscar's sister Gertrude had died in October, of scarlet fever, leaving him an only child. Then, on the sixteenth of December, Oscar, restless, bored, rides his horse out east of Helena, where there is a camp of Indians and Métis. Late that afternoon, the horse shies, Oscar's foot goes through the stirrup, off he goes, he is kicked, and he dies. The horse drags the boy for quite some distance. . . ."

Pallas tapped something into the keyboard. She looked at the screen.

"Hoeft's wife is sinking, there is nothing that can be done for her. Hoeft is beside himself with grief and rage. He can contend with anything, his power is immense, but he cannot save his wife or his son . . ." said DuHoux.

"So he blames the Métis," said Du Pré.

"So he blames the Métis," said DuHoux. "The Republicans have the White House, William Howard Taft sits there, all four hundred pounds of him, and Hoeft's power does reach that far. He demands that the Métis be arrested and deported . . .

"So Pershing and his soldiers are sent. They are hard men. They have been chasing Mexican bandits, ignoring the fact of the border. They fight the first of seven pitched battles with the Yaquis, October 1909."

"There!" said Pallas. "Look here, Granpapa. . . ."

She spun the computer around so Du Pré could see the screen. DuHoux didn't try to look.

"Before that they are in the Philippines," said Pallas, "where U.S. troops killed maybe a quarter of a million Moros and Igorotes."

"Theodore Roosevelt, he liked them doing that," said Du Pré.

DuHoux nodded. "But one Métis band gets away and has the bad luck to run right past Hoeft's home ranch. The man is both crazy and powerful. He gathers a posse, neighbors who owe him, and when they find the Métis, they disarm the soldiers and they kill all in the band but the little girl. . . ."

"Amalie," sail Du Pré. "She dies ver' young, tuberculosis. Another young woman, gets out of jail for assault and theft, takes her name."

"Amalie Montagne," said DuHoux. "Takes her story, lives her life, and when she is old, and very bored, why here comes Gabriel Du Pré, who busts her out of the old folks' home, brings her down here, and causes Homeland Security much embarrassment. . . ."

"That is my granpapa," said Pallas.

"The Canadians, at least, are amused," said DuHoux.

Du Pré got up, went to the bar. Madelaine was beading, keeping her eyes on the little doeskin bag she was holding in the good light. Du Pré made himself a drink.

"How 'bout me, Granpapa?" said Pallas.

"You are fifteen," said Du Pré. "You drink that rotgut Hervé and Nepthele are making out of worms and bugs. . . ."

"I am amazed," said Pallas, "you remember how old I am. . . ."

"Lucky guess," said Du Pré. He came back and sat down.

"It would be a fine book," said DuHoux, "but the whole thing makes me so sad now I don't know if I want to write it. . . ."

Du Pré nodded. He drank half of his tall glass of whiskey and water.

He rolled a cigarette, lit it, blew smoke at the ceiling.

There were ancient dollar bills stuck to the lapped wood.

"You put those in a fold with a quarter and a thumbtack," said DuHoux, "and toss them up there . . ."

Du Pré laughed.

"My father, Catfoot, he used to come in here with Roland

and Black Jean, and they would do this, try a hundred times, finally one of them would stick. Then my maman would come out, the kitchen, with a mop handle, pound them in," said Du Pré.

"Ah," said DuHoux.

"Then she would say 'Crazy Métis, always gambling. So I make sure there is no gambling, when they will fall off,'" said Du Pré. He finished his cigarette, stubbed it out in the ashtray.

"So," said DuHoux, "the Métis are slaughtered, and then . . . there was a good deal of shame—and some fear—I expect. . . ."

Du Pré nodded.

"Hoeft had nothing to do with moving the bodies," said DuHoux, "did he?"

Du Pré shrugged.

"So some group of them takes all the bodies to the dry creek and knocks the bank down on top of them. . . ." said DuHoux.

Du Pré nodded. "Drop the hayhooks, there," he said. "They don't want, use them again. . . ."

"And there they stay," said DuHoux.

Du Pré nodded.

"I went to the old man's cabin," said DuHoux. "Benetsee. Took the wine and the tobacco. He didn't come. . . ."

Du Pré laughed. "Take more," he said, "he know you were there. . . ."

"This comes back to him, doesn't it?" said DuHoux.

Du Pré shrugged.

"Granpapa," said Pallas, looking up from the computer screen, "these people, they try to block information but they are no good at it. . . ."

DuHoux stood up. "I can go and try Benetsee again, I suppose," he said. "That's really all I can do? You can't help?"

Du Pré shook his head.

"Old man will talk," he said, "if he wants to. . . ."

Chappie and Eleanor came in.

She was laughing. Chappie was looking down and shaking his head. They stopped by the table where Du Pré and Pallas sat with DuHoux standing, who nodded to them.

"He is going, try to see Benetsee," said Pallas, "take wine and tobacco. . . ."

Chappie laughed. "If you see a coyote," he said, "that is him. . . ."

"I did see a coyote," said DuHoux. "He was just there, one moment, like he popped out of the ground. . . ."

"Scar on his face?" said Du Pré.

"Yes," said DuHoux, "come to think about it. . . ."

"He is writing, a book about Bitter Creek," said Du Pré.

Chappie nodded.

"Goddamn!" said Madelaine. She squinted at a finger where the needle had stuck.

"I don't suppose that you would come with me?" said DuHoux, looking at Du Pré.

Du Pré shook his head.

"Him, Benetsee," said Du Pré, "if he want me, he will let me know. . . ."

"Granpapa," said Pallas, "these people are idiots. . . ." She tapped at the computer keyboard. She returned to peering intently at the screen.

"Just who is Benetsee?" said DuHoux. "I mean, has he always been here?"

"Long time," said Du Pré.

Chappie and Eleanor walked on, took seats at the bar. Madelaine smiled at them.

"Anything but wine and tobacco I could bribe him with?" asked DuHoux.

Du Pré shook his head.

Pallas tapped at the keyboard.

"Ah," she said, "there. Pret' amazing. . . ."

She stretched.

"What are you looking for, anyway?" said DuHoux.

"Granpapa," said Pallas, "him, ask me how many Congressional Medals of Honor were given out, one battle. . . ."

DuHoux nodded.

"Seven," said Pallas. "Twelve were recommended, but seven awarded."

"Gettysburg?" said DuHoux.

"Oh no," said Pallas. "Wounded Knee. . . ."

· Chapter 44 ·

FATHER VAN DEN HEUVEL LOOKED with distaste at the fancy vestments. "What is wrong with my good old cassock?" he said. "Better yet, jeans and a nice comfortable sleeveless shirt. . . ."

"You are talking crap," said Madelaine. "There will be hundreds of people here. It is *showtime. . . .*"

"This is the sort of thing the bishop should be doing," said Father Van Den Heuvel.

"The bishop, the rest of them, off molesting children," said Madelaine. "Besides, they send you here to forget about you. They are not going to remember you now. . . ."

"I should have run up into the Wolfs," said Father Van Den Heuvel, "and hid out."

"I just send Du Pré," said Madelaine.

"Here they are," said Father Van Den Heuvel.

Two of the big pickup trucks from Bart's ranch pulled up near the churchyard.

Father Van Den Heuvel and Madelaine went out to the six sawhorses set beside the open grave, a wide deep hole. The dug earth had been piled on one tarpaulin next to the grave and covered with another.

Du Pré and Bart and Booger Tom and Chappie got out of the vehicles. They pulled down the tailgates and they slid out wooden coffins, plain pine, the pale wood gleaming in the sunlight.

They set six coffins on the three sets of sawhorses. A TV crew walked toward them, the cameraman peering through his lens, the sound woman flicking the microphone on her short boom with a finger.

Du Pré and Madelaine, Booger Tom, Chappie, Bart, and Father Van Den Heuvel ignored them.

"Could you answer a few questions?" said the reporter, a young redhead in a suit and heels.

Du Pré shook his head, pointed back in the direction they had come from.

"Go," he said, "or the deputies will take you. . . ."

They turned their backs on the TV crew then, and Madelaine set a pie tin on each of the coffins. Du Pré pulled sweetgrass twists, thick ropes of the stuff, out of a canvas bag. He lit the ends of the twists. Benny Klein and four deputies showed up and they put down posts set in steel bases and then they ran yellow plastic tape between them. The TV crew approached Benny.

The reporter said something and Benny shook his head. "You folks behave," he said. "Nerves are a bit raw here and it won't take much fer you to find your teeth are missing and your faces ain't put together like they was. . . ."

The TV crew retreated.

Benny turned and winked.

Cars and trucks pulled as close to the church as they could get and parked, and people in Sunday dress, some in black, got out and waved to each other, formed knots, talked.

"Danged good thing we had to postpone this," said Booger Tom. "Want to have all the gawkers able to come here, a hunnerd miles around. . . ." The old cowboy narrowed his washed-blue eyes.

"And so they should come," said Father Van Den Heuvel. "You old bastard, you're gonna tear up later and you know it. . . ."

"Danged lie," said Booger Tom. "I got no senniments."

"Shut up, both," said Madelaine, "or I get mad."

They both shut up.

A motor home with a news logo on the side pulled in, blocking the road.

Benny walked over.

A nationally known talking head got out and he began to yell at Benny, who backed up a few feet and waved his right hand, *come on.*

The talking head kept talking.

Wilbur's tow truck backed up to the rear of the motor home. It was the big truck, the one used to right logging trucks and eighteen-wheelers. Wilbur got out, hooked chains, stuck his thumb up. The talking head quit talking when his mobile studio moved off, backward.

"Why don't somebody shoot that little prick?" said Booger Tom.

"Why do a kindness, him?" said Madelaine, sweetly.

A big drum started throbbing, off in the thick grove of cottonwoods across the street. Several drummers were at work. Then the singing began.

. . . hair on my neck stands up, I hear that . . . Du Pré thought.

. . . feel it in my blood, heart of the people . . .

The talking head sprinted after his motor home, shouting. The noise faded into the sound of the drums.

A huge man dressed in black got out of a Cadillac, as did some others. Rudabaugh waved to Du Pré. One of the men with him was Bonner Macatee.

More cars pulled in, more trucks, all with the license plates of Bitter Creek's county.

"We'll do Communion after the burial," said Father Van Den Heuvel.

"These people are not all Catholic," said Madelaine.

"They all came here to bury the Métis," said Father Van Den Heuvel. "What lot of superstitions they prefer doesn't concern me."

"Bishop have a stroke, him, hear you say that," said Du Pré.

"If I thought he would," said Father Van Den Heuvel, "I'd say it in his office."

Hundreds of people stood, heads bowed, hands clasped, while the big priest spoke.

"Let us pray," he said, his voice very loud, "that the hate and fear that caused these deaths be cast out, and that we remember one another in the love of Christ. We commit these bones to the earth, and may their souls rest. . . ."

Father Van Den Heuvel motioned to Du Pré, who with Booger Tom and Bart and Benny and other men standing nearby lowered the six coffins into the grave, letting them down on ropes, carefully, and quickly. The people formed lines, passed by, throwing flowers into the graves, Du Pré tossed the ropes of sweetgrass, still smoldering, down on the pine coffin tops.

The priest set up his bread and wine on a trestle table and offered it.

Some people came, others did not. The drumming and singing went on.

The crowd shifted, broke apart, headed back to the cars and trucks they had come in.

They broke around an old man in a wheelchair, pushed by General La Salle. The crowd thinned, and then La Salle pushed the wheelchair forward.

The man in it was black and ancient.

La Salle brought him to the side of the grave.

The old man put his hands to his eyes.

Du Pré and Madelaine went over to them.

"This is Sergeant Boden," said La Salle. "Tenth Cavalry. . . ."

They stood silently while the old man wept.

Then he fished a handkerchief from his coat, dabbed his eyes, and blew his nose. He straightened up in the wheelchair and put his old clawlike hand to his forehead, saluting.

Du Pré knelt next to him.

"Sergeant," said La Salle, "this is Gabriel Du Pré. I told you about him. . . ."

The old man turned to look at Du Pré. A fierce intelligence burned in his old eyes. "Thank you," he said. "My daddy told me this story and hasn't been a day since then I didn't think about it. We was good soldiers, we never would have done this. . . . Tenth Cavalry, my daddy was in it too and he was here when them people was killed. It haunted him. . . . It haunted him bad."

Du Pré nodded.

"Lieutenant Albert, he was a good man," said Sergeant Boden. "When them crazy white men was all pointing their guns at them, my daddy's soldiers, they would have fought 'em. Lieutenant Albert, he said no, put your rifles down, we don't want to get in a fight with these people. . . ."

Du Pré nodded.

"Crazy people," said Sergeant Boden. "Daddy said about all you could see of their eyes was the whites. Like sometimes in battle. They was that hopped up. . . ."

"Hoeft?" said Du Pré. Sergeant Boden nodded.

"He was yellin' how the Indians killed his boy," he said, "and any man didn't do his duty, Hoeft would ruin him. I guess he owned most everything round there. . . ."

Du Pré nodded.

The old man looked down at the coffins. He inhaled deeply. "What is that," he said, "smokin' there?"

"Sweetgrass," said Du Pré.

"I smelled that time to time," said Boden. "Never knew what it was. I'd dream about that day and I'd wake up and smell that. You don't smell in dreams, not usually. . . ."

"They took the soldiers' guns?" said Du Pré.

The old man shook his head.

"After the shootin' stopped, that crazy Hoeft come back and said they had to go and shoot too. Lieutenant Albert ordered his men on in. They come to the place, them people was all dead. He set the men to firing at the bodies. They was out in a skirmish line. . . ."

. . . the piles of .30-40 shells . . .

"They was all already dead," said Boden.

"One little girl lived," said Du Pré.

The old man nodded.

"They rode through after they were done shootin'," he said, "and my daddy saw her crouched down in the brush. 'Course he just went on. You say she lived?"

"Yes," said Du Pré.

The old man nodded.

"They was good soldiers. . . ." he said.

· ABOUT THE AUTHOR ·

Peter Bowen (b. 1945) is an author best known for mystery novels set in the modern American West. When he was ten, Bowen's family moved to Bozeman, Montana, where a paper route introduced him to the grizzled old cowboys who frequented a bar called The Oaks. Listening to their stories, some of which stretched back to the 1870s, Bowen found inspiration for his later fiction.

Following time at the University of Michigan and the University of Montana, Bowen published his first novel, *Yellowstone Kelly*, in 1987. After two more novels featuring the real-life Western hero, Bowen published *Coyote Wind* (1994), which introduced Gabriel Du Pré, a mixed-race lawman living in fictional Toussaint, Montana. Bowen has written fourteen novels in the series, in which Du Pré gets tangled up in everything from cold-blooded murder to the hunt for rare fossils. Bowen continues to live and write in Livingston, Montana.

OPEN ROAD
INTEGRATED MEDIA

CPSIA information can be obtained at www.ICGtesting.com
Printed in the USA
BVOW03s1627200515

401200BV00004B/134/P